MᴄNALLY'S
PUZZLE

McNALLY'S PUZZLE

LAWRENCE SANDERS

G. P. PUTNAM'S SONS
NEW YORK

G. P. PUTNAM'S SONS

Publishers Since 1838

200 Madison Avenue

New York, NY 10016

Copyright © 1996 by Lawrence A. Sanders Enterprises, Inc.

Published simultaneously in Canada

ISBN 0-399-14135-9

Book design by Julie Duquet

Printed in the United States of America

M c N ALLY'S

P U Z Z L E

1

S<small>HE SLAPPED MY</small> face.

I have mentioned in previous accounts of my adventures that I am an absolute klutz when dealing with a weeping woman. I am even klutzier (if there is such a word) in coping with a person of the female extraction who commits an act of physical aggression upon the carcass of Archy McNally, bon vivant, dilettantish detective, and the only man in the Town of Palm Beach who owns a T-shirt bearing a portrait of Sophie Tucker. (She once hefted her voluminous breasts and said, "Hitler should have such tonsils.")

But forgive these digressions and allow me to return to the problem of being the victim of a lady's wrath: to wit, a sharp blow to my mandible. I mean, what was a gentleman to do?

1. Grit one's molars and stiffen one's upper lip in silence?
2. Return the slap while muttering a mild oath?
3. Bow politely and say, "I deserved that"?

Actually, the third choice would have been the most fitting but I was too startled by the sudden attack to make any reasonable response. Let me explain:

Her first name was Laura and her last name is of no consequence to this narrative. She and her wealthy husband of three years had recently finalized what was described as an "amicable divorce"—if there is such an animal, which I doubt.

Laura received a humongous cash settlement. Her ex-hubby retained possession of their Palm Beach mansion with all its rather atrocious furnishings and, of course, his personal property, including a famous collection of sports memorabilia. It had occasionally been exhibited in local museums which could not snare a traveling Monet show and had to be content with a display of ancient gutta-percha golf balls and a stained leather helmet once worn by Bronko Nagurski.

The star of the collection was a 1910 Sweet Caporal cigarette card bearing a likeness of Honus Wagner, famed shortstop of the Pittsburgh Pirates. It was believed only thirty-six of these rare baseball cards still existed, and one recently sold at auction for $450,000.

You can imagine the husband's fury and despair when, shortly after his divorced wife decamped, he discovered his beloved Honus Wagner card had decamped as well. But he had no proof his ex had filched his most valuable curio. And so, rather than create a foofaraw with the local gendarmes, he brought the problem to his attorneys, McNally & Son.

My father, Prescott McNally, is the lawyer. I, Archibald Mc-

Nally, am the son. I do not hold a legal degree due to a minor contretemps resulting in my being excommunicated from Yale Law. But I direct a small department (personnel: one) devoted to Discreet Inquiries. I do investigations for clients who would prefer to have potentially embarrassing matters handled with quiet circumspection instead of seeing them made public and possibly detailed in a supermarket tabloid next to an article entitled "I Am Pregnant with Elvis's Love Child!"

It took only a bit of nosing about to discover the lady was a member of the tennis club to which I belong—although my dues are frequently in arrears. Soon thereafter we were confronting each other across the net. I am not an accomplished tennist, although I do have a ferocious backhand, and it didn't take long to discover Laura was a calm and cool expert. To put it bluntly, she creamed me.

An after-set gin and tonic led to my inviting her to a luncheon and eventually a dinner. Working my wicked wiles, I capped a week of gastronomic seduction with a feast at the Chesterfield (rack of lamb and then a Grand Marnier soufflé). Replete and giggling, we returned to her quarters in a West Palm condo rental. By this time we were sufficiently simpatico that I do not believe either of us doubted how the evening would end.

And so it did. In my own defense I can only plead I was as much seductee as seducer. I mean this was an inexorable progression betwixt a frisky lass and an even friskier lad. What was one to do? Kismet.

But I did not neglect my motive for engineering this joyous occasion. And when the lady scampered into the bathroom after our frolic I scampered to the chest of drawers in her bedroom. And there, under a stack of perfumed undies, I found the stolid portrait of Honus Wagner, his baseball card sealed in plastic. I slipped it into my wallet, delighted with such a triumphant night.

But then, as I was dressing, she came trotting out, naked as a needle, and went directly to her store of flimsies. She discovered my theft almost immediately. She stalked over to me and I fancied even her satiny bosom was suffused with indignation—if not fury.

That was when she slapped my face.

After recovering from my initial shock, I launched into an earnest and detailed explanation. It was not actually larceny, I pointed out; I was merely recovering property illegally removed from the possession of the rightful owner. And as an employee of her ex-husband's attorney it was my duty to reclaim that which was undeniably his. Besides, I argued, my act of pilferage had been to her advantage since it would prevent her ex from filing a complaint of her alleged crime with the polizia.

I prided myself on speaking sincerely and eloquently. As readers of my previous discreet inquiries are aware, I am rarely at a loss for words. Glib, one might even say. Laura was obviously impressed, listening to my persuasive discourse in silence. When I concluded she drew a deep breath. Lovely sight.

"I guess you're right," she said. "But I want you to know I didn't intend to sell the stupid thing or profit from it in any way."

"Then why did you take it?"

"I just wanted to teach him a lesson," she said.

I shall never, never, *never* understand the gentle sex.

It was pushing midnight when I tooled my red Miata back to the ersatz Tudor manse on Ocean Boulevard housing the McNally family. It was the first week of November and it would be pure twaddle to describe the night as crisp. The weather in South Florida is rarely crisp, tending more toward the soggy, but I must report the sea breeze that Friday night was definitely breathable and the cloudless sky looked as if it had been decorated by Tiffany & Co.

Lights were out and no one was astir when I arrived home. I garaged my chariot and toed the stairs as quietly as I could to my mini-suite on the third and topmost floor. I disrobed and bought myself one minuscule marc and a final English Oval before retiring. It had been a somewhat stressful evening and I must confess I was plagued by a small tweak of shame. My successful gambit for recovering the Honus Wagner baseball card had not been strictly honorable, had it? Caddish, one might even say.

I occasionally suffer an attack of the guilts and have found the best cure is a good night's sleep, when a mambo with Morpheus dilutes crass behavior to impish mischief. And so it happened once again, for I awoke the following morning with a clear head, a pure conscience, and only a slight twinge in the lower jaw to remind me of Laura's energetic slap the previous evening. She had been entitled, I acknowledged, and decided I was fortunate that in addition to her tennis prowess she was not also a master of kung fu.

I roused in time to breakfast with my parents in the dining room. Our Scandinavian staff, Ursi and Jamie Olson, had whipped up a marvelous country feast of eggs scrambled with onions, ham steaks, fried grits, hush puppies, and coffee laced with enough chicory to afflict us all with a chorus of borborygmus.

"Goodness," my mother, Madelaine, said, "it *is* peppy, isn't it? Just the one cup for me."

My father was dressed for his customary Saturday golf game with the same cronies he had been playing with as long as I could recall. They were known as the Fearless Foursome at his club for they had once insisted on completing the back nine while a category three hurricane was raging.

Prescott McNally, Esq., wore his usual golfing uniform: white linen plus fours and argyle hose. This attire might have appeared ridiculous on a man of lesser dignity but pops, with his grizzled eyebrows and guardsman's mustache, carried it off with casual aplomb, as if he might be heading for a round at St. Andrews.

"Archy," he said as we left the dining room, both of us still rumbling dully from our gaseous breakfast, "a moment of your time, please."

We paused in the hallway outside the door of his first-floor study.

"The baseball card?" he inquired.

"Recovered," I said. "It'll be on your desk Monday morning."

"Excellent," he said. "Any unexpected difficulty or expense?"

"No, father. The lady was most cooperative."

He looked at me and raised one jungly eyebrow, a trick I've never been able to master. But he asked no questions. The pater prefers not to learn the details of my discreet inquiries. I do believe he fears such knowledge might result in his disbarment. He may be right.

"I'm happy the matter has been concluded satisfactorily," he said in his stodgy manner. "Then you have nothing on your plate at the moment?"

"No, sir. My platter is clean."

"Good. Do you know Hiram Gottschalk?"

"He's on our client list, is he not?"

"He is."

"I've never met Mr. Gottschalk personally but I have a nodding acquaintance with his son, Peter. He's a member of the Pelican Club."

"Is he?" father said. "And what is your reaction to him?"

I chose my words carefully. "I find him somewhat undisciplined," I said.

"So Mr. Gottschalk has led me to believe. He is a widower, you know, and in addition to his son he has grown twin daughters, presently vacationing in Europe. Are you also acquainted with them?"

"No, sir."

"Apparently they're due to return shortly, and perhaps you'll have the opportunity to meet them."

"Perhaps," I said. "Father, doesn't Mr. Gottschalk own that store in West Palm that sells birds?"

"Parrots," the sire said. "The shop is called Parrots Unlimited. That's the only species he handles."

"No auks?" I asked. "No emus or kiwis?"

He was startled. "Archy, you seem remarkably well informed about exotic birds."

"Not really," I said. "The names I mentioned are frequently used in crossword puzzles."

"Oh," he said. "Well, in any event, Mr. Gottschalk came in to consult me. We have been discussing for some time his plan to set up a private foundation. He is a wealthy man. Not from his parrot store, I assure you. But he has inherited a considerable sum, the greater part from his deceased wife, and we have been exploring options that might legally diminish his estate tax. But yesterday Mr. Gottschalk didn't wish to talk about taxes. He asked if I could recommend a private investigator to look into a matter that's troubling him. I told him of your employment as our house specialist in discreet inquiries. He seemed happy to hear of it and requested your assistance."

"Ready, willing, and able, sir," I said, resisting a momentary urge to genuflect. "What's his problem?"

Father paused a beat or two. Then: "He fears someone is trying to kill him."

"Surely not a maniacal macaw," I said.

Mon père glared at me. He does not appreciate my feeble attempts at humor at the expense of clients of McNally & Son. He feels they deserve respect since they put barbecued duck on the McNally table. I do respect them, I really do. But modicum is the word for it since many of our moneyed customers whose problems I deal with turn out to have a touch of sleaze.

"I suggest you visit Mr. Gottschalk on Monday," the boss continued. "I should warn you he is, ah, slightly eccentric."

"Oh?" I said. "In what way?" I remembered the old saw: "The poor are crazy; the rich are eccentric."

"In various ways," he said vaguely. "I'll leave it to you to make your own judgment. It's possible his fears are completely ground-less, but I feel it's a matter deserving investigation. There's no point in his going to the police, of course. He has received no written or phone threats. No attempts have been made on his life. It's just a feeling he has. The police could do nothing with that, and rightly so. But please look into it, Archy."

"Of course," I said. "Monday morning."

He nodded and departed for his golf game. I went upstairs to change my duds for what I hoped would be an active and re-warding weekend during which I planned to play the role of a Palm Beach layabout: a bibulous lunch with Binky Watrous, an ocean swim, dinner with Consuela Garcia at the Pelican Club on Saturday night, golf on Sunday, perhaps a visit to Wellington polo in the afternoon. Good food. Good drinks. Jokes and laugh-ter.

I record this trivia to convince you I do not spend *all* my time outwitting villains and righting wrongs. There is a gloomy Hun-garian saying, something to the effect that before you have a chance to look around, the picnic is over. I have no intention of ignoring the picnic, ants and all. Not that I am given to excess. "Moderation in all things," Terence advised. (He wrote, of course, before the invention of the vodka gimlet.)

After a raucous session of poker with three pals on Sunday

night (I won the princely sum of $3.49), I returned home early in the ayem and had a curious and rather unsettling experience.

I was in a beamish mood, a bit tiddly, and as I pulled in to the area fronting our three-car garage I saw in the headlight glare an enormous black bird stalking slowly across the gravel. Lordy but he was huge, and for one wild moment I thought I had spotted the last pterodactyl on earth.

It was a crow of course and not at all spooked by finding himself in the limelight. He turned his jetty head and gave me what I can only describe as a don't-mess-with-me look. Then he resumed his deliberate walk.

There was something disconcerting, almost ominous in the insolent parade of that funereal fowl. I watched him until he vanished into shadows as dark as he and my élan disappeared with him. I cannot say I felt menaced but I was slightly unnerved by the brief glimpse of that feathered phantom. He seemed so sure of himself, y'see, and totally indifferent to everything but his own desires.

If I wished to anthropomorphize I'd have said the bird personified evil. That's a mite much, you say? I'd be inclined to agree but Mr. Thomas Campbell was soon to be proved correct when he penned:

"Coming events cast their shadows before."

2

I OVERSLEPT ON MONDAY, reverting to my usual sluggardly habit. I finally hoisted myself from the pillows, showered and shaved. I dressed with something less than my usual éclat since I intended to meet with Mr. Hiram Gottschalk and wished to convey the impression of a sobersided investigator, a trustworthy representative of McNally & Son. Hey, I even wore socks.

I breakfasted alone in the kitchen and limited myself to only one croissant sandwich of salami and smoked Muenster. Then I set out for the McNally Building on Royal Palm Way. I distinctly recall having selected from my large collection of headgear a Monticristi panama I had recently bought. The purchase of that marvelous hat had put a severe dent in my checking account and I had the original black ribbon band replaced with one of snakeskin. Raffish, doncha think?

I left the baseball card with Mrs. Trelawney, my father's private secretary, and then went down to my own office. It is as commodious as a vertical coffin, and I do believe I have been sentenced to such a windowless cell by *mein papa* so he might never be accused of nepotism. I, of course, thought it prima facie evidence of parental abuse.

I looked up the number of Parrots Unlimited in the West Palm directory and phoned. A woman answered, I identified myself and asked to speak to Mr. Hiram Gottschalk. He came on the line a moment later. His voice was dry and twangy.

"You Prescott McNally's son?" he demanded. "Archibald McNally?"

"That's correct, sir."

"Call you Archy?"

"Of course," I said.

"Call me Hi," he said. "Hate the name Hiram. Makes me sound like a Nebraska farmer."

"Oh, I don't know," I said. "Hiram Walker and I are old friends."

He picked up on it immediately. "Say, you sound like a sharp kid. Want to see me, do you?"

"Yes, sir. At your convenience."

"Right now suits me fine," he said. "Come on over."

"On my way," I told him, and hung up, warning myself to be careful in greeting Mr. Gottschalk. "Hi, Hi" just wouldn't do, would it?

I found Parrots Unlimited with little trouble. It was on Hibiscus Street out west toward Cooley Stadium. I discovered a legal parking space about two blocks away and strolled back, grateful for my panama because the November sun thought it was still July.

The store was larger than I had anticipated and appeared to

be well maintained. There were no live birds behind the plate glass windows as one might expect of a pet shop, but there was an attractive display of framed color photos of macaws, lovebirds, cockatoos, parakeets, and one magnificently feathered Edward's Fig-Parrot. There was also a printed sign: "BOARDING AND GROOMING AVAILABLE AT REASONABLE RATES." And a hand-scrawled notice: "Part-time assistant wanted. Inquire within."

I opened the door and entered, fearing I would be greeted with a cacophony of squawks and an odor that might loosen my fillings. Nothing of the sort existed. The interior was clean and uncluttered, the cool air smelled faintly of a wild cherry de-odorizer, and rather than indignant screeches, all I heard was a subdued peep now and then, leading me to wonder if a wee bit of Valium might not be added to the daily diet of that multicol-ored aviary.

Just inside the door a large, pure-white parrot was perched on a well-pecked branch of soft wood. It was uncaged and untied. I paused to stare at it and the fowl turned its head to stare back. It had beady, red-tinged eyes, reminding me of my own after I have inhaled three brandy stingers.

I was approached by a salesperson, a plump, attractive young lady who was less parrot than robin redbreast.

"May I help you, sir?" she chirped.

(It always depresses me to be addressed as "sir" by a nubile lass. I dread the day when it may become "pop.")

"This bird," I said, gesturing toward the unfettered white par-rot. "Why doesn't it fly away?"

"His wings have been clipped," she explained. "It's a com-pletely painless procedure."

I found that hard to believe. I know I'd suffer if my wings were clipped.

"My name is Archy McNally," I told her. "I have an appointment with Mr. Gottschalk. Would you be kind enough to tell him I've arrived."

"Just a moment, please, sir," she said, and left.

I wandered about examining the extraordinary selection of parrots being offered for sale, some in individual cages but many in communal enclosures where they seemed to exist placidly together. There were also racks of bird feed, grooming aids, books, cages, perches, and toys. It was truly a psittacine supermarket, with one glassed-in corner apparently devoted to the grooming and treatment of birds with the sniffles.

The perky clerk soon returned to conduct me to Mr. Hiram Gottschalk's private office at the rear of the store. It was a smallish chamber with steel furniture and a computer installation on a separate table. The only item rarely found in commercial offices was a large, ornate cage on a stand. Within was a single parrot of a gray-blue color. It turned its head to watch me warily as I entered.

Our client was a short, stringy man sporting a nattily trimmed salt-and-pepper Vandyke. I guessed his age at about seventy, give or take, but his features were so taut I imagined additional years would wreak little damage to that tight visage. His eyes were hazel and alert. Exceedingly alert. A sharp customer, I reckoned.

We introduced ourselves and shook hands. His clasp was dry and firm. He saw me glance at the caged parrot behind his desk.

"Name is Ralph," Mr. Gottschalk said. "Give him a hello."

"Hello, Ralph," I said pleasantly.

"Go to hell," the bird said.

I glared at him and he glared right back.

"Did you teach him that?" I asked Hiram.

"Not me," he said. "Unsociable critter. No manners at all. Pull up a chair."

I sat alongside his desk, trying not to look at Ralph, who continued to eye me balefully.

"Tell me something, Hi," I said. "Do parrots mimic human speech naturally or must they be taught?"

"Generally," he said, "they require endless repetition. Audiotapes help. But then, occasionally, they'll surprise you by repeating something they've heard only once."

"A word or phrase? Something simple?"

"Not always," he said. "Here's a story for you. . . . A few years ago a very proper matron came in with a blue-fronted Amazon. Nothing wrong with the bird—it was gorgeously colored—but she had purchased it from a seafaring man in Key West, and apparently he had thought it a great joke to teach the female parrot to say, 'I'm a whore.'

"Naturally the new owner was much disturbed and asked if there was any way to rid her pet of this distressing habit. I told her it was doubtful but by a curious coincidence we were boarding two macaws belonging to a man of God who was then on a religious retreat in Scranton. The minister's two birds were extremely devout and spent all their time reciting prayers they had obviously learned from their owner.

"I suggested to the matron that her profane bird be placed in the same cage with the two pious macaws, where she might learn to temper her language. The matron eagerly agreed, and that's what we did.

"The moment the three birds were joined, the female blue-fronted Amazon screeched, 'I'm a whore, I'm a whore.' And you know, one of the macaws turned to the other and said, 'Glory be, Charley, our prayers are answered.' "

Mr. Gottschalk stared at me, absolutely po-faced. "Isn't that a fascinating story?" he asked.

"Remarkable," I said, just as solemnly. "Quite remarkable.

And did the three parrots live happily ever after—an avicultural *ménage à trois*, so to speak?"

"Something like that," he said, and we nodded thoughtfully at each other.

"Got a lot of parrot stories," he went on. "Things you might find hard to believe. They're very intelligent birds. Some can imitate a dog barking or a faucet dripping. Many researchers think they're smarter than chimps or dolphins. I've known budgerigars who could recite nursery rhymes or indecent limericks. My daughters are in Europe right now—they'll be home in a few days—and they wrote me how amazed they were to find parrots who spoke French, Italian, or Spanish. What's amazing about that? The birds will imitate the sounds they're taught. I once heard of a lorikeet who could mimic a police siren. But enough about parrots. That's not why you came to see me, is it, Archy."

"No, sir," I said. "My father tells me you feel your life is in danger."

"Not just feel it," he said decisively. "I *know* it. No threatening letters or phone calls, you understand, but several things I don't like."

"Such as?"

"My dear wife departed this vale of tears three years ago. I kept a framed photograph of us on my bedside table. It was taken at an outdoor cafe on the Cap d'Antibes. We were both young then, laughing, holding our wineglasses up to the camera. A lovely photo. I cherished it. The last thing I saw before sleep and the first thing I looked for in the morning. About a month ago I returned home to find the glass shattered and the photograph slashed to ribbons."

I drew a deep breath. "Ugly," I said.

He nodded. "A week later I opened my closet door to find a mass card taped to the inside. You're familiar with mass cards?"

"Yes, sir."

"You Catholic?"

"No, sir."

"Well, I am. Not a good one, I fear, but once tried, never denied. In any event, the name of the deceased on the mass card was mine."

I winced. My father had warned me our client was "slightly eccentric," and after his ridiculous anecdote about the devout macaws I had begun to suspect he might be a total goober. But now, listening to the disturbing events he related, I became convinced he was an intelligent man despite his quirky sense of humor. I believed he was troubled and telling me the truth. I mean, who but a professional novelist could dream up such bizarre incidents as the slashed photograph and the taped mass card?

"One final thing," Mr. Gottschalk said. "When we bought our house my wife very definitely forbade me to bring in any parrots. She thought they were dirty, selfish, and cantankerous—and indeed some of them are. She finally allowed me one male mynah, only because its coloring matched her decorative scheme for our Florida room."

"Surely mynahs are not parrots."

"Of course not," he said crossly. "Members of the starling family. But I love all birds and mynahs are lovable, this one especially so. His name was Dicky and he was beautiful. Extremely intelligent. Mynahs are superior to parrots in mimicking human speech, you know. Dicky could faultlessly recite the first verse of 'Battle Hymn of the Republic.' In addition, he had a delightfully apologetic manner. If he soiled his cage, upset his water, or made a mess of his feeding cup, he'd duck his head and cry, 'Dicky did it.' He said it so often it became a family joke, and if any of us had a minor mishap—spilled a glass of wine or broke a plate—

we'd say, 'Dicky did it.' What a wonderful bird! My wife loved him. I thought we all did."

He paused. I said nothing, dreading the finale of his tale.

"Last week I went down for breakfast," he said, trying to keep his voice steady and not succeeding. "Didn't hear Dicky chirping as he usually did early in the morning. Went into the Florida room to take a look. The door of his cage was open. He was lying dead. Someone had wrung his neck."

We were both silent a long moment, wrenched. I couldn't look at Mr. Gottschalk but gazed up at Ralph behind his desk. The bird appeared to be sleeping.

"Sir," I said finally, "I don't wish to come to any premature conclusion from what you've related but it seems obvious to me—as I'm sure it is to you—that these acts of what I can only term terrorism could not have been committed by an outsider. The culprit must be a member of your household."

"Yes," he said, his voice muted with an ineffable sadness. "I'm aware of that. It hurts."

3

H E HAD OBVIOUSLY been brooding on the matter, for he had prepared a list of all the family members and staff of his home, their names and relationship to him or their duties. I glanced at it briefly.

"A good beginning, Hi," I said, "but I'll really need to meet these people without their knowing of my assignment. Can you suggest how that might be done?"

He pondered a moment, then brightened. "My daughters are returning from Europe tomorrow. We're planning a welcome-home party on Wednesday night. Family, friends, and neighbors. Open bar and buffet dinner. Very informal. No starch at all. Begins around six or so and runs till whenever. Why don't you show up simply as a guest, a representative of my counselors-at-law."

"Excellent suggestion," I said. "I'll be delighted to attend. Have you also invited the employees of your store?"

He paused to look at me curiously. "I haven't," he admitted. "Do you think I should?"

"How many workers do you have?"

"Four full-timers. The manager, Ricardo Chrisling, and three clerks. And we're trying to find a part-timer for scut work."

"Invite them all," I advised. "I want to meet everyone you deal with on a daily basis. In addition, you'll score brownie points as a kindly employer."

He gave me a wry-crisp smile. "I was right; you *are* a sharp lad. All right, I'll ask them."

I pocketed his list and rose to leave. We shook hands again. This time I thought his clasp was weaker, as if the recital of dreadful events recently endured had enfeebled him.

"Give Ralph a good-bye," he said.

"Good-bye, Ralph," I said, knowing what was coming.

The bird opened its eyes. "Go to hell," it said.

And on that cheery note I departed.

There were several customers in the store and I waited until the young lady I had first encountered completed the sale of a bag of cuttlebone to a scrawny, bespectacled teenager who looked as if he might also profit from an occasional snack of calcium.

"Hello again," I said, giving her the 100-watt smile I term my Supercharmer, since I feared she was too innocent to withstand the power of my Jumbocharmer (150 watts).

"Hello yourself," she said brightly. "Arnold McIntosh, isn't it?"

How soon they forget! "Archy McNally," I repeated clearly. "Now you know my name but I don't know yours."

"Bridget," she said. "Bridget Houlihan."

"Mellifluous!" I said admiringly. "Comes trippingly off the tongue. Bridget, I see you have a notice in the window advertising for a part-time assistant. I have a friend who might be interested. If he decides to come in, may I give him your name? Perhaps you could then direct him to the proper person for an interview and questions about his competence."

"Oh, sure," she said. "Tell him to ask for me and I'll take care of him."

"Thank you so much," I said. "Have a grand day."

"I mean to," she said pertly. What a delightful bubble she was!

I exited into the sunshine and boarded the Miata. But before starting up I buzzed Binky Watrous on my cellular phone.

"Save me!" he cried piteously.

"Save you?" I said. "From what?"

"The Duchess wants me to accompany her to a charity luncheon followed by a two-hour film on the mating habits of emperor penguins. Apparently the males incubate the eggs by balancing them on their feet."

"I wish you hadn't told me that," I said. "I really didn't want to know. Listen, old boy, tell the Duchess you've received an emergency call concerning your on-the-job training to become the Nick Charles of Palm Beach. It's of vital importance you meet with me immediately to discuss a case of criminal conspiracy threatening the very existence of Western Civilization."

"Gotcha," he said happily. "Where and when?"

"Pelican in half an hour. I'll be at the bar."

"Of course," he said. "Naturally."

The Pelican Club is a private home-away-from-home for many of the glossier thirty-somethings of the Palm Beaches. It is located in a decrepit freestanding building out near the airport and offers a bar area, dining room, dartboard alley, and all one could wish for in the way of raucous fellowship, generous drinks, and a menu that disgusts cholesterolphobes.

As one of the founding members, I can testify we were close to bankruptcy when we had the great good fortune to put the fate of our club in the capable hands of the Pettibones, a family of color. Simon, the patriarch, became club manager and bartender. His wife, Jas (for Jasmine), was our den mother who saw to housekeeping chores, preserved limited order on unruly weekend nights, and was capable of gently ejecting members whose conduct exceeded her generous standard of decorum. Daughter Priscilla served as waitress and son Leroy as chef.

Under the aegis of the Pettibones the Pelican Club had flourished and its fame had spread. We now had a long list of wannabes (m. and f.) eager to wear on their jackets the club escutcheon: a pelican rampant on a field of dead mullet. It had certainly become my favorite watering hole in South Florida, and if my monthly tabs were shocking I consoled myself with the reminder that I conducted more business there for McNally & Son than I did in my emaciated office. Thus I could rightfully claim a goodly portion of my expenditures for beer and cheeseburgers on my expense account. Our treasurer, Raymond Gelding, frequently disagreed—but we all know what treasurers are like, don't we.

It wasn't quite noon and the club was deserted when I removed my panama, swung aboard a barstool, and relaxed in the dim, cool interior that always smelled faintly and delightfully of Grand Marnier.

"Mr. McNally," Simon Pettibone greeted me, "I haven't seen you in a long time."

"I know," I said. "It must be almost forty-eight hours. Mr. Pettibone, it is unexpectedly warm and steamy out there—a theme park called Sauna World—and I am in dire need of something tall, frigid, and refreshing. Suggestions?"

"You know," he said, "last night a young lady asked for a Tom Collins. Haven't mixed one of those in years. She seemed to enjoy it. Like to try one?"

"The ticket!" I cried. "I knew I could depend on you. Please make sure the ice is cold."

"I'll try," he said, not changing expression. Mr. Pettibone and I have an understanding.

He really is an expert mixologist and I watched with admiration as he constructed my Tom Collins and added the fruit.

"No straw," I warned.

"Wouldn't think of it," he said.

I sipped and rolled my eyes. "Elixir," I said. "Mr. Pettibone, are you familiar with a member named Peter Gottschalk?"

"I am," he said shortly.

"My father asked my opinion of him and I said I thought he was rather undisciplined. Do you think I was being unduly censorious?"

"No," he said. "On target. He's a wild one. Jas has booted him out a few times. Not for intoxication, mind you. He doesn't drink all that much. But occasionally he starts talking in a loud, irritating voice. Practically shouting. Butts in where he's not wanted. Becomes a real nuisance."

"What does he shout about?"

"Nonsense. Crazy stuff. No rhyme or reason. He just goes off. No control."

"Could it be physiological?" I asked. "Mental?"

"Could be," Mr. Pettibone said. "One minute he's nice as pie and then suddenly he's raving. Maybe it's a brain thing and a pill could straighten him out."

"Maybe," I said. But at that moment Binky Watrous came

scuttling in and I was faced with the case of another man with a brain problem. Binky lacked one. He and a female companion had once been arrested for playing hopscotch in the Louvre.

He slapped my shoulder and slid onto an adjoining stool. "I'll have a fresh cantaloupe piña colada," he declared.

Mr. Pettibone and I glanced at each other. "Sorry, Mr. Watrous," he said. "No fresh cantaloupe available today."

"No?" my pal said. "What a shame. In that case I'll have a double Cutty Sark."

Typical Binky. The would-be Philo Vance was a complete goof.

I ordered a refill and we carried our drinks to the dining room before the luncheon crowd came charging in. We grabbed a corner table for two and Priscilla sauntered over. She was wearing a T-shirt, splotched painter's overalls, and a baseball cap with the visor turned jauntily to one side.

"Well, well," she said. "The Dynamic Duo. Batman and Robin."

"Enough of your sass," I said. "What's Leroy pushing today?"

"Vitamins," she said. "He's on a one-day health kick. A gorgeous seafood salad with fried anchovies."

"That's for me," I said. "Binky?"

"I'm game," he said. "But go easy on the lobster. It gives me a rash."

"Yeah?" Pris said. "Men have the same effect on me."

She bopped away and Binky took a yeomanly gulp of his Scotch. He was a palish lad who looked as if he might shampoo with Clorox. He sported a mustache so wispy one feared for its continued existence in a strong wind. But despite his apparent effeteness—or perhaps because of it—he was an eager and successful lothario, and I hesitated to estimate the limit of his conquests if his mustache had been black and long enough to twirl.

After the accidental death of his parents when he was a toddler, Binky had been raised, educated, and generously supported by a maiden aunt known to Palm Beach society as the Duchess. She was not an actual duchess of course but could have played one on *Masterpiece Theatre*. It was said she had once fired a butler for sneezing in her presence.

The Duchess had heretofore financed Binky's travels, brief romantic liaisons with ladies who sometimes made greedy demands, and his gambling debts. But recently she had brought her largesse to a screeching halt and demanded Binky seek gainful employment. But he had no experience in any practical occupation. His sole talent was birdcalls and there are very few, if any, Help Wanted ads headed "Birdcaller Wanted."

In desperation Binky had approached me with the request I take him on as an unpaid assistant in my Department of Discreet Inquiries for McNally & Son. It was to be on-the-job training and Binky had visions of becoming a successful private investigator. I thought he had as much chance of becoming a successful nuclear physicist, since of all my loopy friends he was the King of Duncedom.

Against my better judgment, and only from a real affection for this twit, I had allowed him to assist me on one case and had been pleasantly surprised to find his contributions of value. I had told him only those details of our client's travails I felt he needed to know, and I'm certain that in his ingenuous way he was totally unaware of the significance of the information he uncovered. But he did help me bring the case to a satisfactory conclusion. I mean he hadn't been an utter disaster and the idea of having a nutty Dr. Watson amused me.

"Binky," I said as we awaited our meal, "a new discreet inquiry has been assigned to me, and I feel I may benefit from your unique skills."

He preened. "Of course I shall be happy to assist you," he said formally. "No chance of a paycheck at the end of the week, is there, old sport?"

"Afraid not," I said regretfully. "The old man wouldn't approve. It must be part of your unpaid apprenticeship."

He sighed. "Better than nothing I suppose. The Duchess has been feeding me a diet of dirty digs lately, asking when I intend to land a job. If I can tell her I'm learning how to become a private eye, even if it's temporarily no-pay, she may stop her grousing."

"Also," I pointed out, "it will provide a perfect excuse for your absences, eliminating the need to accompany the Duchess to charity bashes and those flute recitals you so rightfully dread."

"How true, how true," he said, brightening. "I'm your man."

"You understand, don't you, that I'm to be captain of the ship and you a lowly seaman not allowed to question my judgments."

"Of course," he said. "You lead and I shall faithfully follow. What is it, Archy?"

"There's a bird shop in West Palm. Parrots Unlimited. That's all they sell—parrots. And accessories for their care and feeding. They're looking for a part-time assistant. I want you to apply for the job and do your best to obtain it."

He was horrified. "Surely you jest."

"I do not jest."

"Jiminy crickets, Archy, they'll have me cleaning out the cages."

"That will probably be part of your duties," I admitted.

"I know nothing about parrots."

"But you're—" I started, but caught myself in time. I had been about to say "birdbrained" but changed it to, "You're bird-minded. Your imitations of birdcalls are famous in South Florida. Your mimicking of a loon is especially admired."

My flattery didn't succeed.

"I really wasn't destined for a career of cleaning birdcages," he mourned.

"You'll be paid for your labors," I reminded him. "It won't be much, granted, but it'll be walking-around money. That should make both you and the Duchess happy."

He was wavering but still not wholly committed and so I played my trump card.

"There is a young lady who works there," I mentioned casually. "Quite attractive. You may be interested."

He blinked his pale eyes twice. "Oh?" he said. "A cream puff?"

"A charlotte russe," I assured him. "A mille-feuille. Possibly even baklava."

He sighed. "All right," he said. "I'll do it."

Many people have accused me of being devious. They may be right.

4

OUR SALADS WERE served and those fried anchovies proved so salty I was forced, *forced* to order a carafe of the house chardonnay. And dreadful plonk it is, its only virtues being that it's cold and wet.

As we munched our greeneries I offered Binky a few suggestions anent his assignment.

"If you are interviewed by Hiram Gottschalk, the owner," I said, "I advise you to regale him with the recitation of your birdcalls. He is a confessed bird lover and I think your unusual talent may convince him to hire you on the spot."

"Oh sure," Binky said. "I'll give him the cry of the yellow-thighed manakin. That'll impress him. Say, Archy, this is really awful wine. Can't we have a bottle of Piper-Heidsieck?"

"No," I said. "When you arrive at Parrots Unlimited seek out the young lady I mentioned. She'll aid your application for employment. You may mention my name; I've already alerted her to the possibility of your coming in. Her name is Bridget Houlihan."

"Oh?" he said. "Of Irish descent?"

I looked at him. "Possibly," I said. "Or perhaps Estonian. Binky, if you are hired—and I'm confident you will be—I want you to lavish all your multitudinous charms on the other employees. Learn their names, details of their private lives, observe personal habits, note relationships with fellow workers, including the manager, and especially sound out how they feel about their employer, Hiram Gottschalk."

"In other words, you want me to snoop."

"Exactly."

"That'll be fun," he said happily. "I enjoy snooping, don't you, Archy?"

"I prefer to consider it unobtrusive investigation," I said stiffly. "But yes, snooping is what I require of you. I should also mention Mr. Gottschalk's twin daughters are returning from a European trip tomorrow and will be feted at an informal welcome-home bash at the Gottschalk residence on Wednesday evening. Employees will be invited, so if all goes well I may see you there."

"Hey," he said, brightening, "this case is beginning to sound like one continuous round of merriment."

I didn't believe it would be but didn't wish to disabuse my eager helot. We finished lunch and, feeling contrite about that blah chardonnay, I treated him to a Rémy Martin at the bar. He finished his pony in two gulps—Binky is definitely not an accomplished sipper—and he departed in a blithe mood, vowing to apply for part-time employment at Parrots Unlimited as soon as he had enjoyed a postprandial nap.

I drove directly home in no mood to return to my claustro-phobic office, which I always imagined had originally been de-signed as a loo for pygmies. What a delight it was to reenter my air-conditioned aerie where every prospect pleased and only I was vile. I shucked off those fuddy-duddy threads I had donned to impress Mr. Gottschalk, lighted my first English Oval of the day, and got on the horn.

My first call was to Consuela Garcia, the young lady with whom I am intimate when she is not accusing me of real or fan-cied infidelities. Connie would, I knew, be hard at work as a so-cial secretary to Lady Cynthia Horowitz, one of the wealthiest chatelaines of Palm Beach. Lady Cynthia has six ex-husbands, mayhap a PB record, and at least six hundred enemies she zeal-ously enrages with her acidic wit and political clout. I am thank-ful she considers me a friend.

Connie was happy to take a moment off from organizing a re-ception Lady Cynthia was planning for a visiting Zimbabwean griot.

We gibbered a few moments about such vital topics as Con-nie's new recipe for spicy sautéed trout and a curious dream I had a few nights previously involving Irene Dunne, Akim Tamiroff, and a Ferris wheel.

"Listen, dear," I said, "I have a problem."

"The dream?"

"No, it concerns a chap named Peter Gottschalk. You know him?"

"Do I ever!" she said. "He's always hitting on me at the Peli-can. A real dingbat."

"So I understand. You know I chair the Membership Com-mittee, and we've had several complaints about his acting in an irrational way. We could throw him overboard of course and let him founder, but that seems cruel. Besides, he might sue. Simon

Pettibone thinks it may be a mental disability and the poor boy needs professional help. Are you acquainted with his parents?"

"No, but I've met his twin sisters."

"Have you now," I said.

The reason for my subterfuge is obvious, is it not? If I had started candidly by asking, "Do you know the Gottschalk daughters?" Connie would immediately assume I was casting covetous eyes on one or both and demand to know the reason for my interest. I hadn't lied, you understand, just dissembled. I'm rather crafty at that.

"What kind of females are they?" I asked casually. "I mean, do you think they're sympathetic and understanding? Would they be willing to urge their brother to seek help for his crazy behavior?"

"I don't know," Connie said doubtfully. "Sometimes they act like a couple of ding-a-lings themselves. Maybe it runs in the family."

"Maybe," I agreed. "Well, it wouldn't do any harm to attempt to enlist their assistance. I'd hate to chuck Peter Gottschalk from the Pelican Club simply for not acting in a reasonable manner."

"That's right, kiddo," Connie said. "Set that requirement and you'll be the first to go." She hung up giggling.

I hadn't learned much, had I? But that's the way I work most of my cases: a slow, patient accretion of facts, observations, opinions, surmises, and sometimes apparently inconsequential details such as grammar, dress, and knowledge of how to eat an artichoke.

My second phone call was to Lolly Spindrift, who writes a gossip column for one of our local gazettes. Lol and I have had a profitable quid pro quo relationship for several years. Occasionally I feed him choice tidbits of skinny about my current cases (without compromising client confidentiality) and in return Lol gives me tasty morsels from his consummate knowledge of the high jinks and low jinks of Palm Beach residents.

"You swine!" he shrieked. "Hast thou forsaken me? Things have been so dull! My stable of tattletales seems to be infected with an epidemic of discretion. A horror! I have to struggle—*struggle*, darling!—to fill each day's report. Tell me you have something juicy for dear old Lol."

"Nothing exciting," I admitted, "but it may be worth a line or two if you promise not to mention his name. Call him the scion of a wealthy Palm Beach family. He's about to be booted out of an exclusive private club for improper behavior."

"Name of scion?" Lol demanded. "Name of exclusive private club?"

"Peter Gottschalk," I said. "The Pelican Club."

He sighed. "Peter is a world-class nitwit and the Pelican is about as exclusive as Diners Club. Look, sweetie, this scoop you're offering doesn't quite rival the sinking of the *Titanic.*"

"I know, Lol, but I hoped it might be worth an item."

"Only because I have nothing better. Now what do you want?"

"Do you have anything on the Gottschalk daughters?"

"Oh-ho," he said, and I heard the sudden interest in his voice. "Do I detect a preoccupation with the Gottschalk family? Something going on there, luv?"

"Possibly," I said. "If so, you'll be the first to know."

"I better be. The daughters are Judith and Julia. Identical twins. Two wildebeests. Not as fruity as their brother but almost. Maybe it runs in the family." (Cf. Connie's remark.)

"Unrestrained, one might say?"

"One might," he agreed. "They're very attractive, ducky, which may tickle your id, but they're not my species, as you well know. The girls are remarkable look-alikes. Their favorite caper is to date the same man, separately and alternately, without revealing their deception. The poor stud thinks he's bedding Judith. He might be. Or it might be Julia. They're practically indistinguishable and think gulling their lovers is the funniest hoax in the world."

"Surely they don't dress alike."

"Oh no, they don't carry their twinship that far."

"Ever married? Either or both?"

"Not to my knowledge. Only to each other."

"Thank you, Lol," I said gratefully. "You've been much help, as usual. I'll stay in touch."

"Do that," he warned. "Or I may be forced to publish an entire column on the romantic peccadilloes of Archibald McNally."

"Perish the thought."

"I shall," he said. "Temporarily."

Although interested by what I had learned, I called a halt to sherlocking for the remainder of the afternoon. I tugged on cerise Speedo swimming trunks, added a terry Donald Duck cover-up and leather sandals, grabbed a towel, and went down to the sea for my daily dunk.

I did the usual two miles, south and back, flogging my flaccid muscles into action. Truthfully it was more of a wallow than a swim but I finished with a great sense of accomplishment, hoping *mens sana in corpore sano* really applied to me but with a lurking suspicion I flunked the *sano* part.

I returned to my den, showered away salt water and sand, and dressed casually in time to attend the family cocktail hour. This is not an hour of course, more like thirty minutes when the McNally tribe traditionally gathers in our second-floor sitting room for a pitcher of gin martinis mixed by the lord of the manor. After one wallop—and occasionally a small dividend—we all troop downstairs for dinner.

Dinner that night was sautéed yellowtail snapper with potato patties Ursi Olson had made with a few tablespoons of sherry. Good for Ursi! Dessert was a chocolate cheesecake. Ursi hadn't made that; it was store-bought. It was excellent but so rich I could feel my arteries slowly hardening. I could scarcely finish a second slice.

Back in my digs I kicked off my mocs and donned reading glasses. Yes, despite my tender age, I do need specs for close-up work. I never wear them in public of course since they make me look like a cybernetic nerd and would utterly destroy my sedulously cultivated image of a cavalier, a dashing combination of D'Artagnan and Bugs Bunny.

I sat at my arthritic desk and started a fresh page in my journal. This is a professional diary in which I keep notes of my discreet inquiries. I am not yet a resident of la-la land, you understand, but now and then I do forget things and find a scribbled record an invaluable aid.

I wrote rapidly in my crabbed hieroglyphics, which even I sometimes have trouble deciphering. I started with my father's alert: Hiram Gottschalk feared for his life. Then I added everything that had happened since: my visit to Parrots Unlimited, interview with the client, enlisting of Binky Watrous, and what I had learned from Simon Pettibone, Connie Garcia, and Lolly Spindrift.

Finally I dug out the list Mr. Gottschalk had given me of members of his household: family and staff. I was copying their names when one caused me to pause. His housekeeper and apparently mistress of the Gottschalk ménage was Yvonne Chrisling.

I distinctly recalled Hiram telling me the name of the manager of Parrots Unlimited. It was Ricardo Chrisling, an uncommon surname. I had to assume Yvonne and Ricardo were related. Wife and husband? Sister and brother? Mother and son? I found it intriguing and determined to seek a solution at the Gottschalk welcome-home party on Wednesday night.

It was close to eleven o'clock when I completed my labors and I was pouring myself a small marc as a reward when my phone rang. The caller was Sgt. Al Rogoff of the Palm Beach Police Department. Al and I have joined forces on several cases in the past. He provides me with official assistance when he can and I act as his dragoman to the arcane complexities of Palm Beach society.

Our relationship is, I truly believe, one of genuine friendship. But it does not lack on occasion a certain competitiveness. I mean when we're cooperating on an investigation the sergeant doesn't tell me all he knows, or guesses, and I return the favor. But that just adds a little cayenne to the stew, does it not?

"How's it going, old buddy?" he asked.

"Swimmingly," I replied. "And you?"

"Existing. The last squeal I had was an old dame boosting avocados from a local supermarket. Pretty exciting, huh? You working anything?"

"Nothing important. Dribs and drabs."

"Oh sure," he said. "Because if you were on something heavy you'd tell me about it, wouldn't you?"

"Of course."

"When shrimp fly," he said. "All right, I'm just checking in. If anything intriguing—your word, not mine—comes up, give me a shout. I'm bored out of my gourd."

"Aren't we all?" I said, and we disconnected. It wasn't time to bring Al into the Gottschalk inquiry. Not yet it wasn't and I hoped it never would be. But I was troubled by—what? Not a premonition—I rarely have those—but by a nagging unease caused by the three frightful accidents that had befallen Hiram Gottschalk. I did not take them lightly.

I like to go to sleep in a merry mood and so that night before retiring I listened to a recording of Tiny Tim singing "Tip-Toe thru the Tulips with Me."

It helped.

5

I AWOKE THE NEXT morning knowing exactly what I intended to do. This was a rarity since I usually regain consciousness in a semibefuddled state, not quite knowing where I am or even *who* I am. I recall awakening one morning with the firm conviction that I was Oscar Homolka. I am not, of course, and never have been.

What I intended to do requires a smidgen of explanation.

A few years previously Sgt. Al Rogoff had introduced me to Dr. Gussie Pearlberg, a psychiatrist who had her home and office in Lantana. Dr. Pearlberg did not specialize in forensic psychiatry but on several occasions had provided local police departments with tentative psychological profiles of serial thieves, rapists, and killers. Her predictions had, in most cases, proved remarkably prescient.

She was a wonderful woman, eighty at least although she would only admit to being "of a certain age." It was said she had been psychoanalyzed by Dr. Sigmund F. himself but I cannot vouch for that. She had outlived two husbands and three children but her grandchildren and great-grandchildren were her joy. She had absolutely no intention of retiring, and why on earth should she, since her mind was twice as nimble as shrinks half her age.

After making her acquaintance I had mentioned her acumen to my father and several times he had recommended her to clients or the relatives and friends of clients in need of psychiatric counseling, always with satisfactory results. The woman really was a blessing and it was she I intended to consult as soon as possible. Not in regard to my own shortcomings, I assure you; they're incurable.

I called her office at ten o'clock and, as usual, she answered the phone herself.

"Dr. Pearlberg," she said in her raspy voice. She has, I regret to report, a two-pack-a-day habit.

"Dr. Gussie," I said, "this is Archy McNally."

"Bubeleh!" she cried. "You have been neglecting me shamefully, you naughty boy."

"I have," I admitted, "and I apologize. How is your health, dear?"

"I am alive," she said, "and so my health is excellent. And you? Your family?"

"All in the pink," I assured her. "Doctor, when may I see you?"

"Personal?"

"Not me," I protested. "I'm the most normal and well-adjusted of men."

She coughed a laugh. "Let's just say you've come to terms with your madness. So it's professional?"

"Yes. One of my discreet inquiries. To be billed to McNally and Son. Can you fit me in?"

"I have a cancellation this morning at noon. You can make it?"

"Of course I can and shall with great pleasure. The couch won't be necessary."

She laughed again in her rattly voice. "Don't be so sure, bubeleh. Remember: The older the violin, the sweeter the music."

I had plenty of time to stop at a gourmet bakery and buy a pound of raspberry rugalach, which I knew Dr. Gussie dearly loved. Then I pointed the Miata's nose southward. It was a day designed for convertibles, for the sky was unblemished and a ten-knot breeze smelled faintly of salt. I don't remember singing but if I did, it was probably "It's a Most Unusual Day." Or it might have been "I've Got a Lovely Bunch of Coconuts."

The psychiatrist's office in Lantana always reminded me of the New York aphorism: "If I had my life to live over again, I'd like to live it over a delicatessen." Not that Dr. Pearlberg worked over a deli, but her second-floor office was atop an antique shop. Rather fitting, wouldn't you say, since they were both dealing with the past.

In fact, her office might have been furnished by her downstairs neighbor. It was all flocked wallpaper, dusty velvet drapes, lumpy brown furniture, and a couch covered with what appeared to be crackled black horsehide. Dim diplomas hung on the walls and there were chipped plaster busts of Freud, Beethoven, and one I could not identify but which looked unaccountably like Zero Mostel.

The entire chamber resembled a photo of a Viennese psychiatrist's consulting room of the 1920s. Adding to this illusion was the light, for no matter what time of day I visited, the office seemed suffused with a sepia tone, everything gently faded. That room deserved to be preserved in an album, the way things were in the bygone.

"Bubeleh!" Dr. Pearlberg said, and, as was her wont, kissed the tip of a forefinger and pressed it against my cheek. "What a delight to see you again. How handsome you look!"

I proffered the box of pastries. She ripped it open immediately and popped one into her mouth, groaning with contentment. "Thank you, thank you, thank you," she said. "What a treat for a relic like me."

"Nonsense," I said. "Dr. Gussie, you're getting younger as I get older. Do you think that's fair?"

"What a scamp you are," she said, "fooling a fat bobbeh. Now sit down and light a cigarette so I can have one."

I did as she directed. I sat in a sagging armchair alongside her elephantine desk. We both lighted up, blowing plumes of smoke toward the stained ceiling.

"So?" she said. "What's the problem?"

"A client, who shall be nameless, thinks his life is being threatened. I believe his fear is justified."

I then described the three untoward acts to which Hiram Gottschalk had been subjected: the slashed photo, the mass card, the strangled bird. Dr. Pearlberg listened to my recital intently. She finished her cigarette and lighted another from the butt of the first.

She was a squatty woman, almost as broad as she was tall. Pillowy face. Her wig was a virulent orange and she did have a hazy but discernible mustache, neither of which bothered her or anyone else who knew and admired her. She may have looked like a granny but she had a mental prowess that made the rest of us feel like village idiots.

When I had concluded, she said, "I don't like it."

"Nor do I," I said, and told her that although I had only started

my investigation I had come to a preliminary conclusion: The
threat against our client came from a member of his staff or his
family.

"The family," she repeated, her harsh voice a mixture of scorn
and sadness. "Always the family."

"Doctor," I said, "regarding the three incidents I have described, can you discern any pattern?"

"Perhaps," she said. "Usually in cases of this nature there is a
progression from the subtle to the obvious. An acceleration of
disturbed passion. The slashing of the photograph of the client
and his deceased wife appears to be an attempt to destroy a happy
memory, demolish a remembered relationship. The posting of
the mass card with the client's name I interpret as a warning he
is in danger if he does not mend his ways. The third act, the
killing of his beloved bird, escalates the pressure. This, the bird
strangler is saying, will be your fate if you persist in doing what
you are now doing."

I sighed. "Not a happy prospect," I said. "In effect you're saying the client's death may be the only option left to his enemy."

"Yes, Archy," she said. "That is what I feel. The client has received no written or phoned threats?"

"No. None."

"Then there is little the police can do."

"But what can *I* do?" I said desperately.

"Do what you do best," she advised. "Pry. Meet everyone he's
connected with. Ask questions. Get to know them all. Then
come back and we'll talk again. This troubles me."

"Yes," I said. "Me, too."

I rose to depart but she grasped my arm, stared with those lucid
hazel eyes.

"Sonny, you haven't asked the most interesting thing."

I was startled. "Oh? What is it?"

"Is the psychopath responsible for these acts of aggression a man or a woman?"

I looked into those knowing eyes. "Which do you think, Dr. Gussie?"

"Either," she said. "Or both."

And I had to be content with that Delphic utterance.

I drove home in a mood somewhat less than gruntled. Dr. Pearlberg had told me little more than I had already suspected but her reaction to Mr. Gottschalk's predicament had raised my anxiety level. And I was grateful for her suggestion that the perpetrator might possibly be female. I am such a romantic cove I usually leap to the conclusion that practicers of viciousness are limited solely to the masculine sex. Alas, dear reader, 'tis not so. Consider the career of the charming lady who made lampshades of human skin during the Holocaust.

Ursi was puttering about the kitchen when I arrived. She was preparing a bouillabaisse for our dinner and if you could have bottled that fragrance your fortune would be made. Call it Eau d'Poisson and every trendsetter in the world would put dabs behind the earlobes.

She interrupted her labors long enough to construct a towering Dagwood for me. Thick slices of sour rye served as bookends, and the literature within included slices of smoked turkey, beefsteak tomato, and Bermuda onion: all with a healthy dollop of Ursi's homemade mayo containing a jolt of Dijon mustard. I carried this masterpiece up to my suite, silently giving thanks to John Montagu, 4th Earl of Sandwich. I also lugged two bottles of chilled Dos Equis.

I was seated at my desk, devouring my delayed lunch with eye-rolling rapture, when the damn phone shrilled. I was tempted to let it ring itself to smithereens, but then I imagined it could be an invitation to a social affair during which I might meet the current Girl of My Dreams who bore a remarkable resemblance to Theda Bara. No such luck. The caller was Binky Watrous.

"Archy," he said excitedly, "I got the job at Parrots Unlimited!"

"Delighted to hear it," I said, munching away.

"They hired me around noon and I started work immediately!"

"Excellent. And how are you getting along?"

"Wonderfully!"

"Meet everyone?"

"Uh-huh. Archy," he added soulfully, "I'm in love."

"Oh?" I said. "Which parrot?"

"No, no. It's Bridget Houlihan."

"Ah," I said. "The Hibernian crumpet. Fancy her, do you?"

"She's such a marvelous female," he enthused. "Sweet and charming. And talented. She plays the tambourine."

"Binky," I said, "I'm not sure one can *play* a tambourine. Don't you just shake it or bang it? I mean Brahms never wrote a lullaby for tambourine, did he?"

"Oh, you can play it," he said with great certainty. "Bridget and I are thinking of getting up an act. I'll do my birdcalls while she accompanies me on her tambourine."

I hastily finished my first beer. For some unexplainable reason I recalled the comment of a Hollywood wit who remarked on the natural affinity between Rin-Tin-Tin and Helen Twelvetrees. In my relationship with Binky I seemed to be playing the actress. But I resolutely put this nuttiness from my mind.

"What about the other employees?" I asked him.

"There are two clerks in addition to Bridget. Young kids. Boy and girl. Tony Sutcliffe and Emma Gompertz. I think they may have a thing going."

"Cohabiting?" I suggested.

"What does that mean?"

"Living together."

"Like me and the Duchess?"

"Not quite. Living together as husband and wife."

"Oh," he said. "Well, yes, they may be cohabiting. Did you ever cohabit, Archy?"

"No," I said.

"I did," he said. "Once. For a weekend in Glasgow."

"What on earth were you doing in Glasgow?"

"Cohabiting. And drinking Glenlivet."

"Binky," I said, sighing, "can we get back to business? What about the manager?"

"Ricardo Chrisling? A very slick character."

"Slick? In what sense? Slippery?"

"Oh no, I wouldn't say that. More like sleek—you know? Hair carefully brushed and shining. Silk suit and all that. Might even have a manicure."

"Handsome?"

"I suppose impressionable dolls might think so. I find him a bit on the gigoloish side."

"Smooth?" I suggested.

"Very smooth," Binky said. "Exceedingly smooth."

I asked him if employees had been invited to attend the party welcoming home Mr. Gottschalk's twin daughters.

"We have indeed," he said happily. "Even I, the most recent and lowliest of the peons. You'll be there?"

"Wouldn't miss it," I assured him. "Don't get hammered, Binky. Behave yourself."

"So I shall, old boy," he vowed. "I'll be the very soul of decorum. By the way, while I was being interviewed by the owner he told me the most amazing story about two macaws who prayed all the time. It seems this woman had bought—"

"Stop right there," I said. "He told me the same tale."

"Do you believe it, Archy?"

"Of course. Indubitably."

"I do too," he said. "It just proves what incredible creatures birds are. Equal or superior in intelligence to many humans."

"How right you are," I agreed. "Keep up the good work, Binky. See you at the bash tomorrow night."

We hung up and I hastened to add the names Tony Sutcliffe and Emma Gompertz to my journal before I forgot them. I doubted if this young couple had any connection with the threats against Hiram Gottschalk. But one never knows, do one?

Then I finished my lunch and because the radio and TV had warned about riptides I skipped my ocean swim that afternoon. I took a nap instead and slept fitfully, troubled by wild images: a black crow stalking into the shadows, a strangled mynah, a beady-eyed parrot condemning me to Hades.

I blamed the nightmarish snooze on the smoked turkey in my luncheon sandwich. All those damnable fowl seemed determined to make my life miserable. My discomfiture, I decided, was definitely for the birds.

6

Mr. Gottschalk had told me this party was to be informal, without swank, and so I dressed accordingly. I had recently purchased a lightweight wool sport jacket in a houndstooth check of olive, gold, and blue. Sounds rather citified, does it not? Dullsville in fact. But it had suede buttonholes. It's the details that seduce me.

I perked up my subdued jacket with a pink Lacoste and slacks of a lemonade shade. Plus loafers in a hellish vermilion. No socks. When I inspected the complete ensemble in the bathroom door mirror I decided the effect was twee but not too. The stodgy jacket marked me as a man of substance but the accoutrements proved I was capable of frivolity. Oh lordy, how we deceive ourselves.

The client's home was located in an upscale neighborhood of

Palm Beach which appeared to be a small territory inhabited solely by fanatic horticulturists. I mean, I have never in my life seen such a profusion of tropical foliage. It was like driving through a South Florida rain forest, and if I had heard the chattering of monkeys and the snorting of wild boars I wouldn't have been a bit surprised.

The Gottschalk manse was quite a sight. It had been built, I judged, in the 1930s as a Mediterranean-style villa. More recently, additions had been made that were more Lake Okeechobee than Mediterranean. There were two wings, a guest house, an enlarged garage. The original edifice had also been embellished with bays, turrets, a widow's walk, and a tall, battered cupola which seemed to have no reason for existence other than providing a comfort station for migrating fowl.

It was an eccentric dwelling and, I thought, probably suited the owner just fine.

There were several cars already parked in the slated driveway. One of the vehicles, I noted, was Binky Watrous's dinged 1970 Mercedes-Benz 280 SE cabriolet. Trust my loopy Dr. Watson to be early when free booze and tasty viands were available.

I entered into a brightly lighted interior, a circus of bustle, loud talk, hefty laughter, and the recorded voice of Tony Bennett singing "It Don't Mean a Thing." I was somewhat taken aback by this jollity only because I was privy to the grave problems of the host. The dichotomy was disturbing and I decided my wisest course was to dull my unease with a dram or two of suitably diluted ethanol at the earliest possible moment.

I had those two drams during a chaotic party. But my libations were minuscule—infinitesimal one might even say—and I assure you the McNally mental faculties were not hazed. I smiled, conversed, joked, and followed Dr. Gussie Pearlberg's instructions to pry, ask questions, get to know them all.

It was a kaleidoscopic evening and I shall not attempt to give it a linear or temporal sequence.

I was standing at their modest bar, adding a bit of aqua to my 80-proof, when I felt a light touch on my shoulder. I turned to face a smiling woman, mature, stalwart, and not much shorter than I. She was quite dark: tanned complexion, jetty hair, black eyebrows that looked as if they had been squeezed from tubes.

"Good evening!" she said in a hearty contralto voice. "I'm Yvonne Chrisling, Mr. Gottschalk's housekeeper. And you?"

"Archy McNally, representing McNally and Son, attorneys-at-law. I'm the Son."

"Of course," she said, offering a hand. "So nice of you to come."

"So nice of you to invite me." Her handclasp was dry and surprisingly strong. "You have a lovely home, and it appears to be a joyous party."

She laughed. "Well, thank you. The occasion is to welcome the girls home from Europe. As for our home, I'm afraid it may seem somewhat, ah . . . ."

"Disheveled?" I suggested.

She laughed again, a throaty sound. "Exactly. You do have a way with words, Mr. McNally."

"Archy," I said. "And may I call you Yvonne?"

"Of course. Everyone does."

"Now that we have a first-name relationship, may I ask a personal question?"

Her face didn't freeze but I did detect a sudden wariness. "Ask away," she said.

"I know the manager of Parrots Unlimited is Ricardo Chrisling. Your son?"

"Stepson," she said rather stiffly. "By my husband who is now deceased. Do enjoy yourself, Archy, and don't forget the buffet. We don't want you going home hungry."

She gave me a nothing smile and moved away. She was wearing a very chaste long black skirt and severely tailored jacket. Her costume reminded me of a uniform: something a keeper in an institution might wear. "*Und* you *vill* obey orders!" Silly, I admit, but that was my impression.

Wandering about, glass in hand, I found Binky Watrous and Bridget Houlihan seated close together on a tattered velvet love seat. They were gazing into each other's eyes with a look so moony I wanted to kick both of them in the shins.

"Hi, kids," I said, and they looked up, startled.

"Oh," Binky said finally. "Hello, Archy. Have you met Bridget?"

"I have indeed," I said. "Good evening, Bridget."

"The same," she said dreamily, not releasing Binky's paw. "Honey, do the call of the cuckoo again."

I hastily departed.

I found the host putting another LP on his player and was happy he had not switched to CDs, which are too electronically perfect for me. I cherish those scratches and squawks of old vinyls. Mr. Gottschalk was about to place the needle on an original cast recording of *Guys and Dolls*.

"Excellent choice, sir." I said.

He looked up. "Hello, Archy. Glad you could make it. Enjoying yourself?"

"Immeasurably."

"Like old recordings, do you?"

"Very much."

He paused to stare dimly into the distance. "I do too. And so did my dear wife. On our tenth anniversary she gave me an ancient shellac of Caruso signing '*Vesti la giubba.*' "

"What a treasure!" I said. "Do you still have it?"

He gave me a queer look. "I don't know what happened to it. I'll try to find it."

The record started and I listened happily to "Fugue for Tinhorns." Hi lowered the volume and turned to me. "Have you met my daughters?"

"Not yet. How shall I tell them apart?"

"Very difficult. But one of them has a mole, a small, black mole."

"Oh?" I said. "Which one—Judith or Julia?"

He grinned mischievously. "I'm not allowed to tell."

"Well, where is this small, black mole located?"

His grin broadened and he tugged at his Vandyke. "You're an investigator, aren't you?" he said. "Investigate and find out."

What an aging satyr he was!

The buffet was really nothing extraordinary: a spiral-cut ham, cocktail franks in pastry cozies, chilled shrimp, crudités, cheese of no particular distinction, onion rolls a bit on the spongy side, and, for dessert, petits fours I suspected had been stamped out in a robotized Taiwan factory.

There was, however, one dish I sampled and found blindly delicious. Cold cubes of *something* in a yummy sauce. At first I thought it might be filet mignon, but it lacked the meat's texture. I ate more, entranced by the flavor and subtle aftertaste. Finally, determined to identify this wonder, I found my way into the Gottschalks' kitchen.

There I met a plumpish couple identified in Hiram's list of his staff as Mr. Got Lee, chef, and his wife, Mei, who apparently functioned as a maid of all work. They were wearing matching skullcaps of linen decorated with beads and sequins, and I've never encountered more scrutable Orientals in my life. Both giggled continually; they either enjoyed high spirits or had been hitting a gallon jug of rice wine.

I introduced myself and we all shook hands enthusiastically.

"Ver' happy," Got said in a lilting voice.

"Ver' ver' happy," Mei said, topping him.

"My pleasure," I assured them. "You have prepared a marvelous party."

They both bowed and I was treated to another chorus of "ver' happy's" interspersed with giggles.

"Tell me," I said, "what is that excellent cold dish in a spicy sauce? It tastes somewhat like broiled steak but I'm sure it's not. What on earth is it?"

More giggles and a lengthy explanation in English so strangled I could scarcely follow it. The treat turned out to be thick chunks of portobello mushrooms grilled with seasoning, cooled, and then marinated in lots of swell stuff for an hour and served chilled.

"Well, it's wonderful," I told them, and they beamed. "You enjoy working here, do you?"

The beams faded and they looked at each other.

"Ver' happy," Got said.

"Ver' ver' happy," Mei said.

But the lilt was gone from their voices. The giggles had vanished. They were not, I decided, quite as scrutable as I had first thought.

I was heading for the bar to refill my empty glass, since the contents had unaccountably evaporated. Ahead of me was a trig young man pouring himself a pony of Frangelico.

"Wise choice," I remarked.

He turned to look at me. "I think so," he said, with emphasis on the "I."

"Archy McNally," I said, proffering a hand. "I represent McNally and Son, Mr. Gottschalk's attorneys."

"Oh?" he said, and gave me a brief, rather limp handshake. "I'm Ricardo Chrisling. I manage Parrots Unlimited."

I had already guessed since he was everything Binky Watrous had described: handsome, sleek, possibly "gigoloish." Binky had been accurate but he had not caught the lad's finickiness: every shining hair in place, a shave I could never hope to equal, the three points of his jacket pocket handkerchief as precise and sharp as sword points. I wondered if the soles of his shoes were polished and the laces ironed.

I must confess my description of Ricardo Chrisling might be tainted by envy. He was, after all, about ten years younger than I and closely resembled Rodolfo Alfonzo Rafaelo Pierre Filibert Guglielmi di Valentina d'Antonguolla, a/k/a Rudolph Valentino. I mean he was a *beautiful* man, features crisp and evocative. He really should have been out in Hollywood filming *The Return of the Sheik* instead of futzing around with parrots.

"Nice party," I observed.

"Isn't it?" he said rather coldly. I didn't think he was much interested in me. And why should he be? I wasn't a female. "Meeting everyone?" he said casually.

"Gradually," I said. "I haven't yet come upon the guests of honor."

"The twins?" he said. "You will. They're not shy."

I didn't know how to interpret that. "How does one tell them apart?" I asked.

"One doesn't," he said, gave me a bloodless smile, and moved away.

He left me with the feeling he considered me a harmless duffer of no importance. That suited me. I didn't want anyone in that household to suspect I was a keen-eyed beagle tracking a miscreant threatening the life of the lord of the manor.

There were other guests in addition to Mr. Gottschalk's immediate entourage. There must have been twenty or thirty—friends, neighbors, business acquaintances—and I found them an odd but pleasant lot, all eating and drinking up a storm.

I met Yvonne Chrisling's masseuse, the Got Lees' greengrocer, a morose Peruvian who was apparently a parrot wholesaler, and one shy chap, barely articulate, who appeared awed by his surroundings. He finally admitted he mowed Mr. Gottschalk's lawn and this was the first time he had been inside the house. We had a drink together and got along famously because this seemingly inarticulate fellow could sing "Super-cali-fragil-istic-expi-ali-docious." I can't even pronounce it.

I also introduced myself to the young clerks from Parrots Unlimited—Emma Gompertz and Tony Sutcliffe—the twosome Binky Watrous reported had a "thing" going and might possibly be cohabiting. They appeared to be an innocuous couple, agreeable and polite, but really not much aware of anyone but each other. Their behavior—hand holding and dreamy stares—was remarkably akin to Binky's conduct with Bridget Houlihan.

Romance was rife that night, positively *rife*.

I finally spotted the twins, Judith and Julia Gottschalk. I then experienced a moment of panic, fearing I was suffering an attack of double vision.

Nothing of the sort of course. They were simply twins but so alike one could only marvel at their oneness. They were, I guessed, in their early thirties. Both had deep brown eyes and brown hair with russet glints, cut quite short. They were dressed differently, one in a silk pantsuit, the other in short leather skirt and fringed buckskin jacket. I suspected they shared a common wardrobe; their physical proportions seemed identical.

They were chatting animatedly with each other and I wondered if twins ever became weary of their mirror images. They certainly didn't seem bored at the moment, for they laughed frequently, occasionally leaned close to whisper, and once shook hands as if sealing a private pact. I thought them enormously attractive young ladies and hastened to join them.

"Welcome home!" I said heartily, giving them my Jumbocharmer smile for I felt they were mature enough to withstand it.

"Thank you," they said in unison, and Pantsuit asked, "And who might you be?"

"I might be Ivan the Terrible," I said, "but I am not. My name is Archy McNally, and I work for your father's attorneys."

"You're a lawyer?"

"Not quite. More of a para-paralegal. And you are . . . ?"

"Judith," she said. "I think." She turned to her twin. "Am I Judith, darling?"

"I thought you were this morning," Leather Skirt said. "But now I'm not so sure. You may be Julia."

"Which would make you Judith."

"I suppose. But I can't be certain. I don't *feel* like Judith."

Both looked at me with wide-eyed innocence. I realized this was a routine that amused them greatly and they used frequently to befuddle new acquaintances. They obviously had inherited their father's quirky sense of humor.

"I think I have a solution to this difficult problem," I said. "Suppose I address each of you as Mike. Won't that make things a lot simpler?"

Both clapped their hands delightedly and gave me elfin grins.

"Well done," Pantsuit said.

"Good show," Leather Skirt said. "I love the idea of us both being Mike."

Their voices were identical in pitch and timbre.

Pantsuit stared at me reflectively. "Archy McNally," she repeated. "We've heard that name before. Are you a member of the Pelican Club?"

"I am indeed."

"Peter has mentioned you. We've never been there, have we, Mike?"

"Never, Mike," her sibling said. "Take us there to lunch, Archy."

"I'll be delighted. When?"

"Tomorrow. Is twelve-thirty okay?"

"Twelve-thirty is perfect."

"How should we dress?" Leather Skirt asked.

"Informally. Laid-back. Funky. Whatever."

"That's cool," Pantsuit said.

"You know how to find it?"

"We'll ask Peter. Thank you for the invite, Archy."

Mike #1 leaned forward suddenly to kiss me briefly on the lips. Her buss was sweet and tangy as a Vidalia onion. Ah-ha! Now,

I reckoned, I'd be able to tell them apart. But then Mike #2 duplicated her sister's action. Her kiss was sweet and tangy as a Vidalia onion.

Archibald McNally, the master criminologist, flummoxed again.

7

GUESTS BEGAN LEAVING an hour before midnight. I looked about for Binky Watrous and his Celtic knish but they had already departed. I decided it was time to make my adieus and sought the host to thank him for a pleasant evening. But Hiram was nowhere to be found and so I delivered my farewell to Yvonne Chrisling.

She was in a more relaxed mood than at our initial meeting. At least her handclasp was warm and she seemed reluctant to release me.

"Thank you so much," I said. "It was a lovely party."

"It was sweet of you to come," she said. "I'm glad you had a good time and I hope you'll visit again. Did you meet the twins?"

"I surely did."

"And what did you think of them, Archy?"

"Very personable," I said carefully.

She gave me a cryptic smile. "They're not as scatterbrained as many people think. Quite the contrary."

Then she turned away to exchange good-byes with other guests, giving me no opportunity to ask what she meant by her last oblique comment.

I exited into a sultry night, the air close and redolent of all that gross vegetation. I found my Miata and there, lolling in the passenger's bucket, feet up on the dash, was Peter Gottschalk. He was smoking something acrid and I hoped it might be tobacco.

"Good evening," I said as calmly as I could. I do not appreciate my pride and joy being occupied without my permission, especially by irrational acquaintances.

He patted the door. "Nice heap," he said.

"It is," I agreed. "And now I intend to drive it home. By myself. Alone."

It didn't register. I wasn't certain he heard what I said.

"How was the party?" he asked.

"Very enjoyable."

"Bloody bore," he contradicted me. "I cut out fast. All those phonies."

I was standing alongside the passenger door wondering if I would be forced to drag him out by the scruff. But his last denouncement intrigued me.

"Phonies?" I repeated. "You're referring to the guests?"

His laugh was more of a snort. "I don't even *know* all those stupid guests. I'm talking about the family and staff. Hypocrites, every one of them."

"Surely not your father."

"Him, too," he said bitterly. "Maybe the worst. They think I don't know what's going on. I know damned well what's going on." He suddenly straightened and flicked away the butt of his cigarette. "Hey, let's you and me make a night of it. We'll go to the Pelican first for a couple of whacks and then take it from there."

"Some other time," I told him. "I'm getting audited by the IRS in the morning so I better get a good night's sleep."

I was afraid he might flare but he accepted the rejection equably. I suspected he was accustomed to rejection.

He climbed out of the car and stood on the slated driveway, swaying gently. He was a thin, almost gaunt chap with hollow cheeks, sunken eyes. His hair was a mess and it was obvious he hadn't shaved for at least two days. But he was decently dressed in denim jeans and jacket. A cleaner T-shirt would have helped, but you did not expect to find him sleeping in a cardboard carton under a bridge. I mean he was reasonably presentable if you didn't gaze too intently into those stricken eyes.

"Now I feel great," he declared. "Just great."

"Glad to hear it," I said.

"Maybe I'll cop the old man's car and make a run to the Pelican Club myself."

"Don't you have your own wheels?" I asked.

"Nah. They grounded me. And took away my license," he added.

I wanted to warn him, but what was the use? He'd never listen to me. I doubted if he'd listen to anyone.

"See you around," he said lightly, and went dancing off into the darkness.

I drove home slowly in a weighty mood. The evening had left me with a jumble of impressions. It resembled one of those Picasso paintings in which all the figures seem to have six limbs and three eyes. And you view them frontally and in profile simultaneously. A puzzlement.

It was still relatively early when I arrived at my very own mini-abode. I could have spent an hour or so recording the evening's events in my journal but I needed to sort out a plethora of reactions and try to find significance in what I had seen and heard. I disrobed and treated myself to a small marc and an English Oval to aid my ruminations.

After thirty minutes of heavy-duty brooding the only preliminary conclusion I arrived at was that when it came to dysfunctional families the Gottschalks were candidates for world-class ranking. It was a hypothesis given confirmation when my phone rang shortly before I retired.

"Archy?" the caller asked, and I recognized Hiram Gottschalk's dry, twangy voice.

"Yes, Hi," I said. "I tried to find you to offer thanks for a delightful evening but I couldn't locate you."

"You know that Caruso record I told you about. The one my dear wife gave me on our tenth anniversary."

"Yes, sir, I remember. The old shellac of Enrico singing *'Vesti la guibba.'* "

"After I mentioned it to you I was bothered because I couldn't remember where I had put it. So I went searching. I finally found it about ten minutes ago. Someone smashed it. Now it's just junk."

"I'm sorry," I said softly.

"That record meant a lot to me. A gift from the woman I loved."

"I understand, Hi," I said. "Would you like me to come over now and we'll talk about it?"

"No, no," he said. "Thank you but that won't be necessary. I just thought you should know."

"Of course. Hi, I don't wish to be an alarmist but you should be prepared to find yourself a victim of similar acts of terrorism or viciousness before I can discover who is responsible."

"You think you can find out?"

"Absolutely," I said stoutly. There are some situations demanding unbridled confidence with all dubiety ignored. This was one of them.

"Thank you, Archy," he said gratefully. "You make me feel a lot better."

I went to bed that night wondering if the future would prove me Sir Galahad or Sir Schlemiel.

By the time I clumped downstairs on Thursday morning my parents had long since breakfasted. I found Jamie Olson sitting alone in the kitchen. He was sucking on his old briar (the stem wound with a Band-Aid) and clutching a mug of black coffee I was certain he had enlivened with a jolt of aquavit. His chaps were definitely fallen.

"What's wrong, Jamie?" I inquired.

"That damned raccoon again," he said indignantly. "Got the lids off both trash cans. Made a mess. I'm going to catch up with that beast one of these days and give him what for. You want some breakfast, Mr. Archy?"

"I'll make it. Anything left over?"

"A cold kipper."

"Sounds good to me. I'll toast a muffin and slide it in with a bit of mayo. Enough hot coffee?"

"Plenty."

I had a glass of V8 Picante, prepared my kipper sandwich, and poured a cup of inky caffeine. I sat across the table from our houseman.

"Jamie," I said, "ever hear of the Gottschalk family?"

The Olsons, our staff of two, are part of a loose confederacy of butlers, maids, chefs, housekeepers, valets, and servants of all species who minister to the needs of the wealthier residents of the Palm Beaches. Experience had taught me that this serving but by no means servile class knew a great many intimate details about the private lives of their employers. It was information they would never divulge except, occasionally, to others in their profession when a good laugh was wanted.

"Gottschalk?" Jamie repeated. "Nope. Never heard of them."

"They have a live-in Oriental couple, Got and Mei Lee, chef and maid. Do you know anyone who might be acquainted?"

He relighted his charred pipe. My father also smokes a pipe. His tobacco is fragrant. Jamie's is not.

"Mebbe," he said finally. "I know Eddie Wong, a nice fellow. He buttles for old Mrs. Carrey in West Palm. You want I should ask Eddie if he knows—what's their names?"

"Got and Mei Lee. Yes, please ask him. I'd like to know if the Gottschalks have a happy home. And if not, why not."

Jamie nodded. "I'll ask."

Before I left for the office I slipped him a tenner. Pop would be outraged, I knew, since the Olsons were more than adequately recompensed for keeping the McNally ship on an even keel. But I didn't feel their salaries included Jamie's personal assistance to yrs. truly in my discreet inquiries. Hence my pourboire for his efforts above and beyond the call of duty.

I had two messages awaiting me when I arrived at my cul-de-sac in the McNally Building. I answered Sgt. Al Rogoff's call first.

"Heavens to Betsy," he said. "You're at work so early? Why, it's scarcely eleven o'clock."

"I do work at home, you know," I replied haughtily. "Sometimes with great concentration for long hours."

"You also sleep at home. Sometimes with great concentration for long hours. But enough of this idle chitchat. You know a guy named Peter Gottschalk?"

I hesitated for a beat, then: "Yes, I know Peter. Distantly. He's a member of the Pelican Club."

"That figures. Is he off-the-wall?"

"I really couldn't say. From what I've heard, he's been known to act occasionally in an outré fashion."

"Outré," Rogoff repeated. "Love the way you talk."

"Why are you asking about Peter Gottschalk?"

"Because early this morning, about two or three, he outréd his father's car into an abutment on an overpass out west."

"Holy moly. Anyone hurt?"

"Nah. He didn't hit anyone. Just plowed into the concrete doing about fifty. All he got were a few bruises and scratches. God protects fools and drunks—which makes you doubly blessed."

"What about the car?"

"Totaled. A new Cadillac Eldorado. His blood test showed alcohol a little above the legal limit. Nothing definite on drugs. Maybe he just fell asleep."

"Maybe," I said, not believing it for a minute.

"Uh-huh. Archy, the guy doesn't have any suicidal tendencies, does he?"

I swallowed. Sgt. Rogoff is no dummy. Trust him to come up with an explanation for Peter's accident that matched my own.

"Not to my knowledge, Al," I said faintly.

"Well, his license has been pulled but he didn't hurt anyone and his father isn't preferring charges, so we're squashing the whole thing. But I think the kid needs help."

"Could be," I said cautiously, and that was the end of our conversation.

I sat there a moment, shuddering to think of what might have happened but didn't. I wondered just how long Peter Gottschalk could go his mindless way depending on God's mercy. Not too long, I reckoned. Ask any gambler and he'll tell you there's one sure thing about luck: it always changes.

Since I'm firmly convinced life is half tragedy and half farce,

I decided I needed a bit of the farcical and so I answered the second message. It was from Binky Watrous, my very own harlequin.

"Why aren't you at work?" I demanded.

"Because I clean cages only four days a week," he explained. "Hey, Archy, I like that job."

"And the fringe benefits, no doubt. Super party last night, wasn't it?"

"I guess. Bridget enjoyed it."

"Oh-oh," I said. "Do I detect a slight note of discord?"

"Well, that's why I called. Bridget wants to get married."

"To whom?"

"To me," Binky said gloomily.

"Congratulations."

"Archy, I don't know what to do and I need your advice. I am smitten but do you think a man can be satisfied with one woman?"

"At a time?" I said. "Surely."

"No, no. I mean one woman, the same woman, forever and ever."

"Ah, now you're entering the realm of philosophy—if not cosmology."

"I suppose," he said. "I was never much good at that sort of thing."

"Think about it, Binky," I advised, "before you come to any decision." I knew full well that urging this dweeb to think was similar to cheering on a three-toed sloth in a decathlon. "First of all you must consider if you are financially able to provide for a wife and perhaps eventually a family on the income from tidying up parrot cages."

"Yes," he said, "that is a problem, isn't it? I don't know how the Duchess would react to my getting hitched. She might even turn off the cash faucet. That would hurt. I've got to rack the old brain about this, Archy."

"Do that," I said. "But don't forget the only reason you're working at Parrots Unlimited is to assist me in a discreet inquiry."

"What?" he said. "Oh. Sure. I remember."

"For the nonce, I'd like you to concentrate your snooping on Ricardo Chrisling. That handsome lad interests me. See if you can find out where he lives and with whom, if anyone. Does he have a consenting adult companion, or does he play the field? Any unusual habits or predilections? I want you to provide a complete dossier on Ricardo. I suspect he may be more than just another pretty face. Find out."

"Listen, Archy," my henchman said distractedly, "do you think it's really necessary I marry Bridget? I mean, couldn't we, you know, uh, what's that word?"

"Cohabit?" I suggested.

"Yes!" he said eagerly. "Couldn't we cohabitize?"

I groaned and hung up. If I were a cat Binky would be a hair ball.

8

I HAD DRESSED WITH special care that morning, preparing for my luncheon with the Gottschalk sisters. I hoped they might be impressed by careless elegance, so in addition to a silver-gray jacket of Ultrasuede, black silk slacks, and a faded blue denim shirt I sported an ascot in a Pucci print and used a four-in-hand as a belt, à la Fred Astaire. No socks of course.

I had suggested the twins dress informally and so they did: one in a rumpled suit of white sailcloth, the other in a magenta leotard under a gauzy blouse and open skirt. They looked smart enough but I had the impression they were dressing down and their garments had been adapted from street styles by frightfully pricey French designers. They were wearing trendy costumes as foreign to their taste and nature as the sari.

The arrival of these two lovely look-alikes at the Pelican Club occasioned startled reactions from members in the bar area. Even Priscilla in the dining room was so surprised by the entry of doubles she tempered her sassy impudence and treated us with solicitous politesse. I imagined the sisters were accustomed to the stir their appearance caused and took it casually as their due.

I wish I could describe our luncheon in lip-smacking detail but I confess my remembrances are vague. My recollections are hazy since all my attention was concentrated on how they looked, what they said, and trying to follow Dr. Gussie Pearlberg's injunction to pry and ask questions.

Mike #1 swung about to examine our surroundings. "Rather grotty, don't you think?" she asked her sibling.

"Yes but comfortably so," Mike #2 replied, and they both gave me pixieish grins.

They surely must have noted my discomfiture, for I truly believe the Pelican to be the ne plus ultra of all private clubs in the Palm Beach area. Grotty, yes. Raffish, undoubtedly. Unconventionally stylish, true. But where else could I leap upon a table late Saturday night and attempt to sing "Volare"?

"Archy," one of the sisters said, "this game has gone on long enough and we've decided to come clean with you. I'm Julia."

She was wearing the sailcloth suit.

"And I'm Judith," the other said.

She was wearing the magenta leotard.

They both looked at me as if expecting gratitude.

I dimly recall we were drinking Kir Royales at the time. And I definitely remember their stares of wide-eyed innocence. I didn't totally believe them or totally disbelieve them. I was willing to suspend judgment since I had an ace in the hole or rather—from what Hiram Gottschalk had revealed—a mole in the hole.

"Julia and Judith," I repeated, nodding to each in turn. "Yes, that does simplify things, and I thank you for your confidence in me. I swear I won't tell a soul."

"Tell them what?" Julia asked.

"Which of you is which."

"And how could you possibly do that?" Judith asked.

This was, I believe, my first indication that I was not dealing with bubbleheads and that these two females had more than lint between their ears.

I sighed. "You have a point," I admitted. "Which means every time the three of us meet you must identify yourselves again. What a drag! Couldn't one of you agree to a small tattoo? Perhaps the symbol of pi engraved on one earlobe."

They stared at each other, then stared at me.

"Are you completely insane?" Judith demanded.

"He is," Julia said. "Absolutely bonkers."

I believe at the moment we were working on an enormous seafood salad and demolishing a bottle of sauvignon blanc.

"Happy to be home from Europe?" I asked. "Or devastated?"

"We had a marvelous time," Julia said. "But we're glad to be back. Aren't we, Judy?"

"Oh yes. Definitely. Daddy needs us."

It was at that exact point the tenor of our conversation changed. Up to then it had been breezy silliness, a lighthearted exchange of nonsense. But Judith's comment, "Daddy needs us," signaled a switch of gears. I began to wonder if this luncheon had been requested with a motive other than to examine the flora and fauna of the Pelican Club.

"I'm sure your father was happy to see you return safely," I said, deciding to let them reveal what they obviously intended with no urging from yrs. truly.

It came out with a rush.

Julia: "He worries us."

Judith: "He's acting so strangely."

Julia: "He thinks his personal possessions have been stolen when he's probably just misplaced them."

Judith: "He's convinced there's some kind of a crazy plot against him."

Julia: "But he's not senile."

Judith: "Oh no, nothing like that. Just these absurd notions."

Then they looked at me as if I might be Dr. Kildare ready to deliver an instant and perceptive diagnosis.

"You feel all his fears are delusions?" I asked.

"Oh, absolutely," Julia said.

"No doubt about it," Judith added.

"It could be quite innocent, you know," I said. "Your father is getting along in years and many older people suffer from short-term memory loss. But he seems to be functioning admirably as an efficient and successful businessman. Surely you don't think he needs professional help."

"Oh no," Judith said.

"Definitely no," Julia said. "He's not that bad. Yet. But because you represent his attorney we thought you should be told of how irrationally he's been acting lately."

"Oh yes," Judith said. "Quite irrational."

"Could you give me some specifics?"

"He thinks someone in the house destroyed an old photograph of him and mother."

"And most recently he claims someone broke an ancient phonograph record he treasured."

"I admit they don't sound like much," Judith said, "but they worry us."

"And he thinks someone killed our mynah," Julia put in. "Poor Dicky died a natural death but daddy won't admit it."

"I see," I said, although I really didn't. Not then.

"Well anyway," Judith said with a brave smile, "we thought you should know."

"About the way he's been acting," Julia said. "So you might tell your father."

"I'll certainly do that," I promised, and thanked them for their revelation. They seemed satisfied they had accomplished what they had set out to do.

"If he does any more nutty things we'll let you know," Judith said.

"By all means do," I told them. "His actions may be a temporary aberration or may be an indication of a much more serious psychopathological condition." I said this with a straight face. Is there no limit to my dissembling?

The sisters looked at me with admiration. I had obviously reacted in the manner they had wished.

We finished luncheon and moved to the bar, where I introduced them to Mr. Simon Pettibone. If he was awed by meeting such comely twins it didn't interfere with his preparation of three excellent vodka stingers, enjoyed by one and all.

I then accompanied them out to the parking lot. They were driving a new pearlescent-blue Mercedes-Benz SL500 coupe. I looked at it in amazement.

"This incredible sloop is yours?" I asked, my founded being dumbed.

"It's ours," Julia said lightly. "We like to travel first-class."

"Nothing but the best," Judith said just as gaily.

I was the target of two identical kisses and then they were on their way. I watched them depart, trying to analyze my reaction.

Willie S. came to my aid as he so often does. He wrote: "Double, double, toil and trouble . . ."

I drove directly home. The McNally nous was astir and I was eager to bring my professional diary up to date. A great many things had occurred since the last entry and I knew it would take an afternoon of scribbling to record events, conversations, impressions, and conjectures. Surprisingly, the anticipation of this donkeywork didn't daunt me.

I worked determinedly for more than three hours, skipping my usual ocean swim. I finished my journalism in time to shower, change my duds, and join my parents for the family cocktail hour.

Father seemed in an expansive mood and I deemed it an opportune moment to bring up again a request I had made several times. The McNally household once had an additional member: a magnificent and noble-hearted golden retriever. Max had gone to the Great Kennel in the Sky but his doghouse still existed alongside mother's potting shed.

Since his demise I had suggested the McNally mini-estate would be enlivened by the patter of canine feet, but the only reaction I could extract from the Don was, "I'll think about it." Over martinis that evening I repeated my plea and added that a smart hound might assist Jamie Olson in locating the whereabouts of the rapacious raccoon raiding our trash cans.

"All right," father said unexpectedly. "Find a dog you like but don't buy until mother and I get a look at it."

"Yes, sir," I said happily. "I'll find a winner."

"Not a Chihuahua, Archy," mother said firmly. "They always look so *naked.*"

"Definitely not a Chihuahua," I promised.

Dinner that evening was far from haute cuisine but nonetheless enjoyable. We had a down-home feast of grilled turkey franks, baked beans with brown sugar, and heaps of sauerkraut

tinted with cumin. Cold ale, of course. Nothing fancy but lordy
it was delicious. Ursi Olson provided warmed frankfurter rolls
and a mustard from hell. You had to be there.

I plodded groggily upstairs after dinner and began reviewing
the notes I had jotted on the Gottschalk inquiry. My reading re-
sulted in no epiphanies but did indicate three areas I felt deserved
continued and intensified investigation. To wit:

1. Why was such a handsome and apparently sophisti-
cated chap as Ricardo Chrisling utterly without duende and
working in a parrot emporium? And what was his personal
relationship with his stepmother, the redoubtable Yvonne,
housekeeper of the Gottschalk ménage?

2. Why were the twins, Julia and Judith, so intent on
convincing me of the growing looniness of their father?
Were they correct, or did they have a veiled motive I wot
not of?

3. Was Peter Gottschalk so mentally and/or emotionally
disturbed that he might be the perpetrator of all the acts of
terrorism threatening his father?

I was musing on these puzzles and a few minor ones—such as
why Binky Watrous thought Johann Sebastian Bach was a dark
German beer—when the ringing of the phone roused me from
my reveries.

"Not one but *two!*" Consuela Garcia said accusingly.

Well, of course I knew she'd find out eventually—but so soon!
I knew it hadn't been Priscilla who tattled—she doesn't blab—
so it was probably one of Connie's many informants who was
present at the Pelican Club during my trialogue with the
Gottschalk twins.

"Connie," I said sternly (I can do stern), "those ladies are the daughters of one of McNally and Son's most valued clients. They requested a meeting to discuss personal family matters which I cannot and shall not reveal. But I assure you it was strictly a business conference."

"Including champagne cocktails, wine, and a stop at the bar afterward," she said darkly.

"I tried to be an accommodating host."

"Did you accommodate one by going home with her later? Or making plans for a cozy evening of three?"

"That is an unjust suggestion," I said hotly. "You are accusing me of behavior of which I am totally innocent."

"But you're thinking about it, buster," she said. "Aren't you?"

It infuriated me because, of course, it was true.

"I resent your unreasonable suspicions," I said, "and I refuse to endure them. I think you owe me an apology."

"It'll be a cold day in Key West when I apologize for thinking you're cheating on me or planning it."

"Your delusions are your problem. My conscience is clear."

"Like the Miami River," she said. "Don't call me; I'll call you—which may be *never!*" She hung up.

I replaced the phone with a quavery hand. Connie and I had engaged in many squabbles in the past, most of them concerning my real or imagined infidelities. But none had the virulence of our latest controversy, and it left me shaken.

It was such a complex enigma. I was honest in claiming I had not misbehaved with one or both of the Gottschalk twins and had no firm plans to do so. Connie was correct in divining that I had lust in my heart. But if males can be punished for their illicit fantasies, there aren't enough prisons in the world to hold us all.

When I went to bed that night I punched the pillow angrily

several times. It wasn't my light-o'-love Consuela Garcia I was striking. It was an ineffectual attack against sardonic, implacable destiny. Men are men and women are women, and never the twain shall meet.

Who said that? I did.

9

I WISH I COULD write Friday morn dawned bright and clear. Actually it dawned dull and murky with a sky resembling a sodden bath mat. The kind of day designed to convince one of the utter hopelessness of rising and facing life's demands.

But when duty's bugle sounds the charge, McNally is not found skulking. I resolutely completed the usual morning drill and arrived at my office less than an hour late after stopping at our cafeteria for a container of black coffee and two glazed doughnuts. My abstemious breakfast at home (one skimpy scone) hadn't dulled a hunger I feared might be the first indication of serious malnutrition.

I lighted an English Oval for added nourishment and phoned Lolly Spindrift.

"Lolly," I told him, "let me be perfectly frank."

He giggled. "Darling, I've known two Franks in my life and neither was perfect, believe me."

"Then let me be perfectly honest," I said. "I need to tap your inexhaustible reservoir of inside skinny but at the moment I have nothing to offer in return."

"The story of my life," he said, sighing. "All right, luv, what do you need?"

"Do you have anything on a dazzling bloke named Ricardo Chrisling?"

Brief pause. "No, I—wait half a mo. The name rings a distant bell. I know I don't have him in my personal file but let me dig into the paper's database."

I sipped my coffee, nibbled a doughnut, puffed my ciggie, and tried to relax while Lol made his computer search.

"Got him!" he said triumphantly. "Which proves the Spindrift total recall is not weakening. Probably due to those memory pills I pop every morning."

"Memory pills? What are they called?"

"I forget. Anyway, about a year ago there was an imbroglio at one of our local boîtes. A private party of six South American gents. Voices were raised, fists were brandished, and eventually a pistol was drawn and fired several times. When the police arrived one of the *sudamericanos* was dead, thoroughly riddled. Our reporter asked an investigating officer how the deceased had perished. 'From an excess of holes,' the cop said. Isn't that delightful? All the other partyers were questioned. One of them was your boy, Ricardo Chrisling. But apparently he wasn't held or charged—just questioned. That's all I've got."

"Thanks, Lolly," I said. "I owe you one."

"Keep it firmly in mind," he advised. "You know what happens to people who stiff me, don't you? I reveal their innermost secrets in print."

"Makes me shudder. I shall eventually pay my debt. I am, after all, a man of honor."

"Hah!" was all he said.

I hung up with the conviction I had been correct in deciding Monsieur Chrisling deserved intensive investigation. Not that attendance at a private party resulting in a homicide condemned him, but it did make one question the traits of his friends and associates. I have been present at many, many parties, as I'm sure you have, at which the waving of a pistol and the resulting ventilation of one of the guests would be considered bad form. I mean it's just not done, is it?

Part of my interest in Ricardo Chrisling, I reckoned, came from an innocent faith common to us all that beautiful people, women and men, possess natures as felicitous as their physical attractiveness. It always comes as a shock, does it not, when these gorgeous folk turn out to be wicked wretches.

In any event, I imagined that while Hiram Gottschalk was a client of McNally & Son, it was possible Ricardo Chrisling was a client of Skull & Duggery.

I was still musing on the role Ricardo might or might not be playing in the program of threats against Hiram when I received a phone call from Yvonne Chrisling. It made me wonder if it was mere coincidence or if I was being played as the schnook du jour by a gang of slyboots for reasons of which I was totally ignorant.

"Archy," she said in her brisk contralto, "Mr. Gottschalk and Ricardo are flying up to Orlando to attend a convention of exotic bird dealers. The twins are going to a charity dinner and one simply can't depend on Peter. So I fear I must dine alone, which always depresses me. I was hoping it might be possible for you to join me tonight. Short notice, I admit, but if you can make it I'd love to see you again."

"Delighted," I said without hesitation. "What time?"

"Seven-thirty?"

"I'll be there. Not formal I trust."

"No," she said, laughing, "definitely not formal. Thank you for responding to the plea of a lonely old lady."

We disconnected. Responding to the plea of a lonely old lady? And I am Richard Coeur de Lion. The Gottschalk party proved Yvonne had a plenitude of friends and neighbors she might have called in to assuage her alleged loneliness. But she had selected *moi*. Even my gargantuan ego could not accept that. It wasn't my ineluctable charm, tousled locks, or Obsession cologne that inspired her invitation; Madam Machiavelli had a dark motive for wishing to feed my face.

Doodle was flapping at the Chez Gottschalk.

I spent the next hour scanning ads in the Yellow Pages and phoning kennels and pet shops requesting information on how I might acquire a canine of pleasing disposition but with an inborn prejudice against marauding raccoons. I discovered I could purchase any breed, ranging from Afghan to Rottweiler, which met my requirements. And all, I was told, were purebreds possessing AKC diplomas.

Finally it occurred to me a purebred wasn't absolutely necessary. I mean I'm not a purebred. Are you? So then I called a few charity pounds offering stray, lost, and cast-off dogs for adoption. They weren't selling their boarders but asking for a contribution. They assured me the would-be adoptees were healthy, with all the proper inoculations. I selected one particular shelter to visit only because the young lady who answered my queries sounded exactly like Jean Arthur.

The pound, a mile or two west of I-95, turned out to be a reasonably clean establishment devoted only to finding homes for vagrant dogs; no cats, rabbits, monkeys, snakes, or gerbils need apply. The husky-voiced lady I had spoken to on the phone turned out to be a bit older than I had anticipated but quite attractive in a healthy outdoorsy way. She had a bronzy suntan (her nose was peeling) and wore a rumpled khaki safari suit: jacket and shorts. Her bare legs were muscled and magnificent. We investigators are trained to observe such things.

She introduced herself as June August—which made me hope her middle name might be July. We got along famously. She led me down row after row of cages, all mercifully shielded from sun and rain, and pointed out the fenced area where her tenants were taken for a run or a frolic. There was a lot of barking, yapping, and howling going on but the decibel rate didn't seem to disturb June.

"Where have they all come from?" I asked her.

"Some are runaways," she said. "Or just lost. Some were deserted by owners who relocated. A few are brought in by young couples who can't handle a big dog anymore because they have a new baby. Sometimes they're dropped off by old people who are going into a hospital or nursing home. They cry. It's very sad. Listen, my partner is off today and I want to stay close to the phone. Why don't you just look about and see if you can find the hound of your dreams."

She flashed me a toothy smile and strode back to the ramshackle office. I did as she suggested and wandered down the rows of cages inspecting the inhabitants. I reckoned there were few purebreds present, if any, but all the mutts seemed in good health, with clear eyes and glossy coats.

As I came close I was occasionally snarled or growled at, but most of the dogs reacted as if they were delighted to see me. They jumped up against their cage doors yipping or, once or twice, whimpering piteously. I interpreted this behavior as the "Take me! Take me!" syndrome you've probably noticed if you ever looked at a pack of eager puppies in a pet shop window.

There was one fellow who caught my eye. He wasn't making any noise but as I passed slowly by he grinned at me. You think animals can't grin? Nonsense. Dogs grin, cats grin, dolphins grin, and as for chimps—gold medal grinners.

I completed a tour of the occupied cages and returned for another look at the peaceable one. He was still sitting on his haunches, apparently content with the world and his fate. I looked at him and he looked at me. A mixed breed, no doubt about it, but I thought he might have a lot of Jack Russell in him. Definitely a terrier type, with dark brown ears and head, white muzzle, chest, and legs, and dark brown patches on his short-haired back suggesting a map of the British Isles.

"Good afternoon, sir," I said to him politely. "Enjoying life, are you?"

He yawned.

I was still marveling at his aplomb when June August came up and laughed. "You found Hobo, did you?" she said.

"Is that his name—Hobo?"

"That's what we call him. State troopers picked him up trotting north along I-ninety-five."

"Probably heading for the Westminster Kennel Club show in New York. No one advertised his loss or distributed fliers?"

"Not to our knowledge, and we always check those things."

"How old do you guess him to be?"

"The vet we use estimates two to three years. Not a pup but not full-grown either. The vet says he probably won't get much taller or longer but he'll fill out through the chest and shoulders."

"Fixed?" I asked.

"Oh yes, he's been neutered."

"No wonder he looks so content. Would you object if I asked you to let him out so I may see how he moves?"

"Not at all. We'll take him to the run."

She began to unlatch the cage door, and I said, "Won't you need a collar and leash?"

"Nah," she said. "Not for Hobo. He's a perfect gentleman."

Cage opened, the dog jumped down onto the ground and enjoyed a slow, languorous stretch. June and I headed for the fenced exercise enclosure and he came along. He didn't precede us or follow but trotted alongside as an equal. I thought he moved smoothly with no sign of an infirmity. His head was up and his trot was almost a bounce. A very pert hound.

Once inside the fence, he paused to look up at the leaden sky, apparently decided it was of no interest—which it wasn't—and began to wander about sniffing at the sand and at spots where other dogs had marked their territory. He moved nimbly and once, startled by the appearance of a small chameleon, he leaped suddenly sideways, then returned to paw at the intruder a few times until it scuttled away.

He gave us a glance over his shoulder and then began running as if to prove what he could do. I mean he really raced around the interior of the corral, flat out, ears back and legs pumping. What a display of speed that was! He skidded to an abrupt stop and resumed his placid sniffing, not at all winded by his exultant dash. He halted at a far corner of the run.

"Call him," June August suggested.

"Hobo!" I yelled. "Here boy!"

I held up a hand; he looked and trotted over to us immediately. I leaned down. He nosed my fingers and allowed me to fondle his ears. He seemed to like it. I know I did.

"Did you train him to do that?" I asked June. "To come when called."

"Nope," she said. "He caught on from the start or maybe he had been trained by a previous owner. Whatever, he's one brainy dog."

"I agree," I said. "I'm going to make you an offer you can't refuse. I can't take Hobo at the moment because the final decision rests with my parents. I'll persuade them to come out here as soon as possible and take a look at him. I'll give you twenty dollars now as a sort of option. You keep Hobo until a final decision is made. If he's rejected, you keep the twenty. If he's accepted we'll make an additional hundred-dollar contribution to your organization. Done?"

"You've got it," she said happily. "Come back to the office and let me fill out some papers. I have to ask questions about your ability to care for one of our orphans."

Hobo was returned to his cage with no obvious objection on his part. June and I repaired to her disordered office, where I handed over my business card and a double-sawbuck. I also provided the names of two references and described the McNally property: a few partially wooded acres on Ocean Boulevard in Palm Beach.

"With a doghouse already on the premises," I added. "It's a comfortable condo formerly occupied by a golden retriever we owned who passed away from the ravages of old age. But his home still exists and is large enough to shelter Hobo, I assure you."

"Sounds wonderful," she said, sighing. "I do hope your parents like Hobo."

"What's not to like?" I said. "The kid's a charmer."

Before I departed I returned to Hobo's cage to take another look. He was still awake, sitting placidly, observing the world and thinking dog thoughts. We stared at each other a moment, and you may think me a complete nut but I swear he winked at me. He did, he really did.

What a rascal!

10

I DECIDED TO DRIVE home rather than return to the office. After all, it was Friday afternoon, not a period when any self-respecting entrepreneur initiates new projects or even furthers the old. It is a time for exhaling and contemplating a weekend of relaxation, entertainment, wassail—whatever turns you on.

But en route I was suddenly stricken by a fearsome hunger, a craving for calories that could not be denied. I stopped at the first fast-food factory I encountered, parked, and rushed inside. I ordered their half-pound hamburger, medium rare. A mistake. It was touted on the menu as being made of one hundred percent top-grade ground beef. After one bite I was convinced it was one hundred percent top-grade minced galoshes.

I ate less than half of this abomination, tried a few spears of greasy french fries, took one sip of an acidic cola, and then fled. I continued my journey homeward in a surly mood. I realized my taste buds had taken a terrible whumping that day and I could only hope the dinner offered by Yvonne Chrisling would restore the McNally palate to its customary vigor.

It seemed to me a leisurely ocean swim might help dispel the morning's gustatory longueurs, and I was donning beach duds when Binky Watrous phoned from Parrots Unlimited. He was in exuberant spirits.

"Ricardo and Mr. Gottschalk have gone to a bird show in Orlando," he explained. "So today I'm selling along with Bridget and Tony and Emma. I've already flogged a macaw, three parakeets, and a peach-fronted lovebird. Isn't that fantastic!"

"Excellent," I said. "This could become a lifelong career for you, Binky."

"Well, I'm not sure," he said cautiously. "When Ricardo returns I'll be cleaning cages again. I don't much dig that guy, Archy. He has all the charisma of Grant's Tomb."

"Well put," I told him. "My sentiments exactly."

"Listen, the reason I called is that Tony and Emma are having an after-dinner open house Saturday night. It turned out they are living together and they're having this informal party. BYOB. Bridget and I plan to be there and I asked if I might invite you and they said of course, the more the merrier. Would you like to attend?"

"Sure," I said. "Sounds like fun."

"Maybe you could bring Connie."

"I don't think so. She and I are not communicating."

"Oh?" he said. "A tiff?"

"The mother of all tiffs."

"It'll pass," he said breezily. "Now grab a pen and I'll give you the address. Anytime after eight o'clock tomorrow night. Archy, bring a good vodka, will you? At the moment I seem to be tapped out."

I jotted down the information. Binky went back to extolling the merits of budgies and I went to immerse myself in the Atlantic Ocean. My slow swim had the desired effect: it calmed me, soothed me, and convinced me that one day I might learn to write haiku or play the bagpipes.

At the cocktail hour that evening I informed my parents I would not be joining them for dinner since I had accepted an invitation to dine with Ms. Yvonne Chrisling, housekeeper for Mr. Hiram Gottschalk.

"That's nice, Archy," mother said.

Father gave me a swift glance but said nothing.

I then described my visit to the animal shelter that morning and how I had selected a dog which, with their approval, I felt would make a happy addition to our household.

"Pedigreed?" father asked.

"No, sir. A mixed breed; he has no papers. Terrier type. I'd guess he's part Jack Russell. Brown and white. Very trim. Very attractive. Strong and fast."

"What's his name?" mother said.

"Hobo," I replied, and waited for one of the pater's hirsute eyebrows to elevate. It did.

"Ah," he said. "An aristocrat."

"Please," I urged, "take a look at him. I think you'll be as impressed as I am."

"He doesn't chase birds, does he?" mom asked anxiously.

"He won't if we tell him not to," I assured her. "This is a very intelligent canine; he knows which side his kibbles are buttered on."

The senior McNallys looked at each other. "We could go out

Sunday morning after church," mother offered. "Will there be someone there on a Sunday?"

"I'm sure there will be," I said, "but I'll phone to make sure."

We waited for our liege to announce his decision.

"Very well," he said, after a short spell of mulling. "We'll take a look at Hobo."

I drained my martini. "Thank you, sir," I said. "I think you'll be pleased with him."

He gave me a wry smile and uttered something I never in a million years would have expected him to say. "But will he be pleased with us?" he asked.

I bade my parents an enjoyable evening and a good night's sleep. I then set out for the Gottschalk home, stopping at a liquor store along the way to splurge on a bottle of Duckhorn Vineyards merlot. I figured if dinner turned out to be indifferent, or worse, a choice wine would ease my anguish.

Yvonne met me at the door with an air kiss and a warm hand-clasp. She was wearing silk hostess pajamas in a cantaloupe hue, quite striking on a woman with her darkish coloring. Her dangling earrings were a primitive creation of beads and stones. Her hair was drawn tightly back and fastened with a silver barrette also in a native design. The total effect was somewhat assertive. She seemed more chatelaine than housekeeper.

I proffered my gift of wine. She thanked me and inspected the label with interest. "Will it go with Oriental food?" she asked.

"It will go with *anything,*" I assured her. "Except possibly chili dogs and sauerkraut."

"I think we can do better than that," she said, laughing. "Come along."

She preceded me, tittupping into the dining room where one corner of the long table had been set for two. Lighted candles flickered in frosted hurricane lamps. I discerned a faint odor of an exotic incense—but this being South Florida, it might have been roach spray.

"I thought we'd start with a little hot sake," Yvonne said. "Not too much; it's powerful stuff. Just enough to wake up our appetites. You approve?"

"Sounds wonderful," I said manfully, even though my appetite is always on the *qui vive* and I would have preferred something icy and astringent.

I don't know if Yvonne had a floor buzzer or if the maid had been lurking, but Mei Lee suddenly appeared bearing a black lacquer tray that held a small pot and two wee vessels no larger than eyecups.

"Good evening, Mei," I said, smiling at her.

"Ver' ver' happy," she said, giggling.

She poured us tiny tots of the warmed sake and padded away. We sampled and Yvonne looked at me inquiringly.

"Excellent," I said—only a slight exaggeration. "But not something I'd care to drink all evening if I hope to remain vertical."

"Oh, no," she said. "Just an aperitif. We'll have your wine with dinner. Archy, I can't tell you how grateful I am you could join me. With everyone gone for the evening I'd have been forced to endure a lonely meal—very depressing. Thank you so much."

I thought she was laying it on with a trowel, but perhaps she was sincere. Perhaps. But there was no doubt she was playing the gracious hostess and I couldn't fault her for that.

"My pleasure," I told her. "Will Mr. Gottschalk and Ricardo be gone long?"

"They'll be back tomorrow afternoon. It's really a buying trip. All the bird wholesalers show what they have to offer and retail stores like Parrots Unlimited make their selections."

"Are you interested in parrots?" I asked her.

"Not much," she admitted, and gave me a bent smile. "I prefer chickens, ducks, capons, quail, and pheasants. Roasted of course."

"Of course," I agreed. "You and I think much alike."

"I know we do," she said, so firmly that my original impression of this woman was confirmed: she was Ms. Resolute. I suspected even her whims were inviolable.

I wish I could describe the dinner served that evening in precise detail but I cannot since all the dishes were foreign to me. I had to depend on Yvonne to tell me what we were eating. To the best of my recollection this was the menu:

Seaweed rolls with black mushrooms, green onions, and minced baked ham in a paste of chicken breast, dry sherry, and other disremembered ingredients.

Eight-treasure winter melon soup with lean pork, crabmeat, and shrimp.

Spicy chilled noodles.

Steamed ginger chicken with mandarin pancakes.

Crispy nut pockets with pitted dates, roasted peanuts, and honey.

A pot of steaming tea was available but both Yvonne and I went for the merlot.

I enjoyed that meal, I think, but I was more perplexed than delighted. I had never eaten such food before and so I could not judge whether it was excellently or poorly prepared. I could identify such seasonings as ginger, fennel, and cinnamon. But when Yvonne casually mentioned star anise, lotus seeds, and fuzzy melon, she lost me.

Our exotic dinner completed, we moved to a comfortable corner of the blowzy living room. Yvonne brought out snifters of Armagnac, which was exactly what I needed to relax my uvula. We sat close together on the tattered velvet love seat.

"A remarkable feast," I said to her. "And I thank you."

"You enjoyed it?" she asked, and I thought her glance was mischievous.

"It was different," I admitted. "Something I've never had before and I'm still trying to sort out my reactions. At least it makes me question if a meat-and-potatoes diet is not dreadfully limiting."

"It is," she said decisively. "I wish Mr. Gottschalk would learn that. Got Lee rarely gets a chance to practice his art. He really is an excellent chef, you know, but Hiram insists on red meat and perhaps a baked potato slathered with sour cream and chives. I hate to think of what it's doing to his arteries."

I smiled but said nothing. If Mr. Gottschalk, at his age, preferred a broiled sirloin to stir-fried veggies it was surely his choice to make and should be respected.

"But he simply won't listen to me," she continued, staring into space. "Even though he's aware of the unhealthy effects of his favorite foods." She paused to turn her head and look at me directly, unblinking. "But then he's been behaving so strangely lately."

She stopped and waited for my response. I didn't say, "Ah-*ha!*" aloud of course, nor did I even *think*, Ah-*ha!* But mommy didn't raise her son to be an idiot and I knew very well we had now arrived at the nub of the evening; to wit, why I had been invited for dinner à deux.

"Behaving strangely?" I repeated. "How so?"

"He has these wild ideas," she said. "Delusions really. He misplaces things and believes someone in the house has stolen them. He breaks things accidentally and accuses others of their destruction. Our mynah, Dicky, died a natural death but Hiram is convinced the bird was killed. Archy, I'm telling you these things only because you represent Mr. Gottschalk's attorney and I felt you should be aware of his increasing . . . his increasing . . ."

I suspected she wanted to say craziness but thought better of it. "Irrational behavior?" I suggested.

"Yes," she said gratefully. "Exactly. His increasing irrational behavior."

"Do you believe he needs professional help? A psychotherapist perhaps or even a psychiatrist?"

"I don't know," she said, frowning. "I really don't. But his conduct troubles me. Sometimes I fear he is not all there, if you know what I mean. Archy, I hope you'll repeat what I've told you only to your father. After all, he is Mr. Gottschalk's attorney and I think he should be made aware of his client's condition."

"Of course," I said. "I shall certainly inform him."

Then, having accomplished what she had obviously planned, she relaxed. We spent a pleasant final half hour chattering about saloon singers of the past we had both heard, live or on recordings: Tommy Lyman, Helen Morgan, Nellie Lutcher, and many others long gone but not forgotten.

Finally, my Mickey Mouse watch edging toward eleven, I rose to take my leave and thank her again for her hospitality.

"And you won't forget to tell your father?" she said. "About Hiram."

"I won't forget," I promised. "Father should know of this unhappy development."

"Good boy," she said, patting my cheek, and I wondered if the moment I left she would hasten to her record of pupils' deportment and paste a small gold star next to the name of A. McNally.

But teacher relented at the door to grasp me close and bestow a firm if brief smooch on my lips. "Thank you so much for the wine," she breathed. "And just for being here. You made my evening, darling."

If she was acting she deserved a tin Oscar at least.

11

ONE OF SGT. Al Rogoff's favorite jokes, oft repeated, is: "Last night I slept like a baby; I woke up crying every two hours." My slumber on Friday night wasn't quite as disturbed but it was fitful enough. I simply could not relax but kept flopping about like a beached mackerel.

It wasn't all those spicy viands I had consumed that were causing my distress; it was a mental malaise I could not identify. I had a vague feeling of unease, as if vile plots were astir at the Gottschalk manse I was powerless to foil. I had a disheartening suspicion I was being used, manipulated, for what purpose I could not imagine.

Finally, the dark at my window just beginning to gray, I sank into a deep sleep, mercifully dreamless. When I awoke and glanced at my bedside clock it was pushing ten-thirty. I had all the symptoms of a racking hangover, which was outrageous since my alcoholic intake the previous evening had been if not minimal then certainly restrained.

It required a shave and a long hot shower followed by a cold rinse to restore the McNally carcass to any semblance of normalcy. I pulled on my usual Saturday morning costume of T-shirt, jeans, and loafers. But before descending for a late breakfast I remembered to phone the dog shelter to ask if someone would be in attendance on Sunday. I was assured they'd be open and would welcome visitors.

I found Jamie Olson in the kitchen brewing a fresh pot of coffee: a welcome sight. I poured myself a tall glass of chilled tomato juice into which I stirred a bit of horseradish. I also toasted two big slices of Ursi's homemade sour rye. Those I smeared with cream cheese allegedly flavored with smoked salmon although I couldn't taste it. Then Jamie and I sat at the enameled kitchen table, sipping cautiously at our steaming coffee mugs.

I told him about Hobo and how my parents had agreed to take a look at him on Sunday after church.

"A terrier?" Jamie said.

"Sort of. A mixed breed but mostly terrier. He looks to be strong and I've seen him run. He's fast."

"Uh-huh. Male?"

"Yes. Short coat."

"Been fixed?"

"Yes."

"How old?"

"Two or three years. Around three."

"He might tree that raccoon."

"I think there's a good chance," I said, "if you urge him on. He's one smart hound."

"We'll see," Jamie said. "Some terriers can be hell on wheels. Others just whimper and go hide."

"Hobo won't whimper," I told him. "He's got too much pride."

"Mebbe," Jamie said, and lighted up his old, pungent briar. And I had my first cigarette of the day in self-defense.

We smoked awhile in silence. Jamie is a taciturn man; he considers small talk a waste of time. So I refrained from commenting on the weather or the high cost of haircuts.

Finally he said, "Those staffers you asked about."

It took a mo to get my brain into gear. The effect of sleep deprivation, no doubt. "Got and Mei Lee, chef and maid for Hiram Gottschalk?"

"Yep," Jamie said. "I asked my friend Eddie Wong about them." He paused.

"And?" I said.

"They're closemouthed, that lot. But Eddie says Got and Mei are looking for a new spot."

"Oh? They want to leave the Gottschalks?"

"Eddie says so."

"Did he say why?"

"Nope. Just they want to go. If Eddie knows why, he ain't saying. But he made a face."

"Thanks for your help, Jamie."

"Not much," he said. "But when people don't want to talk they won't."

A truism if ever I heard one. But Jamie had provided another small piece of the puzzle bedeviling me. I washed up my breakfast things, stacked them in the countertop drainer to dry, and returned upstairs to my dorm. I confess I had a fleeting thought a short nap would be welcome, but I determinedly discarded such a disgraceful notion and continued to function.

For the remainder of the morning I scribbled in my journal, not only noting recent events and intelligence but posing questions to myself which I am certain you are also asking as you follow this chronicle. Nothing at the moment made a great deal of sense. But as I explained to Binky Watrous on one occasion, enduring a temporary mishmash is a challenge to an investigator's patience, determination, and acumen. The reaction was vintage Binky.

"What?" he said.

It was about one p.m. when I finished my grunt work, much too late to call pals for a round of golf, a set of tennis, or any other energetic activity. Besides, I was in no mood or physical condition for strenuous exertion except a jolly game of jacks or a rollicking session of mumblety-peg.

I changed into jazzier threads, including a sport jacket of black and white awning stripes. My father once unkindly remarked it made me look like a fugitive from a chain gang. I didn't dare mention that his sport jackets seemed designed for wear at memorial services for President Millard Fillmore.

I set out for the Pelican Club, my spirits already beginning to ascend. I anticipated a quiet, soothing hour or more, perhaps exchanging philosophical profundities with Mr. Simon Pettibone. I would imbibe an exhilarating alcoholic concoction or two. I might even enjoy one of Leroy's special burgers with a slice of red onion atop. Suddenly life was once again worth living and I found myself singing "I Don't Want to Set the World on Fire." As I recalled, the rest of the lyric went, "I just want to start a flame in your heart." Can gangsta rap compete with that?

The Pelican was almost deserted, as I knew it would be on a pleasant Saturday afternoon. The golden lads and lasses would be cavorting on the courts, links, beach, or mayhap just swinging idly in a hammock for two.

I stopped at the bar to exchange greetings with our club manager.

"Something to wet the whistle, Mr. McNally?" he inquired.

I considered. "Perhaps I'll move to the dining room and have a spot of lunch. I'll see what Leroy is pushing and ask Priscilla to bring me a fitting beverage to sluice it down."

He leaned across the bar and beckoned me close. "Peter Gottschalk is back there," he warned in a low voice. "By himself."

"Ah," I said. "What condition?"

"Sober but quiet. Very quiet. I'd say depressed."

"Tell you what," I said. "Mix me a stiff vodka gimlet now, please, and I'll have a gulp of Dutch courage before I join him. Perhaps I'll cheer him up."

"Or perhaps he'll depress you."

"A distinct possibility," I admitted.

I took a swig of the sturdy gimlet and headed for the dining area. Peter was seated alone at a corner table. There was a half-empty pilsner of beer before him, a basket of salted pretzels, and a saucer of mustard. He was staring moodily at this feast and didn't look up until I spoke.

"H'lo, Peter," I said, trying to sound chirrupy.

"Oh," he said. "Yeah. Hi, Archy."

"May I join you?"

"If you like. I should warn you I'm lousy company."

"I'll take my chances," I said, and slid into the chair facing him.

"I goofed," he said suddenly. "I guess you heard."

"No, I heard nothing," I lied. "How did you goof?"

"Totaled the old man's car. The night of the party."

"Were you hurt?"

"Scratches and bruises. Nothing serious. I was zonked. But things are hairy at home. I'm staying away as much as I can."

"Well, as they say in Alaska, be it ever so humble there's no place like Nome."

He looked at me. "Have you ever been in Alaska?"

"No."

"Then how do you know they say it?"

"Peter," I said gently, "I never intend my nonsense to be taken literally."

"You're right," he said unexpectedly. "Things have been happening to me lately. Losing my sense of humor is one of them. I don't know what's going on."

I feared prying into his personal angst. "May I share your pretzels?" I asked.

"Sure. Help yourself."

I dunked one in the dish of steroidal mustard. "What was your father's reaction?" I inquired.

"Well, he didn't kick me out or anything like that. I guess he was just disappointed in me. It's okay. I'm disappointed in him."

I hadn't the slightest idea what he meant by that and I don't believe he did either.

He took a swallow of his beer. "I've got to do something," he declared.

Now I was curious. "Do what?"

"Something. Anything. Everyone else in that zoo has a plan. I mean they know what they want and they're going for it. That's my problem: I don't know what I want. You never met my mother, did you?"

"No, I didn't."

"A beautiful woman. I loved her so much. When she died

everything fell apart. You know what I'm saying? It all went bad."

I was trying to keep up but this conversation was becoming increasingly incomprehensible. "The family?" I ventured.

"Down the tube," he said portentously. "Kaput. Rack and ruin."

"Your father—" I started, but his rancid laugh cut me off.

"A puppet!" he cried. "That's what I call him—the puppet. I hate my father."

He said this with such despairing venom I wanted to reach out and pat his shoulder. Then, to my astonishment, his mood abruptly changed. A complete flip-flop.

He grinned at me and laughed aloud. "Hey," he said, almost burbling, "let's you and me go have some fun. How about Fort Liquordale or Miami? Find some action. Meet a few kindred souls, preferably female. What say?"

"Some other time," I said with an arctic smile. "I'm on the hook for a family do this evening. Two tables of bridge. Very dull but I promised to take a hand."

"Too bad for you," he said with a foolish smirk. "Then I'm off to explore this great wide, wonderful world we live in."

He jerked to his feet, gave me a floppy wave, and rushed out. I sat there, exhausted by the tension of dealing with such a disordered personality. I ate two more pretzels dipped in mustard and finished my gimlet. Priscilla came over and looked at me sympathetically.

"He's a holy terror, isn't he?" she said.

I nodded.

"He didn't sign his tab."

"I'll pick it up."

"Would you like something, Archy? A burger? Salad?"

"No, thanks," I said. "I seem to have lost my appetite."

"Who wouldn't?" she said. "I feel so sorry for the guy. He's just out of it."

I returned to the bar.

"How did you make out with Gottschalk?" Mr. Pettibone asked.

"Rough going."

He nodded. "I have an old uncle—my mother's brother. Lord, he must be pushing the century mark. He's still got most of his marbles. Most but not all. I visit him and sometimes he says crazy things. Truly insane. I never know whether to correct him and maybe set him off, yelling and screaming, or just go along with what he says to keep him peaceable and happy in his nuttiness. It's a problem. You know what I mean?"

"I know exactly what you mean and it is a problem. I don't know the answer. But Peter is a young man. Too young to give up on."

"Maybe," Mr. Pettibone said. "But I guess that's not for you or me to say. If he can be fixed it'll take more than a smile and a stroke."

I would have liked to continue our conversation but a quartet of members came barging in, two couples dressed in tennis whites. They rushed the bar, boisterous and apparently delighted with their present and with nary a doubt of their future. I envied them. I finished my wallop while our mixologist was creating four different esoteric drinks, all of which seemed to require an inordinate amount of fresh pineapple, maraschino cherries, celery, or key limes.

I drove home in a subdued state, the meeting with Peter Gottschalk having put an effective kibosh on my temporary euphoria. The yearning for a nap returned in full force and I now saw no reason to resist it. I had a miserable night's sleep to repair, and perhaps an hour or so of Z's would recharge the

McNally neurons and enable me to extract a few nuggets of significance from all that puzzling palaver with the junior Gottschalk.

Why on earth would a son think his father a puppet? I considered my own sire a master puppeteer.

12

On Saturday evening I enjoyed a pleasant cocktail hour and dinner with my parents which helped restore my dilapidated esprit. It had not been my customary lollygagging weekend and I set out for the party being hosted by Tony Sutcliffe and Emma Gompertz hoping the informal bash would completely rejuvenate my usual stratospheric gusto.

(Connie Garcia hadn't phoned but I determinedly ignored that disappointment. My Brobdingnagian ego simply would not allow me to make the initial rapprochement. Please do not remind me that pride is the first of the seven deadly sins.)

The two clerks of Parrots Unlimited lived in a cramped one-bedroom condo in West Palm. I had stopped en route to pick up a liter of Sterling vodka as urged by my lunatic Dr. Watson, and by the time I arrived the party was already flaming. It was a bit of a shocker to realize the other celebrants were at least ten years younger than Binky and I. But the gulf between twenty-some-things and thirty-somethings didn't seem to discombobulate my aide-de-camp. And why should it, since his mental age is teen-something?

A card table covered with a bedsheet (mercifully clean) served as a sideboard. There was one large platter of Ritz crackers and cubes of process cheese slowly turning green. Understandably no one appeared interested in this nosh; the stacks of plastic cups and gallon jugs of wine, all with screw tops, were the attraction.

I don't mean to be snooty in this description of Emma and Tony's party. Obviously their income and that of their friends was limited. But they were sharing laughter and companionship and if the wine was a vintage of last Tuesday—so what? In my salad days I attended and hosted many similar revelries and no one ever thought of objecting when the cab or zin was served in Smucker's jelly jars.

Binky grabbed my bottle of Sterling like a cookie addict who had endured a week without his daily Pepperidge Farm fix. He found ice somewhere and came back with plastic cups of chilled and scantily watered vodka for me, Bridget Houlihan, and him-self.

"I'm teaching Bridget to appreciate the glories of eighty-proof," he informed me.

"It tastes like medicine," she said with a shudder after one small sip.

"It *is* medicine," I agreed. "But need not be inhaled or injected. I have found it an effective disinfectant for small wounds as well as an excellent gargle for a raspy throat."

She looked at me doubtfully and I wandered away. I moved through the gabbling throng (it seemed like a throng only be-cause the apartment was so cramped) and found host and hostess. I thanked them for their hospitality and assured them it was a marvelous party. They glowed although I doubted if they recalled who I was. Their memories might have been dulled by the volume of hard rock thundering from two speakers large as coffins.

I decided to have one more tincture of Sterling and then split. But when I went searching for the vodka bottle I saw Ricardo Chrisling standing alone, gripping a plastic cup of red wine. Well, he wasn't alone of course—one couldn't be in that mob— but he was withdrawn, solitary, with a fixed smile that struck me as remote if not supercilious. I moved through the crowd to his side.

He was wearing Armani, naturally, beautifully tailored. The man's immaculacy amazed me. Didn't he ever drop a button or stain a cuff? He was so *complete*. I was absolutely certain he had hairs removed regularly from ears and nostrils.

"Ah," he said. "Archy McNally."

I was pleased he remembered my name. "In the flesh," I said, "sort of. Good to see you again, Ricardo. How was the Orlando trip?"

If he was shocked by my knowledge of his activities he didn't show it. He flipped a hand back and forth. "So-so," he said. "We bought the usual. Nothing very extraordinary except for a magnificent pair of varied lorikeets. Are you interested in parrots?"

"No," I said, and he gave me his glacial smile.

"I promised the kids I'd put in an appearance," he said. "I have and now I'm ready to leave. Are you staying?"

"Actually I was going to have one more small swallow and then cut out."

He looked at me speculatively. "Why don't you have your swallow at my place?" he suggested. "Something better than jug wine. This really isn't my scene."

I accepted his invitation gladly. The unending jackhammering of hard rock was flossing my ears and I yearned for a spell of quiet. We stole away and I am certain our departure wasn't noticed. Certainly not by my fruitcake assistant who was entertaining a fascinated audience with his repertoire of birdcalls, including that of the Slovenian grebe.

I would have imagined a lad as frigidly elegant as Ricardo would be driving something sinuous, foreign, and frightfully expensive. A Lamborghini Diablo? But no, his personal transportation was a white four-door Ford Explorer. Room enough for a troop of tots or cargo—lots of cargo. It was a nice enough vehicle, mind you, but I thought it an odd choice for a man who wore Armani (black label) and favored French cuffs on his silk shirts.

I began to have second thoughts about Ricardo Chrisling. My first impressions are usually accurate—but not always. I once tabbed a chap to be a complete schlub and he later turned out to be a bloomin' genius.

It wasn't only the car Ricardo was driving that made me begin to doubt my incipient evaluation of his character and personality. There was an added factor: the links on those French cuffs were miniature dice. Costly, I'm sure, but more Las Vegas than Paris, wouldn't you say?

I followed Ricardo's truck to a neighborhood not far from where the wine party was still blasting away. But this was an upscale area of West Palm, a quiet section of private homes and low-rise condos, all nicely landscaped with trim lawns and a restrained selection of dwarf palms. It was not an enclave of the *rich* rich, but just as obviously the residents were not financially disadvantaged, if you will forgive my use of the politically correct gibberish *au courant* these days.

Ricardo's dwelling was on the second floor of a modest three-story building. He had not one, not two, but three locks on his front door, and I waited patiently while he found the proper keys.

"Security problems?" I asked.

"No," he said shortly. "And I want to keep it that way."

He flipped on a bright table lamp and I looked about. His one-bedroom condo was high-ceilinged and airy. Now I must give you my first impressions, again after warning they have occasionally proved faulty in the past.

The apartment looked like a model room displayed in a South Florida furniture store. The mirrored wall, the colors, furnishings, lighting—everything was pleasant enough but so pristine and spotless it was difficult to believe the place was actually inhabited.

That was my first reaction. The second was a conviction the condo had been decorated by a woman. The feminine aura of pastels was the tip-off: all those soft shades of aqua, lavender, and the palest of pinks and yellows. I mean the room was totally lacking in vigor. It seemed to have been created with colored chalks.

Of course a female interior decorator may have been hired to create that tinted meringue. Or perhaps Chrisling had purchased or leased the condo fully furnished and never bothered altering it to conform to his personal taste. But it was definitely a womanly apartment, not quite fluffy but so . . . so *delicate* I wondered if Ricardo, even when alone, closed the door of the bathroom when he used it.

I go to such lengths to describe his living quarters because they puzzled me. I simply could not believe a man dwelt there comfortably. *Suffocating!* That's the word I've been seeking.

De gustibus non est disputandum. And if you think that means there is no accounting for tastes you're right on. And who wrote it? Our old friend Monsieur Anon.

"Do you like brandy?" Ricardo asked suddenly.

"Very much," I said.

"Ever have Presidente? It's Mexican."

"No, I've never tried it but I'm willing."

"Nice flavor," he said. "I think you'll like it. I'll get us a glass. I'd appreciate it if you didn't smoke."

He disappeared and I sank into a plumpish upholstered armchair. A mistake. I sank and sank, wondering how I'd ever get out of the damned thing without the aid of a block and tackle.

He returned with the brandy in stemmed liqueur glasses rather than snifters. But that was all right; I can rough it. He handed me a tiny tot and waited until I took an experimental sip.

"Well?" he asked.

"Excellent," I pronounced. "Flavorful, as you said."

"You don't find it a bit sweetish?"

"A bit," I admitted. "But not overwhelming."

"An acquired taste," he said. "Very popular south of the border."

"You've been to Mexico?"

"I have friends there," he replied, which didn't exactly answer my question.

He moved away from me to a couch covered with unspotted periwinkle velvet. He didn't sit but leaned back against one of the armrests. It put him at a higher altitude than I. I was entrapped by that quicksand armchair and so he towered. I recognized it as a common ploy of business executives. If you sit or stand at a higher elevation than your visitor you automatically reduce him or her to an inferior.

"I wanted to get out of that madhouse," he said abruptly. "Also, I wanted to talk to you in private."

"Oh?" I said, and took another sip of Presidente. It was emboldening.

"Let's see if I've got this straight," he said, speaking rapidly now. "Your father is Hiram Gottschalk's attorney. And you are your father's assistant. Correct?"

"More or less," I said. "But I am not a lawyer. If this concerns a legal matter I suggest you speak to my father."

"No," he said firmly. "It hasn't come to that. Yet. But I think you should know Hiram has been acting crazy lately."

"Acting crazy? In what way?"

"He thinks someone has a grudge against him. Smashing his phonograph records, slashing an old photograph, even strangling Dicky, the mynah he owned. It's all a crock of course. Strictly in his mind. What's left of it."

"Is he becoming senile? Alzheimer's perhaps?"

Chrisling shrugged. "Who knows? But the trip he and I just made to Orlando was hard to take. I mean he just wasn't talking sense. Even the wholesalers noticed it. A few of them asked if he was sick."

I was silent. Ricardo took a gulp of brandy that drained his glass.

"His son," he said. "Peter. Have you met him?"

I nodded.

"Then you know he's off-the-wall." His laugh was harsh. "Maybe it runs in the family. Anyway, I thought you might want to let your father know how Hiram's been acting."

"Yes, of course," I said, and finished my own Presidente. "He should be informed." I struggled from the armchair's embrace and stood. "Thank you for the transfusion. I better be on my way." I realized he had nothing more to say to me. He had accomplished his purpose.

"Wait a sec," he said, and left. He reappeared a moment later bearing an unopened bottle of Presidente brandy. "For you," he said with his tight smile. "Enjoy it."

"Thank you," I said, startled. "It's very generous of you."

"My pleasure," he said, but I didn't think it was.

I drove home slowly. It was a reasonable hour, not yet midnight, and I was reasonably sober. And so I was capable of totting up what I had heard the last few days.

1. The twins, Judith and Julia, had told me of their father's nuttiness.

2. Yvonne Chrisling, housekeeper, had told me of Hiram's conduct.

3. And now Ricardo had told me of his employer's erratic behavior.

A chorus of harpies.

There were, I decided, two possibilities. One: Judith, Julia, Yvonne, and Ricardo were joined in a conspiracy to convince me—and through me, my father—that Hiram Gottschalk had gone off the deep end and his mental capabilities were no longer to be trusted.

But if it was a conspiracy, what could be their shared motive? And if such a motive existed I could not believe the members of the cabal would have decided to attempt to enlist my support not once, not twice, but thrice. That, I was certain they would recognize, would be overkill. These were not stupid people.

The other possibility, I had to acknowledge, was that each separately, without knowledge of the others, was speaking the truth, and Hiram Gottschalk had flipped his wig. My father had warned me from the outset the client was eccentric. Perhaps what *mein papa* saw as eccentricity was or had evolved into something approaching lunacy.

My wisest course of action, I concluded, was to have a personal meeting with Hiram as soon as possible. After all, we had only met twice. A one-on-one interview would help me judge his mental condition. If I thought him normal, even if idiosyncratic, I would suspect a vile plot existed involving his children and employees. If he exhibited obvious symptoms of paranoia, then I would certainly suggest to my father that Mr. Gottschalk be urged to consult Dr. Gussie Pearlberg.

Having untied the knot of my doubts and insecurities, I regained the safety and comfort of my own snug den with a feeling of relief. My cave was, I admitted, somewhat grungy compared to Chrisling's immaculate apartment. But my sanctuary is *me*, completely mine, and I grin every time I walk in.

Before I retired I opened the Presidente brandy Ricardo had given me and had a taste. It was nice enough but lacked the punch of marc. But then what doesn't?

I fell asleep wondering why he had gifted me a bottle. I didn't think he was a Greek but I could not forget Virgil's warning.

13

M Y PARENTS WENT to church on Sunday morning, as usual. And, as usual, I did not accompany them. I attended only when my sins become unendurable—a rare occurrence since I customarily find virtuous reasons for misdeeds, as I'm sure you do as well.

They returned and we all piled into mother's nicely restored 1949 Ford station wagon, familiarly known as the Woody. It really is a charming antique, fully operable, with a V-8 engine and side panels and tailgate of finely grained wood.

Father drove since he has an absurd notion that I am a speed demon. I am not, of course, and even if I were I can't see a '49 Ford wagon competing in the Daytona 500, can you? Mother insisted we bring along the collar and leash formerly the property of Max. I agreed because I didn't wish to cause dissension, although I knew Max's collar would go about Hobo's neck at least twice.

June August greeted us at the dog shelter and I introduced her. I think my parents were favorably impressed and I'm sure she was, since they were still wearing their Sunday-go-to-meeting uniforms, the picture of puritan rectitude. We all repaired to the cage harboring Hobo and stood in a semicircle observing him.

He was curled into a ball, sleeping soundly. But becoming aware he had an audience, he opened one eye, examined us, then rose to his feet, yawned, stretched, and pressed his nose against the door of his cage.

"Hiya, Hobo," I said. "Have a nice snooze? I've brought some friends to meet you. Could we have him outside, please, Miss August?"

She opened the door; he immediately jumped to the ground, had another luxurious stretch, and then looked at us more closely. And you know, the villain picked out the one of his four visitors who would determine his fate. Tail wagging, he sidled up to mother and gave her an affectionate ankle rub.

"Why, Hobo," she said, obviously enchanted, "you *are* a friendly pooch, aren't you?"

She leaned to scratch the top of his head and tweak his ears. He writhed with content. That kid must have studied method acting. I looked at father. *Both* his hairy eyebrows were hoisting aloft. He knew Hobo had conquered.

"Would you like to see him run?" June August asked.

"I don't think that will be necessary," I said, and looked to my parents for approval. They nodded and we all returned to the office to sign papers and ransom Hobo.

Twenty minutes later we were on the way home. As I had guessed, there was no need for collar and leash. Hobo bounded readily into the Woody and sat rather grandly between mother and me, making no fuss but viewing the passing scene with calm curiosity. I think father was amused.

"Not a very excitable beast, is he?" he said.

"No, sir," I agreed. "But deep. Definitely deep."

We arrived at the McNally manse and alighted. Hobo leaped down, shook himself, and looked around at his new surroundings. Ursi and Jamie Olson came from the kitchen to join us and examine the latest addition to our household.

"What a cute doggie!" Ursi said.

"Um," said Jamie.

The five of us were standing there, staring at the terrier, when suddenly he took off. I mean his acceleration was incredible. One moment he was still, the next he was a brown-and-white blur. He raced away from us, ears laid back, tail horizontal, and dashed into the wooded portion of our mini-estate.

He reappeared, circled the garage at full speed, and disappeared again. We caught glimpses of him darting through the underbrush, charging around the entire McNally domain, apparently never pausing to take a sniff.

"He's not running away, is he?" mother asked anxiously.

"Of course not," I said, praying my faith in Hobo would be justified.

Finally the scoundrel came skidding to a stop in front of us. He flopped onto his side, panting mightily, tail thumping. I think we were all astonished and puzzled by his behavior.

"Now why did he do that?" Ursi wondered.

Father pressed a knuckle to his bristly mustache, probably to hide a smile. "I suspect he may have been celebrating," he said.

I think it occurred simultaneously to all of us that we had made no preparations to feed and water our adoptee. It was decided a wooden bowl of water would be temporarily provided along with leftovers from our Sunday dinner and supper. Hobo would not suffer from malnutrition for one day, and mother and Ursi promised to go shopping for him on the morrow. They planned to purchase everything a healthy hound might desire: a supply of food, bowls, brush, comb, flea-and-tick spray, and perhaps a rawhide bone to exercise his molars.

"And some treats," mama said happily. "Little biscuits and nibbles. Things like that."

"But no gumdrops," I warned.

She stared at me. "Archy," she said, "I never know when you're joking."

"All the time, darling," I said, and hugged her.

My parents and Ursi went indoors. Jamie and I introduced Hobo to his new condo, beckoning him forward to examine the doghouse formerly occupied by Max. The strange dwelling didn't spook him at all and I was convinced the kid was fearless. He poked his head through the doorway, looked around a moment, then slowly entered. I leaned down to see what he was doing. Just sniffing, inspecting the premises he had inherited. Then he came bouncing out, tail wagging.

We took him on a tour of the McNally domain and he followed along happily, occasionally frisking ahead. He explored the garage, potting shed, and greenhouse. Apparently he found nothing to which to object. We have a low stone wall bordering Ocean Boulevard and he could have leaped it easily. I pointed to the traffic speeding by and said, "No! No!" as sharply as I could. I hoped he understood he was not to venture onto the highway to chase cars.

We returned to the main house and I left him in Jamie's care. The two seemed to have formed an instant rapport, and I wondered how long it would be before Hobo was smoking a pipe and drinking aquavit.

I went up to my snuggery to relax before dinner. I was happy the adoption of Hobo had been glitchless. I hadn't mentioned it but I did hope the others would not attempt to teach tricks to our new family member. I mean it's quite sensible to train a dog to obey simple commands such as Stay, Heel, and Sit. Even Fetch. But when it comes to such things as Shake Hands and Play Dead, I object. It's an insult to a dog's dignity, making him exhibit his total serfdom. If your boss commanded you to lie down and roll over, what would be your reaction? Exactly.

Dinner was short ribs of beef, which everyone agreed was a fortuitous choice. The bones, rinsed free of a delightful red wine sauce, would keep Hobo content for the remainder of the day. I even added a single small macaroon just to convince him he had arrived at a canine Ritz.

I postponed the usual après–Sunday dinner nap to add a few lines to my journal describing the curious conversation with Ricardo Chrisling the previous evening. I also jotted a separate note to remind myself to call Mr. Hiram Gottschalk the first thing Monday morning to set up a meeting.

I finished those minor chores and was about to collapse onto the mattress for a few hundred welcome winks when my phone destroyed that hope. Ah-ha! I thought. Connie Garcia is calling to apologize for her unseemly behavior. Not quite.

"Archy McNally?" A sultry female voice.

"I am indeed. And you?"

"Judith Gottschalk."

A short, shocked pause. Then I said, "Judith! How nice to hear from you."

"I got your number from daddy. I hope you don't mind."

"Not at all."

"Listen, you live on the beach, don't you?"

"Practically in the sea."

"It's such a gorgeous day I'd love to take a dip."

"Of course," I said bravely. "And Julia?"

"She's got the sniffles or something. Maybe the flu. She plans to spend the day in bed."

"What a shame," I said, resisting the urge to ask, "With whom?"

"Could I pop over for an hour or so? Just long enough to get wet."

"Come along," I said, not terribly enthused at the prospect.

"Got any bubbly?" she asked in a tone implying that if I didn't I was a hopeless dolt.

"I think I might be able to find a bottle," I said, a bit miffed by her peremptory demand.

"Do try," she said. "See you in thirty minutes or so."

She hung up and I sighed. But then I reflected that an afternoon with one of the twins might prove more productive than entertaining both at the same time. Encouraged, I went downstairs to the pantry, found a bottle of Korbel brut, an excellent wine, and popped it into the freezer for a quick chill along with two plastic cups. Then I climbed up to my aerie again.

I changed to swimming trunks imprinted with portraits of the Pink Panther and added a cover-up of aubergine terry. I slid my feet into flip-flops and picked up a beach towel.

I flip-flopped downstairs and waited at the kitchen door until I saw the blue M-B come charging into our driveway, skidding to a halt with a scattering of gravel. Judith Gottschalk alighted, then leaned back inside to retrieve a beach bag and an enormous pagoda-shaped hat of fawny linen. She was wearing a gauzy cover-up beneath which the eagle-eyed McNally discerned the world's tiniest bikini, in a calico pattern. If my father had observed her arrival from his study window I reckoned his eyebrows had ascended to his hairline.

I plucked the Korbel and plastic cups from the freezer and

went out to greet her. She gave me an air kiss and then examined my offering.

"But it's *domestic*," she said in a snippety tone approaching outrage.

I refused to be offended by her pettishness. I glanced at the label. "Jumping Jehoshaphat, so it is!" I exclaimed with shocked chagrin. "I could have sworn I selected a bottle of an '83 Krug. Well, it's chilled, so I'm afraid we'll have to make do. Shall we go to the beach?"

She pouted. I don't think she was accustomed to having her desires thwarted—or even diluted. The Gottschalk twins, I decided, were enamored of the lush life and expected it as their due.

We went down to the strand and scouted three locations before Judith approved of a spot to spread my beach towel. I saw no difference in any of the places; sand is sand is sand. But that's a characteristic of pooh-bahs and would-be pooh-bahs. Observe their behavior in a restaurant; they will *never* accept the first table offered by the maître d'.

Finally we were settled, I opened the bottle of champers, and we each had a cupful. At least she had the grace to murmur, "Very nice." Then we went down to the sea, which proved a mite chilly but still held just enough summer warmth to be more invigorating than uncomfortable.

Judith was not a swimmer; that was obvious. She was more of a dunker, careful not to get her hair wet. She was also a bobber. You've seen them I'm sure. They stand in waist-high water and bob up and down, occasionally slapping their shoulders and upper arms vigorously.

I did nothing but get my knees wet while I watched Judith cavort. I was, I admit, a bit put out by her behavior and kept my distance. Not exactly Miss Congeniality, was she? She finally emerged from the briny and strigiled water from her torso and legs with her palms.

"That was divine," she said.

I was happy she approved of the Atlantic Ocean.

She strolled ahead of me back to our spread. I studied her lilting walk in the minuscule bikini plastered to tanned and glistening hide. Poetry in motion? Yes indeedy. But whether it was a sonnet or a limerick I could not have said.

We drank more Korbel and she opened her beach bag to extract a package of rice cakes. She offered me one and I politely took a bite.

"Good?" she asked.

"Appetizing," I responded, thinking it was about as tasty as I imagined a coprolite would be.

She lay on her back, stretched out like a gleaming starfish. She placed her hat over face and head. I lay propped on my side examining her attractive carcass with more than prurient interest. I found it: a small black mole, no larger than an aspirin tablet, nestled low on the left side of her flat abdomen. I restrained myself and didn't shout, "Eureka!" or even, "Hoover!" But I believed I had solved one small equation: Mole equaled Judith.

"So, Archy," she said, voice muffled by her hat, "what have you been up to?"

"This and that," I said, and then revealed something I hoped might provoke a reaction. "I had a drink with Ricardo Chrisling last night."

"Whatever for?" she said, disdain curdling her voice. "The man is a viper, definitely a viper." Pause. Then: "I hope you won't tell him I said so."

"Not me," I assured her. "Discretion is my stock-in-trade."

She removed her hat and donned mirrored sunglasses to look

at me. At least I think she was looking at me. With those specs it was hard to tell.

"Archy," she said, "did you talk to your father? About what my sister and I told you—how crazy daddy has been acting lately."

"I haven't had a chance to inform him as yet," I confessed. "But I fully intend to."

"You absolutely must," she said firmly. "We cannot let it go on and maybe get worse."

That had an ominous tone but I made no reply. Shortly thereafter she announced she wished to leave, and so we did. A very perplexing few hours. I mean I really didn't understand the reason for Judith's unexpected visit. It may have been quite innocent; she merely yearned for a brief ocean dunk. I did not think so.

That night before retiring I was still puzzling over our short encounter. Two things gradually surfaced from the bowl of Grape Nuts I call my brain.

First: Judith had referred with obvious malevolence to Ricardo Chrisling as a viper. It would certainly suggest the twins were not joined with Ricardo in some adroit plot against Hiram Gottschalk. Coconspirators rarely malign each other, do they?

Second: Was it really Judith Gottschalk with whom I had spent a not very exciting afternoon? Judith with the abdominal mole. She had said Julia was home with the sniffles. But could I have been deluded and was it actually Julia I had watched bobbing in the sea? Julia with the mole.

It was a crossword puzzle with no clues.

14

MAY HAVE SET a personal record for oversleeping on Monday morning. By the time my dreams of Rita Hayworth had evaporated and I awoke, it was nudging ten o'clock and I muttered a mild oath. I staggered to the window and peered out. A gummy day with a ponderous iron sky pressing down and all the palm fronds hanging limply. I seriously considered returning to Rita for another hour.

But there was work to be done, Western Civilization to be saved, and so I went through my usual morning routine, still somewhat somnolent. I was tugging on a lovat polo shirt that seemed distressingly snug, when my phone pealed. I glared at it, wondering what fool would call at such an outrageous hour. The fool was my father.

"Archy?" The tone was cold.

"Yes, sir," I said, expecting he would demand to know why I had not yet appeared at my place of employment.

"Hiram Gottschalk was killed last night," he said, speaking rapidly. "Sergeant Rogoff informed me a few moments ago. He says it is clearly a case of homicide. He will be contacting you later. I want you to tell him everything you know about our late client's fear for his life and whatever you may have discovered in your discreet inquiry. Is that understood?"

"Yes, father," I said faintly, and he hung up abruptly.

I just stood there, trembling. My drowsiness had vanished to be replaced by a sadness so intense I could scarcely endure it. And guilt of course. If I had worked harder, if I had moved faster, if . . . if . . . if . . . But I had failed and the man was dead.

I collapsed at my desk. I could not bring myself to make a journal note of my failure. Instead I read and reread the note I had scrawled to myself to set up a meeting with Hiram Gottschalk as soon as possible. I was about to destroy that punishing reminder but then propped it up against my rack of reference books. I wanted to view it continually. "Vengeance is mine; I will repay, saith the Lord."

"You better believe it," I saith aloud.

I knew it would be useless to call Sgt. Rogoff. He was probably at the crime scene and would phone when he had completed the details of opening a homicide investigation. I could think of nothing I might do at the moment but mourn. I surrendered to that, had a tasteless breakfast, and drove slowly through a sticky morning to my cubicle in the McNally Building on Royal Palm Way.

I wondered, not for the first time, if I was temperamentally suited for my chosen profession. Perhaps I should open a small haberdashery or seek employment as a waiter in a restaurant with enough chic to offer Grand Marnier soufflé. "Hello! My name is Archy and I shall be your serving person this evening."

Any job would do in which violent death was not routine. I am essentially a peaceable chap with, I admit, a dollop of timidity.

I smoked much too much that morning, remembering Mr. Hiram Gottschalk, recalling our brief conversations, and realizing how much I liked him, really *liked* him. He was capricious, no doubt about it, but there was no malice in him and whatever his sins I did not believe they deserved murder. I hoped Sgt. Rogoff would phone and suggest we get together to exchange information. But my only call came from Binky Watrous, who sounded as shaky as I felt.

"Archy," he said, almost wailing, "did you hear what happened?"

"Yes, I heard."

"It's terrible," he lamented. "Just terrible. He was a *nice* man, Archy."

"I know. Where are you calling from, Binky?"

"The store. We're closed for business of course. But we're all here. The birds have to be fed and the cages cleaned. But it's all so sad. The girls are crying. I feel like joining them. Do you ever cry, Archy?"

"Only at weddings."

"Listen, Ricardo called and told us to close up early. I guess he's in command now. So we're going to lock up and go out to lunch together. Do you want to come along?"

"Thank you, no, Binky. I'm waiting for a phone call."

"Archy, when you told me to get a job at Parrots Unlimited you said it was part of a discreet inquiry. Does Hiram's murder have anything to do with it?"

"Possibly," I said cautiously. "I won't know until I learn more about what happened."

"Then you'll tell me, won't you? I mean I am your lackey, cleaning out cages and all that, so I have a right to know."

"Of course you do," I agreed. "And so you shall. Now get off the line like a good lad and maybe the call I'm awaiting will come through."

He hung up but my phone didn't ring again that morning. I packed it in around one o'clock and went home for lunch. I was in no mood for the conviviality of the Pelican Club. It seemed to me indecent to seek companionship as a quick fix for my melancholia. *Mirabile dictu*, I found a cure on the grounds of the McNally duchy.

I dismounted from the Miata and heard the fast scrabble of claws on gravel. I turned to look and Hobo came racing around the corner of the garage. He skidded to a halt in front of me, panting, and jumped up to put paws on my knees. He seemed happy and he made me happy. What did he know of failure and murder most foul? He was just glad to see me and I blessed him, leaning to stroke his ears and scratch his hindquarters, which made him squirm with delight.

"Hobo," I told him, "you are a canine Samaritan and I thank you."

Jamie Olson came ambling up, gripping his old briar. His creased features wrinkled even more as he gave me a gap-toothed grin.

"That's some beast," he said.

I looked at him. "Don't tell me Hobo found the raccoon."

"Yep."

"Tree him?"

"Nope. Didn't give him a chance. Tell you what, that hound is swift. Set out after the critter. You should have heard Hobo snarl. Scared the daylights out of Mr. Raccoon. He went skedaddling south with Hobo right behind him. I finally whistled the dog back and he came. But I figure that raccoon is in Broward County by now and still running flat out."

I gave Hobo an extra helping of pats. "Well done, sir," I told him. "Keep up the good work."

I went into the house, my sunken spirits somewhat elevated by the tale of Hobo's hunting prowess. Ursi was working in the kitchen and offered to prepare a lunch but I respectfully declined. My appetite was blunted—a *very* rare occurrence, I assure you, and indicative of how deeply I had been affected by the news of Hiram Gottschalk's murder.

Up in my hidey-hole I reviewed all the notes I had made on what I was now fancifully terming the Puzzle of the Patricidal Parrot. I chose the adjective because I was convinced the birdman had been topped by a close relative. But a desperate search of my journal revealed nothing of significance. Just bits and pieces, dribs and drabs.

I existed in a mindless stupor for a half hour or so. I was thinking but it was a chaotic process, skipping from this to that: Ricardo Chrisling's taste in interior decor to Judith Gottschalk's mole, Peter Gottschalk's irrationality to Yvonne Chrisling's dictatorial manner. I mean the McNally cerebrum was in a tizzy with a surfeit of stimuli, whirling like a bloody carousel with the brass ring continually out of reach.

I was saved from total mental collapse by a phone call, finally, from Sgt. Al Rogoff. He was obviously in no mood for idle chatter.

"You going to be home for a while?" he demanded.

"The rest of the day as far as I know."

"Suppose I come over now. Okay?"

"Sure. Hungry?"

"I could use a sandwich and a beer."

"You've got it," I said. "How does it look, Al?"

"The Gottschalk kill? Pretty it ain't. See you soon."

I went down to the kitchen. Ursi had finished her chores and was gone; I played the short-order chef. I made Al two sandwiches, both with luncheon meat: sliced chicken breast with tomato and mayo, and salami with pickle relish. Even preparing this sumptuous repast didn't perk my appetite and I feared I might never wish to eat again. That put me in a better mood; absurdity always does.

Al pulled up outside in his pickup truck. It's not that he couldn't commandeer an official squad car but he has a nice sensibility about how Palm Beach residents feel about having a police vehicle parked in their driveway. Neighbors ask questions or gossip. I couldn't care less, of course, but I appreciated his discretion.

He came lumbering into the kitchen, took off his sagging gun belt, and slumped at the table. He looked more weary than grim and we did nothing but nod to each other. I popped two cans of chilled Coors and gave him one with the sandwiches. I gripped the other as I took a chair facing him.

"Rough morning?" I said.

"Not a barrel of laughs," he said. "Thanks for the feed. You make these sandwiches?"

"I washed my hands first."

"I hope so. Your father says Gottschalk thought someone was after him. Right?"

"Correct."

"Why didn't he come to us?"

"Come on, Al," I said. "Get real. He had received no threatening letters or phone calls. Would you have done anything?"

He picked up the chicken sandwich. "You're right," he admitted. "Until he got snuffed. Now we got to do something. Did you believe him?"

I flipped a palm back and forth. "Maybe yes, maybe no. Here's why he was spooked . . ."

I related what Hiram had told me: the slashed photograph, mass card, dead mynah, shattered phonograph record. Al listened closely while chomping through his first sandwich and picking up the second. I brought him another beer.

"You think he was telling you the truth?" he asked.

"I thought so at first," I replied. "What reason would he have to lie? But then I began talking to his children and employees, and they told me he'd been losing his marbles, had delusions of persecution. They implied senility."

Rogoff stopped scarfing and drinking to stare at me. "Did you ask them if he had been acting nutty, or did they volunteer the information?"

"They volunteered," I said. "They may have been right."

"Do you believe that?"

"No," I said.

"Me neither," he agreed, and started on his salami sandwich and second beer.

"I think they were trying to convince me Hiram was non compos mentis," I said. "They wanted me to tell my father his client's judgment was not to be trusted."

"And why do you suppose they wanted you to do that?"

" 'Ay, there's the rub,' " I said. "Hamlet's soliloquy."

"Thank you so much, Professor," he said. "I learn a lot when I talk to you. It takes weeks of hard work to forget it."

"Al, it couldn't have been an intruder, could it?"

"A masked villain who breaks in, kills, and escapes without stealing anything? I don't think so. But some moron tried to make it look like that. A pane of glass in the patio door was broken and the door was wide open."

"So?"

"All the broken glass was on the outside."

"Beautiful," I said. "Either a moron, as you said, or a murderer so emotionally disturbed by what he had done that he wasn't thinking straight."

"Or she wasn't," Rogoff said, finishing his beer.

"You think it might have been a woman?"

"Possibly."

"Al, you haven't yet told me how Hiram Gottschalk died."

"According to the doc, the victim was probably snuffed while he slept."

"But *how?* Shot, stabbed, strangled, smothered?"

"You don't want to know."

"I *do* want to know," I said angrily. "I want you to tell me."

"He was stabbed through both eyes with a long, slender blade, something like an ice pick, probably a thin stiletto."

I groaned. "I wish you hadn't told me." I found myself involuntarily pressing palms to my own eyes, to make certain they were still there.

"Archy, don't repeat what I just told you: the stabbing of the eyes. We're holding out on that, just telling the media he was knifed to death. We keep a few details back to check fake and real confessions."

"I know," I said. "I shan't repeat it to anyone, I assure you. It's not something I'd care to mention casually at a Tupperware party. Al, I know you've only started your investigation but I'm sure you've met all the whirlybirds involved. Any first impressions?"

"Yeah," he said. "How do you tell the difference between the twins?"

"You don't," I told him. "Think of them as one woman. But what I want to know is if you have any initial feeling or instinct about who might be responsible for Hiram's quietus."

"You know," he said, "I've decided you talk the way you do

because it helps soften the world's nastiness. You can't face crude reality, can you?"

"I can face it," I said defensively, "but would prefer not to. You haven't answered my question. Who is your number one suspect at the moment?"

He sighed. "It's got to be the son, Peter Gottschalk. The guy is such a wacko. I mean we're talking world-class kookiness. He's capable of shoving a shiv into his father's eyes while the old man slept."

"But why?"

The sergeant shrugged. "Maybe just for the fun of it. I don't know whether or not the kid is a druggie—we'll find out—but he sure acts like one. So he's got to be tops on my hit parade. That doesn't mean I'm going to stop looking at the others. Where were they last night? What time did they go to sleep? Did they hear anything? See anything? The usual drill."

He rose, buckled on his gun belt, looked at me. I was still nursing my first beer.

"You going to keep digging?" he demanded.

"You want me to?" I asked him. "Or do you want me off?"

He considered a moment. "Keep nosing," he said finally. "They might tell you things they won't tell me. And I know you'll report anything you learn."

"Of course," I assured him.

"Of course," he repeated.

We smiled at each other.

15

I KNOW YOU'LL BE delighted to learn I regained my appetite on Monday evening. Well, of course it had to happen because Ursi served beef stew Provençale with fettuccine, and what man, woman, child, or werewolf could resist that? Oh, how I gorged! But remember, I had ingested scarcely a morsel all day. It is foolish (and painful) to deny the body's demands.

Dessert, mercifully, was a simple lime sorbet. By the time I waddled from the dining room I had decided that life, despite its eternal frustrations, was indeed worth living. The guv stopped me in the hallway.

"You talked to Sergeant Rogoff?" he asked. "About Hiram Gottschalk's murder."

"Yes, sir. I told him what little I had learned. He wants me to keep nosing about."

The sire nodded approvingly. "Good," he said. "Do it."

And that was the extent of our conversation. I went upstairs to my journal, wanting to find a factoid I dimly recalled. I found it: a scrap of conversation with Peter Gottschalk at the Pelican Club. "I hate my father," he had said.

But now, with Peter being Al Rogoff's chief suspect in a heinous killing, the son's emotional comment took on an added resonance. I debated informing the sergeant but decided not to *pro tempore*. One impulsive utterance was hardly evidence of murderous intent, was it. Was it?

Disturbed about where my duty lay, I deserted my quarters, went downstairs and outside. I wandered over to the doghouse. Awakened by my approach, Hobo emerged slowly, yawning, tail wagging feebly.

"Sorry to disturb your slumber, old man," I said, and leaned down to peer within his shelter.

There was now a square of old carpeting on the ground, and he had been provided with plastic dishes holding food and water. There was also a rawhide bone and a toy that looked like a stuffed cat and already showed signs of enthusiastic gnawing.

"All the comforts of home," I told him. "You've got it made, Hobo."

I sat down on the patch of lawn about his mansion. He came close and curled up alongside. He rested his head on my knee and looked up at me. I am trying very hard not to anthropomorphize too much but I swear that animal knew or sensed I was troubled. His look and manner were concerned and sympathetic. Ridiculous? Possibly.

I stroked him steadily and absently, scratching his ears and head, smoothing his coat down to his tail. He allowed me, although I suspected he might have preferred snoozing within his castle. I don't know why but caressing the dog was marvelous therapy. I suppose I might have achieved the same result with a cat, gerbil, hippopotamus—or even, I thought suddenly, a mynah who responded to all approaches by repeating, "Dicky did it."

I finally arose, gave Hobo a final pat, and returned to the house. I paused at the kitchen door and looked back. He was standing at the entrance to his dwelling, watching me. To make certain I'm safe inside, I fancied, and then recognized it was so loony that if I kept it up I'd soon be inviting him in to join me for luncheon at the Pelican Club.

Up in my den again, I treated myself to an English Oval and a marc, parked my feet on the desk, and surrendered to the gruesome puzzle biting at me since I spoke to Sgt. Rogoff. Hiram Gottschalk had been stabbed through the eyes. Wouldn't your average, run-of-the-mill assassin, anxious to complete the dirty deed and escape, knife a sleeping victim in the heart, or at least the chest, once or many times? But no, the killer had deliberately pierced the eyes. And through those orbs of seeing into the brain. Why?

Obvious, was it not? A deranged slayer sought to make Hiram Gottschalk permanently sightless. He had seen too much, and so he had to perish. I could come to no other conclusion. Could you?

But that judgment solved little. It merely engendered more questions. What had Hiram seen—or what was he seeing? Why did his witnessing have to be abruptly terminated in such a vicious manner? In my brief conversations with the man, I had thought him mildly eccentric but hardly the possessor of dark secrets so ominous they demanded his death. Someone thought otherwise.

I went to bed that night still pondering what Hiram might have viewed that caused his demise. The result of my mulling? Nada.

Connie Garcia didn't phone.

Tuesday might as well have been called Bluesday. Not the weather—that was sprightly enough—but I was feeling far from gruntled. The perplexities of the Gottschalk affair were nagging, of course, and Connie's intransigence was infuriating. Her refusal to make the slightest effort toward a rapprochement was a blow to the McNally ego. After all, who had taught her the complete lyrics of "May the Bird of Paradise Fly Up Your Nose"? *Moi!* And cold rejection was my reward. Maddening!

A breakfast of scones with apricot preserves helped but I was still in a tetchy mood when I drove to work. I decided my megrims could only be vanquished by resolute action. I would make phone calls, ask stern questions and demand answers, pry relentlessly, and by the end of the day I would have Hiram's killer by the heels.

It didn't happen. I found myself slumped at my desk, counting the walls (four) and wondering what to do next. There's a German word for my condition: *verdutzt.* The Yiddish version is *fartootst.* Both mean confused, bewildered. At the moment A. McNally was definitely fartootst. Plussed I was non.

My brain was saved from a total scatter by a phone call from Julia Gottschalk. At least she claimed to be Julia. The voices of the twin sisters were so alike I could not be certain but took the caller at her word.

"Julia," I started, "I want to express my—"

"Yes, yes," she said somewhat testily, cutting my condolences short. "I know how you must feel. We all feel the same way. Archy, I'd like to see you as soon as possible."

"Oh? Sniffles better?"

"What?"

"Your sister said you were indisposed. Cold, flu, or whatever."

"Oh that," she said blithely. "It went away. When can we meet?"

"Lunch?" I suggested.

"No can do," she said promptly. "Judith and I must go shopping. Something suitable to wear at the funeral, you know."

"Of course," I said, amazed at the priorities of Hiram's loving female offspring.

"Around three o'clock," she said firmly. "The bar at the Cafe L'Europe. We'll have some nice shampoo and a cracker or two."

"I'll be there."

"See you then," she said lightly, and disconnected.

I sat staring at the dead phone. Hardly the wail of a grieving daughter, was it? "Shampoo and a cracker or two." Was that her idea of a wake for her murdered father? I wondered if Mr. Gottschalk had been fully aware of the character of his progeny. Parents sometimes do have a tendency to view their kiddies through glasses so rose-colored they're practically opaque. My mother, for instance, firmly believes me to be sterling. Father, on the other hand, is convinced I am tarnished brass.

I was still musing on that curious exchange with Julia Gottschalk when I received another equally puzzling call.

"Archy?" she said. "This is Yvonne Chrisling."

"Oh, Yvonne," Please let me express my condolences for your loss. He was a fine gentleman and I shall miss him, as I'm sure you all will."

"Of course," she said. "And I thank you for your sympathy. The sooner they find the fiend who did it, the better. It was an ugly, despicable crime, and I haven't stopped crying yet."

She didn't sound as if she was weeping, or had been, but perhaps she had herself under control. No surprise there.

"Archy," she said, "the last time we spoke we discussed how strangely Hiram had been acting recently. Did you tell your father about that?"

"No, I did not. I didn't have the opportunity."

"Good," she said. "Because it's all meaningless now, isn't it?"

"Quite right."

"That's a relief," she said, and I thought it was to her—a relief. "There's no point in bringing it up since the man has passed. Well, I must ring off. Things are in an uproar, as you can imagine, with the police, reporters, television crews, planning for the funeral, and so forth. The children have been of no help whatsoever. But I do want to see you again as soon as things settle down."

"If there's anything I can do to help, please let me know."

"I'll do that," she said warmly. "I know you represent Hiram's attorney but I think of you more as a friend. A close friend."

"Thank you, Yvonne," I said, thinking, Close friend? Since when?

"Ta-ta," she said, and hung up.

It was the final "Ta-ta" I found particularly distasteful. I mean it was so frivolous. The woman's employer had been brutally slain, stabbed to death through the eyes, and she said, "Ta-ta."

Suddenly I realized if I had failed to take action that morning as I intended, action had come to me. I had received two communications and though neither was apparently of earthshaking importance, both were what I call nuzzles: little nudges by which fig leaves are raised ever so slightly and nakedness can be glimpsed. My lady callers had intrigued me, not with revelations but with teasing hints of hidden treasures. And both, I reckoned gleefully, had me pegged as a simp. I thought that was just dandy.

I was beginning to regain a measure of the usual McNally esprit when I received my third call of the morning. It was from Binky Watrous but had no deflationary effect.

"Hi, Archy," he said brightly. "I'm at home."

"Bully!" I said. "Whose?"

Short silence. Binky, as I'm sure you're aware, is not too swift.

"Why, I'm at *my* home," he said finally. "I don't work on Tuesdays. Archy, did you know there are more than eighty-six hundred species of birds?"

"Heavens to Betsy!" I exclaimed. "Would you wait half a mo while I make a note of that."

Another short silence. He was actually pausing to enable me to jot a record of his disclosure. What a dweeb!

"And how many species of parrots do you estimate are in existence?" I asked seriously, keeping my prank alive.

"Oodles," he said. "Just oodles."

It was fun diddling Binky but I felt it had gone on long enough. "And this information on the variety of our feathered friends is the reason for your call?"

"I thought you'd be interested," he said somewhat aggrievedly. "It might help our discreet inquiry, mightn't it?"

"A remote possibility."

"Actually," he blathered on, "there's another reason. I phoned Bridget Houlihan at Parrots Unlimited. Just to chat, you know. We've become close."

"Glad to hear it."

"*Very* close," he said in a tone so smarmy his shins would have been endangered had he been within kicking distance. "We've been working on our act where Bridget plays the tambourine accompanying my birdcalls. We thought we might try it out at nursing homes. Bring a little jollity to the oldsters. What do you think, Archy?"

My first reaction was to cry, "Have you no mercy?" But I restrained myself. "A generous impulse," I said.

"Anyway, Bridget told me this morning Ricardo Chrisling had two visitors. Ricardo has moved into Mr. Gottschalk's private office and the poor man isn't even buried yet. Also, Ricardo told the clerks to put Ralph, Hiram's personal parrot, up for sale. That seems rather unfeeling, doesn't it, Archy?"

"You're right, Binky; it does."

"Well, Ricardo had these two visitors, apparently friends or business acquaintances. He gave them a tour through the store and then took them into his office and closed the door—something Hiram never did. Bridget said she didn't like the looks of the two strangers."

"Oh? Why not?"

"Too much flash. That's Bridget's word—flash. Shiny silk suits and lots of gold jewelry. Also, they spoke a foreign language with Ricardo. Emma Gompertz thought it was Spanish but Tony Sutcliffe said it was Portuguese."

"Esperanto?" I suggested. "Or perhaps pig Latin."

"Bridget said that after the visitors left, Ricardo called the staff together and told them he planned to increase the variety of parrots offered for sale, concentrating on rarer, more expensive birds. He said he would give them instructions on their care and feeding. That guy is really taking over, Archy. Can he do that?"

"I don't know the ins and outs of the situation, Binky. I don't know who inherits Parrots Unlimited. I presume it's one of the assets left to his children. If that's true and they want Ricardo to continue managing the store, then he can do whatever he pleases providing it's lawful."

"I guess," he said. "But Bridget doesn't like it and neither do Emma and Tony. They're all upset."

"Change affects some people that way."

"So you think it's okay?"

"I didn't say that. As political pundits like to predict, time will tell. You're working at the store tomorrow?"

"Yep. Nine to five."

"Keep asking questions," I instructed. "You're doing fine."

"I am?" he said happily. "Archy, when can I go on salary as your paid assistant?"

"Time will tell," I told him. "Meanwhile, consider your fringe benefits. You met Bridget Houlihan, didn't you?"

"Oh yes," he said soulfully. "My very own mavournik."

"Your *what?*"

"Mavournik. You know—a lovely Irish missy."

"Binky," I said gently, "the word you seek is mavourneen."

"Whatever," he said dreamily.

I gave up.

16

I HAD A SLOW and solitary luncheon at the Pelican Club during which I indulged in some heavy ratiocination. Oh yes, I am capable of that occasionally even though you may think me just another pretty face. I came to no startling conclusions, mainly because I had so little to go on. But I was convinced Mr. Gottschalk had been put down by a member of his household. And I was certain mischief had been afoot prior to his demise and might well be continuing even after the poor man met his quietus.

Al Rogoff had told me there are two main motives for homicide: sex and money. In this case I suspected money took precedence since it was difficult to imagine the elderly Hiram was the victim of a crime of sexual passion. But one never knows, do one?

I arrived at the Cafe L'Europe on the dot, figuring I'd have a twenty- or thirty-minute wait before Julia Gottschalk appeared, fashionably late. But she was already present, sitting at the bar and sipping a flute of a vintage champagne while nibbling a bit of toast heaped with sturgeon roe. My expense account took a sudden liftoff.

I paused a moment before making my presence known. The grieving daughter of a slain father was wearing a ruby velvet jumpsuit belted with a flowered Hermès scarf. She also flaunted white leather boots and a necklace of multihued Lucite chunks in cages of gold wire. Not exactly sackcloth and ashes, was it?

She turned to greet me. "Hi, Archy," she said with one of the twins' elfish grins. "I started without you."

"So I see," I said, and motioned to the barkeep to provide me with a duplicate of her mini-banquet. "I'm glad to see you're bearing up under the sorrow of your father's death."

I tried to keep the sardonicism from my voice and apparently I succeeded for she said, "Well, things have been in a tizzy but life must go on, mustn't it?"

"Indeed it must," I agreed.

"I think it's hit Peter more than Judith and me. The boy is lost, won't talk to anyone, keeps mumbling nonsense and drinking far too much."

"Ah," I said. "Pity."

"But that's not why I wanted to talk to you. Do you remember when we told you how strangely daddy had been acting before he died?"

"Yes, I remember."

"Did you tell your father what we said?"

"No, I did not. Didn't have the opportunity."

"Good," she said, and her relief was evident. "Because it's unimportant now, isn't it?"

"Of course."

"So we can just forget about the whole thing—right?"

"Right," I affirmed.

"Good," she said again, much assuaged. She motioned and we finished the bottle of bubbly with another spoonful of fish eggs on toast points.

"One other thing," she said, nibbling thoughtfully. "Do you know what's in father's will, Archy?"

I was startled. "Of course not. How on earth would I know something like that, Julia?"

"You're sure?"

"Cross my heart and hope to die. I'm certain you'll learn the details shortly. Probably within a week or so. Why don't you phone my father and ask?"

"We could but we don't want to seem pushy."

It was difficult to refrain from hooting. Pushy? Yes, I would say the twins suffered from a severe case of chronic pushiness, wouldn't you?

Moments later she finished her costly snack and grabbed up her blue leather Louis Vuitton shoulder bag. I received a small cheek kiss. Then she was gone. I was left wondering what her purpose had been in scheduling our brief meeting. Wondering if she really was Julia and not Judith, knowing there was no way of knowing unless she unzipped the jumpsuit and proved she possessed no small abdominal mole.

And wondering, as I examined the tab presented to me, how I could convince Raymond Gelding, treasurer of McNally & Son, that vintage Krug and beluga caviar were a legitimate business expense.

The perplexities of that day had not yet ended. I was in my lair after dinner, scribbling in my journal while listening to a tape of Louis Armstrong playing such wonders as "Anybody Here Want to Try My Cabbage?" and "I'm a Ding Dong Daddy (from

Dumas)," when my phone rang. I grabbed it up eagerly, hoping it might be Connie Garcia calling with a wailing apology—which would make me a ding dong daddy from Palm Beach.

It wasn't Connie. It was Ricardo Chrisling.

"Hope I'm not disturbing you," he said in a tone implying he couldn't care less if he was.

"Not at all," I said. "I was saddened to hear of Mr. Gottschalk's death. Dreadful business."

"Yes," he said. "We're all stunned. Trying to function, you know, but still shaken. A fine gentleman."

"He was," I agreed.

"Archy, the last time we met I happened to mention how crazily Hiram had been acting recently. Really batty. Did you report what I said to your father?"

"No, I did not."

"Glad to hear it," he said, his voice warmer now. "Because with the old man gone it's of no importance, is it? I mean, what's that expression of speaking nothing bad of the departed?"

" '*De mortuis nil nisi bonum.*' Freely translated: 'Say nothing but good of the dead.' "

"Exactly," he said. "We'll let it go at that—okay?"

"Sure."

"Hey, have you tried that Mexican brandy I gave you?"

"I have indeed. Very nice."

"Ready for another bottle?"

"Good lord, no! I have plenty left."

"Well, I have a case of the stuff, so whenever you're ready just give me a shout. Listen, Archy, I like you and hope we can get together for dinner some night."

"Sounds good to me," I said, hoping I effectively cloaked my astonishment.

"Y'see," he went on, very solemnly, "since Hiram was killed

I've been doing a lot of deep thinking. Realizing how short life is and how we should get as much enjoyment as we can while we can."

Now I was doubly astonished. Suddenly he had become one of those grinches who saw life as a terminal illness. Very philosophical. But his superficial maunderings did not square with my impressions of the man. I did not believe him capable of "deep thinking." I suspected he was governed more by physical appetites than by moral principles or reasoned enlightenment.

I could be wrong of course. I have been wrong in the past. For instance, I once assured Connie I was quite capable of consuming two enormous bowls of fried calamari and an entire bottle of Barolo without suffering any ill effects. Fortunately we had exited to the restaurant's parking area before I was stricken. I shan't describe it. Surely you've heard of Krakatoa.

I entered the details of my conversation with Ricardo in my journal—with the fey fancy that God might keep a similar record of us all—and then sat back to review the day's findings.

I started with my nutsy chat with Binky Watrous. Disregarding his moony comments about his Erin-go-bragh poppet, I found his report of some interest. Ricardo now seemed to be the honcho of Parrots Unlimited and was entertaining flashy visitors and speaking a foreign language. In addition, the inventory of birds was apparently to be enlarged by the addition of rare and more costly parrots.

What all that signified, if anything, I hadn't the slightest and put the whole matter on hold.

My exchanges with Yvonne Chrisling, Julia representing the twins, and Ricardo were something else again. All three parties had been intent on convincing me of Hiram Gottschalk's increasing irrationality prior to his murder, requesting I report their revelations to my father. And then, after Hiram's death, all three had been just as eager to confirm I had not repeated their comments to his attorney.

Their actions seemed incomprehensible. But I knew they were not stupid people. Venal perhaps, but not stupid. I mean they were obviously following plans that seemed logical to them. But I could not even guess what their motives might be. I reckoned it had to be greed: a hunger for a healthy share of the deceased's estate.

But whether greed was sufficient reason for his brutal murder I could not say. I doubted it since all concerned were living very well indeed while Hiram was alive. But then again one must never forget the first dictum of accumulating wealth: Enough is never enough.

I went to the sheets that night with a very curious thought: Was I dealing with corrupt people? Corruption exists in a variety of modes of course, ranging from the depredations of Attila the Hun to stealing towels from a hotel. But I sensed the malignity in the Gottschalk household was not as flippant as the latter. After all, a man had been viciously put to death and someone in his entourage had committed the dirty deed. It bespoke of infamy that frightened me.

Why can't we all be nice and love one another? And why can't we all have wings and thus eliminate department store escalators?

I awoke on Wednesday morning in time to breakfast with my parents—and that turned out to be a mistake. Not because of the vittles, you understand. Who could object to mini-waffles with clover honey? Not me. But it was father's mood that dulled the matutinal meal.

He was not surly—he's never that—but he was definitely grumpy, and his sour humor put the kibosh on what should have been a pleasant morning assembly of the McNally clan. The reason for his peevishness was explained when he stopped me in the hallway as we exited from the dining room.

"Sergeant Rogoff called early this morning," he said. "While I was dressing." His tone was indignant, implying a gentleman should never be interrupted in the process of donning his balbriggan underwear. "Apparently yesterday evening Peter Gottschalk did not appear for dinner. The maid was sent to his chamber and discovered him lying on the floor in what was allegedly a comatose condition. The paramedics were summoned and Peter was taken to a hospital. There it was reportedly determined he was suffering from an overdose of barbiturates and alcohol."

He paused. I disregarded his lawyerly "apparently, allegedly, reportedly."

"An attempted suicide?" I asked, my heart shrinking.

"It may be so," the squire said in his magisterial voice. "I suggest you contact Sergeant Rogoff as soon as feasible. Try to learn more details of this distressing matter, the boy's present physical condition, and so forth."

"Yes, sir," I said. And speaking as unemotionally as he, I added, "I'll attend to it at once."

"Good," he said, then mentioned almost absently, "If the son dies it will complicate the settlement of Hiram Gottschalk's estate."

Please don't think my father was oblivious to the human tragedy possibly involved here. But he was not a man much given to an outward display of his feelings. An attorney specializing in wills and estate planning accepts the inevitability of illness, decrepitude, and mortality sooner than most of us and so, as a measure of self-preservation, learns to control his personal reactions. Usually it works. Not always.

I waited until m'lord had departed in his black Lexus. Then I went into his study, sat in his chair, behind his desk, feeling as usual like a pretender to the throne. I phoned Al Rogoff at headquarters but his line was busy. I lighted a cigarette and waited patiently, resisting a desire to sneak a nip of papa's best cognac. Early in the morning for a wee bit of the old nasty, I admit, but I was spooked by the news of Peter Gottschalk.

I finally got through to the sergeant.

"Your father tell you?" he demanded.

"Yes. How is Peter doing?"

"He'll survive. Listen, it's not so easy to croak on pills and vodka. Takes a load of both to do the trick."

"Did he leave a note?"

"No, but that doesn't mean anything. Sometimes they do, sometimes they don't."

"But you're convinced it was a suicide attempt?"

"What else? Another piece of evidence."

"Evidence of what, Al?"

"C'mon, Archy, what've you got between your ears—succotash? The kid ices his father and then tries to end his own life because of guilt."

"Is that how you see it?"

"What other motive for suicide could he have?"

"How about grief?" I said. "Ever think of that?"

Rogoff sighed. "You're a doozy, you are. You remind me of the federal judge riding along a country road with a friend. The pal says, 'Look at that herd of sheep. They've just been sheared.' And the judge says, 'They appear to have been sheared on this side.' That's you—always questioning the obvious."

"Al, you're evidently a devotee of Occam's razor."

"Of *what?*"

"Look it up. Where is Peter Gottschalk now—still in the hospital?"

"No, he's been released. He's probably home. I don't have enough on him for an arrest—yet."

"Would you object if I visited him?"

Long silence. Then: "I can't officially say no. But why do you want to visit him?"

"I really don't know," I confessed. "Just to talk I guess. It can't do any harm, Al."

"I suppose not. You'll tell me what he says?"

"It depends," I said.

"Yeah," he said disgustedly, "I figured that. Thank you for your kind cooperation."

17

I T WAS APPARENT Sgt. Rogoff believed Peter was his father's murderer. Al is rarely wrong in his professional judgments but in this case I thought he was. I simply could not see that poor, disturbed lad as a stiletto-wielding patricide. A weirdo *ja*; a killer *nein*. But I had to admit the son's attempted suicide could be interpreted as an indication of his culpability.

I went back to the desk and phoned Dr. Gussie Pearlberg. Luckily I caught her between clients and we were able to exchange affectionate greetings.

"Dr. Gussie," I said, "I am in Dire Straits, a narrow body of turbulent water between Total Confusion and Utter Despair." I was awarded a croaky laugh. "Is it at all possible you might see me sometime today?"

"Only on my lunch hour, bubeleh," she said. "If you are willing to sit and watch an old lady stuff her fat face, I can see you at one o'clock."

"Wonderful," I said. "I'll be there. Please, may I bring you lunch?"

"No, no," she protested. "Every day I have delivered a nice chopped chicken liver sandwich, a nice kosher dill, a hot tea with lemon, and a nice prune Danish. Listen, sonny, you'll have lunch before you come to see me?"

"Of course."

"Maybe a tuna fish salad with a glass of milk," she suggested.

"That would be nice," I agreed. Never!

I set out for the Gottschalk home wondering if I should bring Peter a get-well gift. But what on earth do you give a would-be suicide? Flowers? Bonbons? A bottle of vodka was obviously out of the question. And so I arrived empty-handed, dubious about this errand of mercy and what it might accomplish.

I was greeted at the door by Mei Lee but before we had time to exchange salutations she was brushed aside by Yvonne Chrisling, whose stern, almost outraged manner softened when she recognized me.

"Oh, I'm so glad it's you, Archy," she said. "The reporters have been driving us crazy."

"I can imagine," I said, and followed her inside. I thought the interior of the Gottschalk manse seemed even more disordered than I recalled from my previous visits.

"How are you coping, Yvonne?" I asked.

"We're surviving," she said with an imitation of a brave smile. "Things are in a horrible stew at the moment but I'm sure everything will soon straighten out."

"Of course," I said, which I didn't believe for a minute. "I was hoping to see Peter. Is he home?"

"He's here," she admitted. "I suppose you heard what he did—

or tried to do. I'm not certain he's in any condition to receive visitors."

"Please try," I urged. "I promise not to upset him or stay too long."

She bit her lower lip and I doubted Peter's physical condition was her main concern. I was suddenly convinced she wanted him kept incommunicado for reasons I wot not of.

"Wait here," she commanded.

I waited for what seemed to me an unreasonably long time. Finally she reappeared and conducted me to a second-floor bedroom.

"He's awake," she reported, "but not quite coherent. Don't believe everything he tells you."

I nodded. Yvonne leaned forward to give me a brief cheek kiss and a frozen smile. I thought that was okay. But then she did something so astounding I hesitate to repeat it, fearing you may believe I'm making it up. She goosed me. It's the truth. I swear it. Then, after her astonishing assault, she stalked away without looking back, leaving me with my flabber totally gasted and wondering if I had strayed into a loony bin.

I had expected to find a wan invalid lying motionless in bed under a sheet, staring vacantly at the ceiling. Instead I found Peter wearing jeans and a T-shirt, bopping around the room barefoot, snapping his fingers to the best of acid jazz thundering from an enormous speaker. He had the courtesy to turn down the volume when I entered.

"Hiya, Archy," he said with a feral grin. "Thanks for stopping by."

"How are you feeling, Peter?" I asked. It was the best I could do.

"Just great," he said blithely. "I can't do anything right, can I?

The problem was I had too much vodka, got so drunk I forgot to gulp enough pills. Next time I'll know better."

This discussion of the mechanics of self-destruction alarmed me. "I hope there won't be any next time."

He shrugged. "Not at the moment," he said, and continued to jive about the room, still snapping his fingers. He seemed more gaunt than ever, eyes sunk deeper, his entire face a portrait of young desolation. Yet he was obviously in a hyperactive mood; even those recessed eyes were bright and glittering.

"Peter," I said, "ever think of taking a trip? Get away from it all for a while. Maybe a European jaunt. Just as your sisters did. South of France and all that. Change of scene. Meet new people."

He stopped dancing to stare at me. "Great idea," he said. "I'll do it. Change my way of living—right? And if that ain't enough I'll even change the way I strut my stuff. But not yet. I've got to see this through first."

"See what through? The settlement of your father's estate? The solution of his murder?"

He wasn't offended by my rude questions. "Everything," he said, nodding, "I know a lot now and can find out the rest."

"Peter, you're talking in riddles."

He laughed so hard he lapsed into a fit of coughing. But gradually he calmed and wiped his mouth with the back of a hand.

"They think I don't know," he said, the savage grin returning. "They think I'm too loopy to know. But I *do* know. The catbird seat. Isn't that what it's called? Sure. I'm in the catbird seat."

I knew further prying would be useless. This conversation had skidded into dementia. But there was something I had to ask.

"Peter," I said, "you're not in any danger, are you?"

"Nothing I can't handle," he said, and then barked a laugh. "Except from myself."

"If you need any help," I told him, "physical assistance or just a listening ear, I'm available. Any hour."

It wasn't a majestic statement of sympathy, I admit, but it devastated him. He began weeping with great heaving sobs, palms to his face, his entire body trembling with anguish. I had absolutely no idea of how to deal with that and so, following my cowardly instincts, I made a hasty departure. So much for my errand of mercy.

I didn't regain any measure of emotional equilibrium until I was seated at the bar of the Pelican Club, frantically gulping a Sterling on the rocks with a smidgen of aqua. Can you blame me? I had just been wantonly mauled by a beetle-browed dominatrix and had witnessed a vastly troubled lad reduced to the weeps by a simple offer of support. It was enough to drive a man to drink—and so it did.

I remained at the bar, hailed Priscilla, and asked her to bring me a gargantuan cheeseburger with side orders of peppered slaw and Leroy's thick garlic potato chips.

"On a diet?" she said, and when I didn't deign to retort to her impertinence she asked, "Still seeing Connie?"

I flipped a hand back and forth.

"Oh-oh," Pris said. "Trouble in paradise. She was in the other day and wanted to know if I had seen you. I figured there was a problem. It's your fault."

"How dare you!" I cried indignantly.

"You're a man, aren't you? *Ipso facto.* Is that the right expression?"

"It is a legal term," I admitted. "But it doesn't apply in this particular case."

"Hah!" she said, and went to fetch my cholesterol à la carte.

By the time I pointed the Miata southward toward Lantana and the office of Dr. Gussie Pearlberg I was in a chipper mood.

All those yummy calories had restored the McNally sangfroid, and no one is sanger or froider than yrs. truly.

A short time later I was slumped in the lumpy armchair alongside Dr. Gussie's bulky desk. I marveled at how this accomplished woman adroitly managed a chopped chicken liver sandwich, kosher dill, container of hot tea, and prune Danish while smoking a filter-tipped cigarette and listening to my concerns.

Actually it was she who ignited our conversation.

"Sonny," she said, "the last time you were here you spoke about a client who feared his life was in danger. He had been the victim of several nasty acts of psychological terrorism. Was he the man who was recently murdered? The owner of the parrot store?"

"Yes," I said. "Hiram Gottschalk. How did you know?"

"I didn't *know*, but I read about it in the papers, heard about it on the radio and television, and I feared it might be your client. I am so sorry."

"Not half as sorry as I. If I had moved faster . . ." My voice trailed away.

"Don't blame yourself, bubeleh," she advised. "Investigations take time; we both know that. Some of mine have been going on for ten years with no resolution. No, there is no reason for you to feel guilty. Some things are inevitable; we simply cannot forestall them. The news reports said only that he was stabbed to death while asleep. Stabbed where? In the heart? Or slashed? How many wounds?"

I drew a deep breath and decided to break my promise to Sgt. Rogoff. "He was stabbed through the eyes with a long stiletto-type weapon."

She seemed more excited than outraged. "The eyes! Now that *is* significant. Indicative. Definitely indicative."

"Of what?" I asked.

She ignored my question. "Who is handling the case?"

"Sergeant Al Rogoff. You know him of course."

"Of course. A good professional policeman with all the talents, experience, and limitations of the breed. Does he have a suspect?"

I trusted her discretion completely. She could be drawn and quartered and never betray a confidence.

"Al does have a suspect," I told her. "The murdered man's son, Peter Gottschalk."

"Oh?" she said, starting another cigarette. "Tell me about him."

I told her everything I knew about Peter Gottschalk: physical description, wild mood swings, laughter and tears, recklessness and accidents, occasional incoherence, attempted suicide and his casual mention of trying it again. And his puzzling remarks about hidden plots within the Gottschalk household, things no one suspected he knew.

Although she didn't interrupt, Dr. Gussie's expression grew increasingly pained during my recital. It may have been the prune Danish but I doubted it.

I finished and asked, "What do you think?"

She stirred, shifting her weight irritably. "It would be unprofessional to venture an opinion without examining the subject personally, Archy; you know that."

"Of course."

"And naturally I would never offer my conclusions in a court of law without many interviews with this Peter Gottschalk."

"Understood, Dr. Gussie. I am merely asking for a snap judgment, *entre nous.*"

She sighed. "Sonny, what you have just told me is almost a classical clinical analysis of bipolar affective disorder. You probably know it as manic-depression. I don't like to term it a psychosis though many professionals do. I prefer to call it a mental illness. Its main characteristic is wild mood swings between elation and despair. From your description, I would guess Peter Gottschalk is a manic-depressive."

"Do they commit suicide or try to?"

"If I told you how many," she said sadly, "you wouldn't believe. But only because their condition is not recognized and they go without treatment."

"What *is* the treatment?"

"Mainly medication. Sometimes neuroleptics. For a long time lithium was the only thing available. But now there are more and better drugs which don't have the side effects of lithium."

"You haven't used the word cure, Dr. Gussie."

"No, and I won't. All we can do at this time is treat the symptoms."

"You mean a manic-depressive must continue to take medication for the remainder of his or her life?"

"Yes, and must be monitored regularly to make certain the results are satisfactory or if the dosage should be altered or another drug substituted."

There was something additional I had to know. "You said suicide is common amongst untreated manic-depressives. Are they also prone to violence?"

"Frequently."

"Homicide?"

She stared at me. "That I cannot tell you because I just don't know. I have seen no studies of murders supposedly committed by manic-depressives."

"But you think it possible they might kill while in a manic or depressed state?"

"Oh, bubeleh, we're talking about people. Human beings. *Anything* is possible."

I knew what must be done but didn't have the courage to volunteer. "Can you suggest a way Peter might be helped?"

She saw through my cowardice at once and gave me a gentle smile. "You know what you must do, sonny. Convince him he must consult me or any other psychiatrist as soon as possible. And I mean *immediately*. If my off-the-cuff diagnosis is correct and he is suffering from bipolar disorder, he is in very great danger every day he goes without treatment."

I groaned. "How do I tell Peter he is mentally ill and needs professional assistance? He's liable to deck me."

"Possibly," she agreed calmly. "He may react with hostility. Or he may simply deny there is anything wrong with him. Or he may surprise you and agree he needs help. Whatever his reaction, you'll have done what you *must* do. The final decision is his."

"All right," I said mournfully. "I'll get through it somehow."

She rose to pat my cheek. "Of course you will," she said. "And you will succeed. You are a very charming, persuasive young man. If I were fifty years younger I would be writing you a billet-doux every day."

"Billy, do?" I said innocently. "But my name is Archy."

"Out!" she said, pointing to the door.

18

DESPITE THE FINAL lighthearted fillip, my conversation with Dr. Gussie left me in a subdued mood. The old chops were definitely in free fall, and a return to my cramped cul-de-sac in the McNally Building was not to be suffered. I needed a spot of alfresco brooding. How does one go about telling a chap he's around the bend? He's liable to reply, "So's your old man," or some other cutting remark, and that would be the end of that.

Dejected by this and other conundrums of the Gottschalk affair, I drove home, pulled in to our graveled turnaround, and alighted from my barouche. My spirits ascended instanter for Hobo came dashing to me. Clamped in his jaws was a short length of what appeared to be a sawed-off broom handle. He dropped the stick at my feet and looked up expectantly.

I laughed. Listen, it was his game, not mine; I hadn't taught him Fetch or any other silly trick. But I picked up his baton and gave it a good toss. He whirled and raced after it. A moment later he came trotting back with the prize clenched in his teeth, dropped it and waited.

We continued our sport for about five minutes and I tired before he did. I think he was disappointed when I stroked his head, told him what a splendid retriever he was, and left him to find other entertainment. I went inside feeling upbucked after my short session with the frolicsome Hobo. He had a gift of conveying joy.

We all have our wonts, do we not, and one of mine is to dither when faced with a difficult decision. I was tempted to delay a confrontation with Peter Gottschalk to another day. Perhaps to the next century when, with luck, I might be dead. But that I realized was an ignoble snivel and so, as the Reverend Spooner might say, I lirded my groins and phoned the Gottschalk residence.

"Hello?" a wary female answered. I thought I recognized the voice of Julia or Judith.

"Hello," I said. "Archy McNally here. Julia?"

"Judith."

"Uh-huh," I said. "How are you enduring?"

"Such a drag," she said. "We'll be happy when it's all over. Julia and I decided we need R and R in Italy to recover. We love Milan. Ever been there?"

"Afraid not."

"Divine boutiques. All the latest."

"I'm sure," I said. "Actually I called to speak with Peter. Is he available?"

"No, he took off."

"Took off?" I said, astonished. "But I spoke with him this morning. I mean he's recovering from an attempted suicide, isn't he. But he's gone? Where?"

"Who knows?" she said. "He's perpetually out to lunch. That young man really should be put away. Thanks for calling, Archy."

She hung up abruptly, leaving me to stare at the silent phone and try to understand her blithe indifference. After all, Peter was her brother, a member of the family. One might expect his condition to be of more concern than Milanese boutiques. I was beginning to get antsy about the Gottschalk twins. Disturbing conduct on their part, wouldn't you say?

I did my afternoon swim in a sea that was chilly but not painfully so. I attended the family cocktail hour, during which nothing was mentioned about the death of Hiram Gottschalk. Mother said Hobo had padded into her potting shed, curled up in a patch of sunlight, and snoozed for almost an hour, waking occasionally to make certain she was still there.

"He's such a dear doggie," she said. "I talk to him and I really think he understands. Do you talk to him, Archy?"

"Frequently," I said. "Although I can't fully agree with his opinion of the International Monetary Fund."

I do believe my father snorted.

Dinner that evening was lamb shanks—one of my thousand favorite dishes. I would have preferred mint jelly but Ursi served it with a ginger sauce. No complaints. Dessert was fresh strawberries drizzled with crème de menthe. A red zin to sluice it all down. Sometimes I imagine my arteries must resemble Federal Highway during the morning rush hour.

I retired to my third-floor digs intending to spend a quiet night adding to my record of the Gottschalk case. Then I might treat myself to a marc and listen to Ella Fitzgerald sing, "Lover, Come Back to Me," and wonder how Connie Garcia could possibly be so cruel as not to phone me. Had I completely misjudged her? Was she totally heartless?

But the revelations and surprises of that confusing day had not yet ended. I received a phone call from my loyal but mentally disadvantaged henchman, Binky Watrous. And even before he spoke I thought I heard the brittle clinking of a tambourine in the background.

"Archy?" he said. "Is this Archy?"

"No," I said, "this is Horace Walpole, author of 'Mysterious Mother' and other wildly popular fictions. Binky, what's *with* you? Of course this is Archy and are you boiled and why do I hear the sound of a tambourine?"

"I am *not* boiled," he said indignantly. "And I am calling from Bridget Houlihan's apartment where we are rehearsing our first appearance at a nursing home in Riviera Beach."

"Excellent," I said. "And that's why you called—to announce your theatrical debut?"

"Not exactly. Archy, something happened at Parrots Unlimited I think you should know about. Discreet inquiry stuff."

"Oh? What happened?"

"Well, you met Tony Sutcliffe, the senior salesclerk there. He knows more about parrots than any of us."

"Of course I met Tony and his companion, Emma Gompertz."

"Sure. Well, ever since Hiram died and Ricardo Chrisling took over, we've been getting some rare and high-priced birds."

"I know, Binky. You told me."

"It seemed to bother Tony. The parrots looked nice to me. Healthy and very pretty. Anyway, this afternoon Tony went into the private office to talk to Ricardo. The door was closed. I don't know what went on. But about fifteen minutes later Tony came out. Archy, he was as white as an umbrella cockatoo and obviously shook. 'I've been sacked,' he told us. That's all he'd say. He began to pack up his personal stuff and Emma started crying.

'Then I'm going too,' she said, and the two of them marched out. Doesn't that boggle the mind?"

"It does indeed," I said. "Did Ricardo offer any explanation?"

"About an hour later. He said Tony and Emma had resigned for personal reasons and he would hire replacements. Meanwhile he asked Bridget and me to cope as best we could until the new people came aboard. It's all so strange. Don't you think it's strange, Archy?"

"Definitely," I said. "Did Tony resent Ricardo becoming the mikado?"

"Well, they never were exactly buddy-buddy but I think it was more than just jealousy. I don't know why Tony got canned and Bridget can't guess either. I mean he knew an awful lot about parrots. But he suddenly got bounced."

"Binky," I said, "you have Tony's phone number, don't you?"

"Of course. Somewhere. And if I can't find it, Bridget is sure to have it. She's very organized. She even makes shopping lists."

"Amazing," I said. "Why don't you give Tony a call and tell him I'd like to buy him lunch. To commiserate on his sacking. You're included of course."

"That would be a decent thing to do," he agreed. "I'll give Tony a buzz and get back to you. Know something, Archy?"

"Know what?"

"I don't think everything is kosher at Parrots Unlimited. I suspect there's hanky-panky going on."

"You may be right."

"I think I'm developing a real talent as an investigator, don't you, Archy? I mean I'm learning how it's done."

"And how is it done?"

"You suspect *everyone.*"

"A good beginning," I assured him. "And as a fledgling detective, what is your guess as to the nature of the wickedness transpiring at Parrots Unlimited?"

He paused a moment, then said portentously, "It is my considered opinion that Ricardo Chrisling is running a white slave ring."

"Uh-huh," I said. "Or perhaps counterfeiting food stamps. Call me after you talk to Tony."

What a twit!

No Ella or marc for me that night. I just sat there, neurons atingle, trying to make sense of what Binky had just revealed and wondering if the goings-on at Parrots Unlimited had anything to do with the murder of its late proprietor. I thought there might be a connection, however tenuous, but could not imagine what it might be.

Now we shall fast-forward a few days in this report on *l'affaire* Gottschalk, for nothing of significance happened in the interim. Actually, things of some importance did occur but were negatives, only meaningful by their absence, which, I confess, I hadn't the wit to recognize.

For instance, Thursday and Friday passed uneventfully, and it was Friday night before I recalled I hadn't heard from Binky anent the luncheon with the dismissed Tony Sutcliffe. Nor had I been able to contact Peter Gottschalk to arrange a meeting during which I would attempt to convince him he was semibonkers and required professional help.

It was a leaden two days and the fact that Connie Garcia didn't phone only increased my angst to the point where I considered I might be happier in a monastery. One with a library including the complete recordings of Bessie Smith. More to my taste than Gregorian chants.

I finally came alert on Saturday morning, which was a puzzle because it was a chill, drizzly day designed for lolling in bed. But no, I felt an ineluctable urge to *do*. I decided some—any—action, no matter how unproductive, was necessary to retain my professional standing as a practitioner of discreet inquiries. And so, about noonish, I phoned Parrots Unlimited.

I recognized Bridget Houlihan's chirpy voice. "Parrots Unlimited," she said. "How may I help you?"

"Polly want a cracker," I said. "Bridget, please forgive a stupid jape. This is Archy McNally. How *are* you?"

"Oh, Archy," she said, "Binky and I are so rushed. Ricardo promised to hire two more people but no one's showed up yet. I guess you heard about Tony and Emma leaving."

"I heard and that's why I'm calling. Binky promised to set up a lunch with Tony but nothing has happened."

"I know," she said, "and it's very odd. We've been calling Tony and Emma two or three times a day and no one answers. And none of their friends have been able to contact them. They just seem to have disappeared."

"A holiday?" I suggested. "A vacation after Tony got canned?"

"Maybe," she said doubtfully. "But wouldn't you think they'd tell someone where they were going and for how long?"

She sounded worried.

"I'm sure they'll turn up eventually," I told her. "I presume Binky is busy at the moment."

"Oh yes. He's selling lovebirds to newlyweds."

"Very fitting," I said approvingly. "Tell me, Bridget, how did your act go at the Riviera Beach nursing home?"

"Oh, it was a great success," she said enthusiastically. "They laughed so hard."

"I can imagine."

"And everyone applauded and cheered."

"A standing ovation, eh?"

"Well, not exactly, since most of them were in wheelchairs.

But they want us to come back again. 'Better than Valium,' one old man said."

"Wonderful. Tell Binky I called, will you, Bridget, and if you hear from Tony and Emma please let me know."

I hung up troubled by what she had told me of the former clerks at Parrots Unlimited. It did seem exceedingly strange a young, gregarious couple would simply take off without telling anyone of their plans. Even if they were stressed by their sudden unemployment they would surely discuss their predicament and options with friends.

I pulled on a liverish nylon golf jacket and my puce beret and went down to the second-floor sitting room where mother was seated at her spindly desk penning chatty letters to her enormous network of correspondents.

"Moms," I said, "may I borrow your wagon? I have an errand to run, it's weeping out, and I hate to put the lid on my chariot."

"Of course, dear," she said. "I think it has enough gas but don't trust that gauge. Are you dressed warmly enough?"

"Absolutely," I assured her. "I'm even wearing socks." And I swooped to kiss her velvety cheek before taking off.

Mother's ancient wood-bodied station wagon is a balky beast. But on that Saturday morning it behaved splendidly, carrying me safely to West Palm Beach. I took along my cellular phone in case I couldn't find Tony Sutcliffe's home and had to call Binky or Bridget to direct me to the cramped condo where the wine-and-cheese orgy had been held.

19

MEMORY SERVED AND I found the place: a rather scuzzy three-tier edifice of chipped plaster, sun-bleached shingles, and with a dismal lawn that appeared to have been cropped by a bulimic goat.

There was a human-type goat propped against the outside doorframe when I climbed out of the wagon. He was wearing a shabby denim jacket atop splotched painter's overalls and was mouthing a toothpick apparently surgically attached to his lower lip. He seemed engrossed by the lowering sky and didn't give me a glance as I approached.

"Good morning, sir," I said.

How slowly he focused on me. His eyes were so pallid I was tempted to break into a chorus of "Jeepers Creepers."

"Yo," he said tonelessly.

"I'm looking for the manager or super," I told him. "Is such a person available?"

"Me," he said.

I was reminded of Jamie Olson. The two of them would be worthy adversaries in a monosyllabicity contest.

"I'm a friend of Tony Sutcliffe," I said. "Do you know if he's home?"

"Nope."

"Could you tell me the number of his apartment?"

"In the lobby."

"Have you seen him about recently?"

Those washed-out eyes stared at me. I sighed, took out my wallet, extracted a fiver, and offered it. An eager claw snatched it away.

"Not for two, three days," he said, toothpick bobbing.

"I'll see if he's in," I said. He didn't much care and returned to inspecting the firmament.

The handwritten register showed Emma Gompertz and Tony Sutcliffe as residents of apartment 2-B. I pressed the intercom bell. Several times. No response. I tried the inner door. Locked. I was ready to return to the taciturn super when the door was jerked open from within.

The lady about to exit was a bit long in the tooth and dressed flamboyantly. She was startled by my presence.

"Hi," she said tentatively.

"Hi," I replied, thinking her lashes were so heavily loaded with mascara she really should have been accompanied by a Seeing Eye dog.

"You live here?" she inquired.

"No, ma'am, I do not. Just visiting."

"Pity," she said. "Have a nice day."

"You, too," I said. "Have a good one."

"I do," she said, "but I don't get much chance to use it." She winked at me and went merrily on her way.

Then I was inside, recalling the route from my previous visit. Up a grungy stairway to 2-B. I leaned on the bell button. No answer or sounds from within. I rapped the door sharply. Several times. Nothing. I tried the doorknob. It turned easily and I stepped warily inside.

"Hello," I called. "Anyone home?"

No reply.

I closed the door quietly behind me and looked about. Deserted. I went through living room, bedroom, bathroom. All vacant. I even peered into closets and glanced behind the shower curtain at the bathtub. I returned to the kitchen.

The wooden table had been set for two. Dinner had obviously been suddenly interrupted. Plates held half-eaten portions of congealed lasagna. Glasses were stained with dried dregs of red wine, only small puddles of liquid remaining. Cockroaches and one humongous palmetto bug were busy. Not a pleasant sight. And the scent was not something you'd care to dab behind your earlobes.

The only indication of what might have occurred was a single chair tipped over and lying on the floor on its back. I could see no other signs of possible violence. The entire scene said so little but implied so much. Very disturbing. Especially the empty silence.

I left the apartment, closed the door softly behind me, returned to my parked wagon. The super was nowhere to be seen. I used my cellular phone to call Sgt. Al Rogoff at headquarters. He wasn't available, they said, and refused to tell me his whereabouts. I tried him at his home.

"Yeah?" he said.

"Archy McNally."

"Call me on Monday. I'm not working till then."

"Sure you are," I said. "You never stop working. What are you doing right now?"

"If you must know," he said, "I just picked up my laundry and I'm folding my shorts. Satisfied?"

"I'm in West Palm," I said. "Not too far from your place. You could be here in ten minutes."

"Why should I be there in ten minutes?"

"It concerns the Gottschalk homicide," I told him. "It may be something or it may be nothing, but you should see it."

"Why?"

"It would take too long to explain on the phone. Al, please do me a personal favor and get over here."

"The last time I did you a personal favor I almost got iced."

"You're stymied on the Gottschalk case, aren't you?"

"We're making progress," he said.

"Don't gull me," I said. "You're stuck and so am I. This could be a break."

"It better be," he said, "or you get promoted to the top of my S-list. What's the address?"

It was almost twenty minutes before Al's pickup came wheeling in to park alongside my wagon. Meanwhile the overalled super had reappeared and taken up his station next to the outside door. He stared at me with a definitely jaundiced glint. Maybe he suspected I was a cat burglar. Maybe he was hoping for another five. Who knew—or cared?

Rogoff came trundling over to me. He was wearing faded denim jeans and jacket and juicing up a fresh cigar. He was not in an amiable mood. "All right," he said, "let's have it."

I gave him the background, speaking rapidly. Tony Sutcliffe and Emma Gompertz. Former clerks at Parrots Unlimited, owned by the defunct Hiram Gottschalk. Tony's apparent altercation with Ricardo Chrisling, the new honcho. Tony's firing and the resignation of Emma. Their recent disappearance with no mention of their plans to friends.

"So I tried to make contact," I finished. "I think you should see their place."

"Anyone file a missing persons report?" he asked brusquely.

"Not to my knowledge."

"They have any close relatives?"

"I don't know."

"There's a lot you don't know, isn't there, sonny boy? Let's go take a look. What's the apartment number?"

"Two-B."

We marched up to the super. Rogoff displayed his ID.

"Sergeant Al Rogoff," he said. "PBPD. I want to take a look at apartment two-B."

The schlub stared coldly at him. "You got a search warrant?" he demanded.

"No," Al said, "I haven't *got* a search warrant. You *got* an operating sprinkler system? You *got* working smoke alarms? You *got* emergency exits clearly marked and lighted? You *got* garbage cans tightly lidded? You *got* rodents and vermin on the premises? I don't have a search warrant. How much you *got?*"

The super turned wordlessly and unlocked the inner door for us. We tramped up to the second floor.

"You're a rough man," I told Al.

"When I have to be," he said. "What did you touch in this joint?"

"Nothing. Except for the doorknobs."

Then we were inside 2-B. I stood stock-still while the sergeant went prowling. I knew he wouldn't miss the half-eaten meal on the kitchen table, the overturned chair. He came back to me a few minutes later. I could not decipher his expression.

"Wait for me downstairs," he commanded. "I'm going to toss the place."

"Hey," I said angrily, "why do I have to go? I gave you this. Can't I help you search?"

"No," he said stonily. "What I'm going to do is illegal. I don't need an eyewitness."

"Don't you trust me?"

"Dummy!" he said scathingly. "Not only am I covering my own ass but I'm covering yours. What if that goof in overalls files a complaint? Then I'm up for internal investigation. You get called to give testimony as a material witness. Probably under oath. Is that what you want?"

"I'll wait for you downstairs," I said hastily.

I sat in the wagon to escape the drizzle and chain-smoked two cigarettes, something I rarely do. Eventually Rogoff came out carrying a small brown paper bag. His chewed cigar was still cold but when he climbed in next to me he lighted up. I lowered the window.

"Anything?" I asked him.

"Some personal letters," he said curtly. "Names and addresses of people who seem to be relatives."

"Anything else?" I persisted.

"You ever hear of the Fish and Wildlife Service?"

"Of course. It's part of the Department of the Interior."

"Gee, Professor, you know everything," the sergeant said. "Well, they have a Division of Law Enforcement. This Tony Sutcliffe had some correspondence with them."

"About what?"

"I don't know exactly," Al said blandly. "I'll go over it when I have the time and see if it means anything."

He was stiffing me of course but that was okay; there were things I hadn't told him. It's the way we work together: a curious mixture of cooperation and rivalry. I know it sounds stupid but it's effective. Usually.

"What about Emma and Tony?" I asked him.

"If no one files a missing persons report, there's not much I can do officially."

"And unofficially?"

"Ask around. Contact the relatives. Talk to neighbors."

We were silent, neither of us wanting to allude to our primal fear. Finally I had to ask.

"Do you think they left voluntarily?"

"No."

"Someone barged in and grabbed them in the middle of their lasagna dinner?"

"Could be."

"Are they still alive?"

He glared at me. "What kind of a sappy question is that? How the hell should I know?"

"What's your guess?"

He stared out at the melancholy sky. "I think they're gone," he said in a low voice, leaving me to wonder if he meant Tony and Emma had simply been abducted for whatever reason, or were now dead. I didn't dare to keep pressing because I didn't want to know, didn't want my own dread to be confirmed.

We parted without further palaver. Al climbed into his pickup and headed out. I finally got the wagon rolling after some asthmatic engine coughs which caused me to suffer a mild panic attack. On the trip homeward I could not help but recall Hamlet's lament: "The time is out of joint; O cursed spite, that ever I was born to set it right!"

I do tend to drivel occasionally, do I not?

You will have noted, I trust, it was latish in the afternoon and I had not yet lunched. This was deliberate on my part for the waistbands of my trousers had become so constrictive of late I feared friends might soon be addressing me as "Porky."

My dreams of an abstemious diet went glimmering when I returned home. The weather was so inclement an ocean swim was not to be attempted and so I had no choice but to eat. The kitchen being temporarily deserted, I hurriedly constructed a sandwich of heroic proportions: two thick slices of pumpernickel clamping a deck of baked ham, a slice of sharp cheddar, another of red onion, another of beefsteak tomato, the whole painted lovingly with horseradish sauce.

I carried this magnum opus with a cold bottle of Heineken up to my den and settled down to feed my face and reflect on the developments of that frustrating day.

As I gorged I became convinced the disappearance of the two former clerks of Parrots Unlimited did indeed have a bearing on the murder of Hiram Gottschalk. The connection was unknowable at the moment but I felt a relation did exist and required some heavy sniffing about.

To do that, I realized, I would to some extent have to depend on the investigative talents of Binky Watrous—which was somewhat similar to a man with a broken leg leaning on a rubber cane. But Binky was capable of making observations and reporting odd or unusual occurrences, and I reckoned his raw data was necessary if I was to arrive at any intelligent analysis of what had happened and was happening in this baffling puzzle.

In addition to giving Binky fresh instructions—couched in the form of a pep talk since the lad needed constant reassurance he was a reincarnation of Hercule Poirot—I intended to dig into the role of the Fish and Wildlife Service. Sgt. Rogoff had mentioned that the missing Tony Sutcliffe had corresponded with that agency. Al's remark had been so casual I was certain the matter was more important than his offhand manner implied. The

sergeant plays his cards very, very close to his vest. And so do I—
if I wore a vest. Will a shocking-pink Izod golf shirt do?

The sandwich and the brew worked their way and I was suddenly overcome by the need of a nap. Not a long one, you understand, but a brief, intense slumber to give my wearied gray
matter (it's really a Black Watch tartan) a chance to regain its customary zip.

But before I drifted off I had a strange epiphany. Because parrots seemed to play an important part in this affair, I had come
to visualize the Gottschalk ménage as an aviary, a cageful of exotic and brilliantly colored birds. Suddenly my fancy was revised
and I imaged it as a zoo crowded with ugly and rapacious beasts.

A curious vision certainly but mental pabulum all the same.

20

BY SUNDAY MORNING the skies had cleared—and I wished I could say that for my thoughts. I was in such a distracted mood I accompanied my parents to church: something, I regretfully admit, I rarely do. The sermon was based on the scriptural dictum "The meek shall inherit the earth." How true, how true, and keep it in mind the next time you're mugged.

We returned home and went our separate ways. Father retired to his study to continue devouring *The New York Times*. Mother hurried to the greenhouse to commune with her begonias. And I went searching for Hobo. I finally found him—or rather he found me. He came trotting out of our small patch of woods and paused for a yawn and a long stretch. I had obviously interrupted a noonday nap but he showed no resentment and greeted my presence with an ankle rub.

I had learned from experience the activity he enjoyed most was what I can only term roughhousing. I crouched before him and we engaged in mock combat. He attacked with snarls and growls, jaws open. I defended myself by cuffing him, pushing him violently away, sometimes even flopping him onto his back.

He never bit me of course but delighted in giving my bare hand or wrist a good gumming. We continued this boisterous play until we both had to pause, panting. Then we went for a short walk about the grounds, Hobo padding contentedly at my heels. Finally I peered into his dwelling to make certain his water dish was filled and bade him a fond farewell, urging him to continue his nap.

I retreated to my own doghouse and shucked off my churchy duds, donning a new cotton robe I had recently bought. Well, it was really a nightshirt and the reason for its purchase was that the back was printed with a photograph of Laurel and Hardy trying to push a piano up a hill. I could relate to that.

I then settled down at my desk, blissfully mindless, and began to browse through the Sunday edition of one of our local newspapers. I found no mention whatsoever of the murder of Hiram Gottschalk, from which I could only conclude the police had made no progress. At least they had the decency not to issue the usual claptrap statement: "The homicide is being actively investigated and important developments are expected shortly."

I flipped the pages to Lolly Spindrift's gossip column. His breezy comments on the deeds and misdeeds of Palm Beach County's *haute monde* are always good for a laugh, or at least an amused smile, but there was one item I found more intriguing than risible. It stated:

"What oh-so-handsome manager of a popular bird supermarket in West Palm is setting new records in the man-about-town sweepstakes, leaving many a female heart atwitter? A word of caution to this lothario's conquests: You haven't got a chance. He may be a gorgeous hunk, ladies, but his heart belongs elsewhere."

I read the item twice. I was certain he was referring to Ricardo Chrisling. But his characterization of Ricardo as a lothario was surprising. I had no idea the lad had so active an avocation. Even more puzzling was Lolly's final remark: ". . . his heart belongs elsewhere." What on earth was the blabmeister hinting? That Ricardo was gay? I doubted it but Monsieur Spindrift would be the first to know. I preferred to believe Lol was implying Ricardo had a one-and-only of the female persuasion.

Another enigma to be unraveled and I knew it might require a champagne lunch to persuade the gossipmonger to reveal more of what he knew or had heard of the passions of Ricardo Chrisling.

The remainder of the day was uneventful except for the dessert Ursi Olson served at dinner. It was zabaglione: whipped cream, brandy, marsala, strawberries, and thin shavings of chocolate.

O cholesterol, where is thy sting?

I started the new week ready for derring-do and hopeful that before the day ended I might accomplish much, perhaps even positively identifying the Man in the Iron Mask. But I began with a more mundane challenge than that.

I must start by telling you McNally & Son, like most legal firms, is computerized. All our attorneys and paralegals have access to databases able to provide almost instant references to laws, judgments, and precedents that would take hours to find in the stacks of lawbooks now mildewing on office shelves.

Everyone at McNally & Son has a PC on his or her desk except for my father and myself. He doesn't need one; clerks do his donkeywork. I don't have one because I am a computer illiterate. In fact, I am a technophobe and have trouble changing a lightbulb without assistance.

Our house cyberflake—every company has at least one—is a dreamy-eyed bloke name Judd Wilkins. He looks more like a 1960s hippie than a 1990s digital nerd, for he wears a long blond pigtail cinched with a butterfly paper clip and sports two earrings in one ear.

Father endures Judd's eccentric appearance and dress (stonewashed jeans and a sequined monkey jacket) because the lad is a certified genius when it comes to the information super-highway, byways, lanes, and trails. I mean he knows everything there is to know about computers, printers, modems, networks, and how they all interface. Is that the correct word?

Anyway, Judd is carried on our employee roll as a paralegal but he is really our interpreter of the Brave New World of Bytes, capable of solving any glitches occurring in our electronic equipment. It is generally known he spends most of his spare time seated before his personal computer in his tiny condo exchanging important messages with strangers ten thousand miles away—messages like, "How's your weather?" I believe Judd is convinced if the Messiah ever returns it will be via Microsoft.

I approached him with a request for info on the Fish and Wildlife Service and particularly their Division of Law Enforcement.

"Government agency?" he asked.

"That's right. Department of the Interior."

"No problem. What do you want to know?"

"What laws are being enforced. What are the penalties if the laws are broken. Prison sentences? Dollar amounts of losses and fines after convictions—if they're available. Number of investigators assigned. The areas most active in criminal activities, whatever they may be. I'm starting from scratch on this. I need anything and everything."

"No problem," he said. "You want names? Addresses?"

"Sure," I told him. "Especially the bad guys."

"They can run but they can't hide," he said. "When do you need this stuff?"

"A week," I said. "Sooner if possible."

"No problem," he said, turned to his keyboard, and began typing.

I left him, wishing I could say "No problem" to every task confronting me.

Back in my very own tomb I phoned Parrots Unlimited and was answered by a male voice I could not identify. I thought I detected a slight foreign accent—Spanish? Portuguese? Icelandic?—but I could not be certain.

"May I speak to Mr. Watrous, please," I said politely.

"He's busy," he said gruffly. "To what does this concern about?"

Beautiful syntax, no?

"I purchased a parrot from him recently," I said, "and the poor bird appears to be molting at a ferocious rate."

"Yeah?" he said. "Okay, hang on; I'll get him."

A moment later Binky picked up. " 'Lo?" he said warily.

"Greetings, son," I said cheerily. "Archy here."

"Shh," he said.

"What do you mean shh?" I said indignantly. "I'm not exactly screaming you know."

"People are lurking," he said darkly.

"Ah. New employees?"

"A married couple. Youngish. Definitely not upper drawer. They lurk."

"Surely they know something about parrots."

"Mucho. Did you know that parrots can die of the fumes from an overheated nonstick frying pan?"

"Why, no," I said, "I don't know that and shall do my very best to forget it. These new people—hostile, would you say?"

"Well, maybe not hostile but, uh, watchful."

"Mistrustful?"

"That's the word, Archy," he said gratefully. "Bridget and I are thinking of deserting the ship."

"Binky, don't do that," I said hastily. "I'm depending on you."

"You are?"

"Absolutely. This is a very important discreet inquiry and you're playing a major role. I want you to observe everything happening at Parrots Unlimited and give me the benefit of your wise perceptions. You've done such a splendid job so far as an investigator and it's of vital importance you continue."

"Well," he said, his voice oozing hubris, "I guess I can stick it out for a while."

"Good man," I said. "Watch, listen, and report. By the way, how are you and Bridget coming along with your theatrical career?"

"A success!" he cried. "We've been invited to perform in three more nursing homes. Our reputation is spreading."

"I can imagine," I said. "Tell me, Binky, do you have a name for your act?"

"Oh yes," he said, preening. "We call ourselves The Busy B's. Bridget and Binky. Get it?"

"I do," I said. "Unfortunately."

I hung up congratulating myself on my fortitude. The Monday tasks I had set were humming along briskly and I resolutely continued. I phoned Lolly Spindrift at his newspaper and found him in an uncharacteristically downbeat mood.

"What's wrong, pal?" I asked.

"Another funeral," he said dully. "I don't know how many more of these I can take. Two this month. About twenty during the past year."

"Close friends?"

"All of them. Not fun, sweetie."

"What time is the funeral?"

"Twelve-thirty."

"Lol, I'm heading for the Pelican Club. I'm not suggesting lunch but why don't you meet me at the bar for a cognac. It will help see you through."

"Yes," he said immediately. "I can use it."

Half an hour later Spindrift and I were seated at the Pelican mahogany. He was working on a double Rémy Martin and I was sipping a tall g&t. Lolly is a small, birdlike chap who usually flashes a chirpy wit. But now he looked wrung out and pinned up to dry. It was obvious sorrow had brought him low; he seemed shrunken and his face was so wrenched I reckoned he was trying hard not to weep.

We drank in silence for a while because I am not very good in the sympathy department. I mean I can feel it and ordinarily I'm glib, but when I try to commiserate it comes out so soppy I can't believe the words are mine.

Finally Lolly perked up and asked, "Why did you phone me, luv?"

"It's not important. It can wait."

"No, no; tell me. Get my mind off the temptation to take a long walk on a short pier."

"The item you wrote yesterday about the bird store manager . . . Ricardo Chrisling, right?"

"Uh-huh. I figured you'd pick up on it since you asked me about him a week or so ago."

"Sparking about is he?"

"Definitely. Hither, thither, and yon–ish. And very success-fully from what I hear. He's a handsome devil."

"Your last comment, '. . . his heart belongs elsewhere.' What did you mean by that? He's gay?"

Lol gave me a wan smile. "Wish he was. No, I think the lad is straight. I keep picking up these hints he has a grand passion."

"What kind of hints?"

"Nothing much really. Weekly orders from a florist delivered to his apartment. Late-night comings and goings, also at his place. A diamond choker bought on Worth Avenue. Things like that, all indicating he may be smitten. No solid evidence, Archy, but you know if I waited for definite proof I'd have to close up shop and get in another line of business. Listen, dear, I've got to dash to the funeral. Can't be late, you know. You'll be on time for mine, won't you?"

I nodded, not trusting myself to speak.

"Thanks for the jolt. Just what I needed. I'll get through it now without blubbering. Keep in touch."

"You betcha," I said.

"And now you owe me one," he said, regaining his sauce.

"Acknowledged," I said.

We shook hands. I don't know why but I was glad we did. Then he departed, squaring his narrow shoulders and lifting his chin. Challenging life—and death.

21

THE DINING AREA was jammed with the luncheon crowd and so I remained at the bar. The next time Priscilla appeared to pick up an order of drinks I asked her to victual me *in situ.* "Something light," I told her.

"Like what?" she said. "A double cheeseburger with home fries?"

I sighed. "It's so hard to get good help these days. Try again but not quite so calorific."

"How about a crock of onion soup and a grilled chicken sandwich?"

"Perfect. By the way," I added faux casually, "have you seen Connie around lately?"

"Ask me no questions and I'll tell you no lies."

"What a brilliant bon mot," I said. "Original?"

"Keep it up, buster," she said, "and there'll be more in your soup than onions." Then she looked at me pityingly. "When are you two going to sign a truce?"

"I'm willing," I said. "Tell her that."

"*You* tell her that, Romeo," she said, and chasséd away.

I was consuming my spartan lunch and reviewing my brief conversation with Lolly Spindrift when a sly thought slid into the McNally cranium. If Ricardo Chrisling actually had an unknown inamorata—and Lol is usually on target when ferreting out private affairs of the heart—could it possibly be Julia Gottschalk, or Judith, or perhaps both, the moled and the moleless? Hey, why not? They were not blood relatives; the twins were attractive ladies; he was a "handsome devil." What a *ménage à trois* that would be!

I was amused by the idea until sobered by a second thought. If such a relationship existed, it might hold the motive for the slaying of Hiram Gottschalk. Three conspirators linked by passion, greed, and amorality. A fanciful plot? Of course. But completely illogical? I didn't think so.

I was in a gouty mood when I finished my solitary lunch. Although I had been active that morning I had the painful notion I was spinning my wheels—or even slowly in reverse. All my initiatives seemed to result in more questions than answers. At the moment I could think of nothing to do but plod on and I am not by nature a plodder, fancying myself more Captain Ahab than Bartleby.

I called the Gottschalk home from the pay phone at the Pelican Club. Mei Lee answered and, after identifying myself and inquiring as to her health ("Ver' happy"), I asked to speak to Peter. It was at least three minutes before he came on the line.

"Hullo?" he said in a voice so hollow it seemed to reverberate.

"Hi, Peter," I said with all the cheer I could muster. "Archy McNally. How're you doing?"

"Surviving," he said. "I think. Why are you calling?"

Good question. I had no good answer.

"I have nothing to do," I said lightly, "and thought we might waste some time together. Gorgeous day."

"I got no wheels," he said. "I'm a prisoner."

"Why don't I pick you up," I suggested. "Take a drive. Go somewhere. Even a prisoner is entitled to fresh air occasionally."

"Yeah," he said dispiritedly. "Go where?"

"How about my place?" I said, the best I could come up with. "I've been to your home but you've never been to mine."

"I don't know. I'm in a lousy mood. Down."

"Give me a chance," I urged. "Maybe I can bring you up. You like dogs?"

"Dogs? They're okay I guess. We never had one. Just birds."

"Well, my family has a new pooch. A real character. You've got to meet him."

He wasn't wildly enthusiastic. "If you say so. You'll come by?"

"Sure. Half hour or so."

"Got anything to drink at your place?"

"Of course," I said. In for a penny, in for a pound.

"I haven't showered or shaved in two days," he reported in his sunken voice. "Do I have to clean up?"

"Nah," I said. "Come as you are." I sounded giggly even to myself but he made no response, just hung up and left me wondering exactly what I was doing—and why.

He was waiting for me when I pulled in to the Gottschalks' slated driveway and he was as cruddy as he had warned: unshaven, hair a snarl, jeans and T-shirt wrinkled and soiled. And he exuded an effluvium I don't wish to describe in detail since you may be reading this after having recently dined. I shall only say I was happy I was driving an open car and wished for a more vigorous breeze.

He was singularly uncommunicative during our trip to the McNally manse, answering questions with monosyllables and offering no comments of his own. He seemed oblivious to his surroundings, staring straight ahead with unseeing eyes. I thought him lost in a dark world where only he existed, in pain and confusion.

When I parked on our turnaround he made no effort to get out of the Miata, just sat there looking about with those dulled eyes. I could discern no reactions whatsoever.

"You live here?" he said.

"I do indeed," I told him. "The house is Tudor manqué but comfortable."

"Nice," he said—his first expression of an opinion. It gave me hope.

"Suppose I get us some refreshment," I offered. "Gin and tonics?"

"Vodka," he said flatly. "Just vodka."

I went into the kitchen, hoping he'd still be present when I returned. I built both of us heavily watered vodkas on the rocks and brought them outside. He was standing alongside the car, hanging on to the opened door as if he feared if he relaxed his grip he might collapse. I handed him a drink and he took a gulp, closing his eyes.

"Nice," he said again. "Yvonne won't give me anything. She's locked up our liquor supply. Bitch!"

His virulence shocked me.

"And all the others!" he added just as venomously.

I didn't know how to respond to such hostility—except to change the subject. "How about taking a stroll about the grounds?" I said. "Then I'll show you the house."

"No," he said.

A stalemate was avoided when Hobo came trotting around the corner of the garage and padded up to us, tail wagging.

"This is Hobo," I said. "The latest addition to the McNally household."

I reached down to stroke the dog's head. He moved to Gottschalk, took one sniff, and turned away. I didn't blame him.

"Does he bite?" Peter asked.

"Hasn't yet," I said cheerfully.

"How about another drink?" he said, holding out his emptied tumbler. "No water this time."

This strained encounter, I realized, was getting precisely nowhere, and if he continued to drink it could only deteriorate further.

"Peter," I said, "may I speak to you as a Dutch uncle?"

"A what?"

"Talk bluntly," I said impatiently. "The hard truth. I think you're ill."

He swiveled his head sharply to stare at me.

"You've got a brain," I said, ready now to tell him what I had to. "For your own sake, man, use it. You know you're not acting normally. Wild mood swings. Periods of euphoria alternating with fits of awful depression when you think suicide is the only way out. And sudden violent urges. You're out of control and you know it."

He made a choky sound, face contorted. He dropped his tumbler onto the gravel. It shattered. Then he reached for me, hands clawing. I didn't know whether he intended to throttle me, rip the tongue from my head, or merely cuff me until my fillings loosened.

But he never accomplished his attack. Hobo had been lying at our feet, curled up but awake and watchful. When Peter made his threatening move the dog bounced upright and stood braced, legs stiff. His fangs were bared and basso profundo growls came rumbling from his throat.

Peter dropped his arms immediately. He slumped and slowly, slowly slipped onto the gravel and broken glass. He sat bent over, legs outstretched, head lowered to his chest.

I knelt beside him, fearing to touch.

"Peter?" I said.

"Sure," he said in a voice so faint I could hardly make it out. "I'm sick. I know it."

Perhaps I should have been saddened by this muttered admission but I was elated. I hoped it was the first step toward recovery or at least amelioration of his condition. He finally raised his head and I helped him to his feet and propped him against the side of the car. His face was bleached and he clasped his hands in a futile effort to conceal his tremors.

"Vodka?" he croaked hopefully.

"No," I said firmly, "not from me. Peter, I'm not going to tell you what ails you is no worse than an ingrown toenail. You and I realize it's more serious than that. But help is available if you're willing to accept it. I know a wonderful doctor, an older woman, who's had a lot of success treating illnesses like yours. She's a marvelous diagnostician—and honest; if she feels she cannot aid you she'll recommend someone who can. Will you go see her?"

He nodded.

"Good man," I said. "I'm going to give you her name, address, and phone number. Then it's up to you. I've done all I can. It's your life we're talking about. You understand?"

He nodded again. "Get in the car," I commanded, "before Hobo decides to gnaw on your shin."

I carried my empty glass back to the kitchen and took a moment to jot Dr. Gussie Pearlberg's name, address, and phone

number on a scrap torn from a brown paper bag. I went back outside to find Peter seated in the Miata, the door latched. I handed
him the scrawled information. He didn't glance at it, just grasped
it tightly.

"Tell her I recommended you see her," I advised.

"You really think she can help me?" he said.

"Guaranteed," I said, deciding it was a moment requiring pos-
itivism.

"Lord," he breathed: possibly the world's shortest prayer.

I drove him home. He was silent and so was I, fearing any additional advice might turn him off. For instance, I wanted to tell
him to lay off the booze and funny cigarettes, but I figured I had
played the guru enough for one day.

I exited the car when we arrived at his place, thinking he might
need assistance in walking. But he navigated steadily enough, still
gripping the scrap of paper I had given him.

"You'll call her?" I asked.

"Sure," he said. "Soon as I get inside."

"I'm not going to ask for a promise or any nonsense like that,"
I said. "It's your decision."

He took a deep breath. "Thank you," he said. It came out tentatively, almost like a foreign phrase, as if he had never before
said, "Thank you."

He went indoors. I returned to my steed and was about to vault
into the saddle when the blue M-B coupe came purring into the
driveway. I waited and watched as the twins popped out. Both
were clad in outfits I deemed outlandish. I had never seen such
a surfeit of vinyl, gauze, leather, and fur. Their costumes may
have been fashionable but style was lacking.

They came bopping up to me, laughing, each brandishing a
corked bottle of Mumm Cordon Rouge. Affixed to the neck of
each bottle was a purple orchid, now slightly wilted.

"Look what we've got," one shouted happily.

"A private trunk show," the other chortled. "And bottles of bubbly were the favors. Isn't that fabulous?"

"It is indeed," I agreed. "I know you'll treasure them unopened as mementos for years to come. And to whom, pray, am I speaking? Mike One and Mike Two just won't cut the mustard anymore."

"I'm Judith," one of them claimed.

"Ah, yes," I said, remembering the abdominal mole revealed by her bikini during our brief session on the beach. "And so," I said to the other, "by process of elimination you must be Julia."

"I was the last time I looked," she said, and the two dissolved in a burst of senseless giggles.

"Got to run," Judith said. "Have some bubbles and prepare for the evening's festivities. A charity bash, isn't it, Julia?"

"Something," her sister said. "Somewhere. Hoity-toity I suspect. We must remember to wear panties."

They had another fit of the tee-hees and I thought they were a bit old for this schoolgirlish behavior. I didn't think they were tiddly—but one never knows, do one?

They paused long enough for each to give me a swift peck on the cheek. Then they scampered up to the doorway, flourishing their bottles. I hoped they would not share their bounty with their brother.

But that wasn't the only thing to disconcert me. When they turned away I noted the twin who identified herself as Julia had a small black mole on the back of her left shoulder. There was no mistaking it. She was wearing a strapless cocktail dress, all froufrou, and the mole was obvious.

So both sisters had a mole, identical in size, shape, and color. Significant? Of course not! I laughed with delight because it was a final example of Hiram Gottschalk's quirky sense of humor.

"One of them has a mole," he had told me, to pique my interest and set in motion an inquiry that would have amused him.

What an eccentric he was! He may have had faults that led to his death but no one with his taste for harmless mischief should be murdered. That's stupid, isn't it? I know it is but it's the way I feel.

22

THE MOMENT I arrived home I went into the pantry to fetch a dustpan. I returned to our driveway, crouched and began picking shards of Peter's broken glass from the gravel. I didn't want Hobo cutting his pads. The hero himself emerged from his house and came wandering over to watch me at work.

"I want to thank you for your efforts on my behalf," I told him. "You behaved admirably."

His tail thumped once: sufficient acknowledgment.

I smoothed the gravel, dumped the glass into one of our trash cans, and went back inside. I judged it too late for an ocean swim and so I spent the remainder of the afternoon detailing the day's activities in my journal. I labored diligently and paused only to join my parents for the family cocktail hour.

After dinner I returned to my desk and completed my scribbling. I sat back and realized I was in a melancholy mood. Definitely an attack of the mopes. I realized it had nothing to do with the Gottschalk case. It had to do with a long-haired, bouncy lady who refused to phone and suggest a reconciliation.

And the worst part of it, the absolute *worst*, was that I could not remember what our disagreement was about. Maddening! Connie didn't call and I wouldn't. Of course it was an ego thing; I admit it. I could not endure crawling, supplicating. I was determined to remain upright, stern, and righteous no matter how much suffering it might cause her.

And so I went to bed, suffering.

I awoke the next morning still assailed by the blue devils. I was tempted to stay in bed for the remainder of my worldly existence, to be fed mush by a hired aide who might occasionally change tapes from my collection of Edith Piaf recordings.

Complete lunacy of course, and I knew it was as I hauled myself groaning out of the sack and stumbled back to reality. I staggered through the morning drill and clumped downstairs to the kitchen, where I found Jamie Olson gumming his decrepit briar and nursing a mug of black coffee.

He seemed to be as much a victim of the megrims as I, for all we exchanged was a listless nod. I fixed myself a meager breakfast of cran juice, a toasted (and buttered) onion bagel, and a cup of black jamoke. We sat across the table from each other, and it was a long time before our glum silence was broken.

"Eddie Wong," Jamie said finally.

I looked up. "Who?" I asked.

"Eddie Wong," he repeated. "I asked him about the staff at the Gottschalks' like you wanted."

"Oh yes," I said. "Sure. Got and Mei Lee. Eddie told you they weren't happy there."

"Yep. Eddie called me yesterday. They left. The Lees. Quit."

"Did they? Better jobs?"

"Eddie didn't know. Says they just took off. Packed up their wok and vamoosed."

"No reason?"

Jamie shrugged.

"Have they been replaced?"

"Yep. A family. Man, woman, two young kids. Spanish-speaking, Eddie Wong says. Called 'em furriners."

"Aren't we all?" I said. "Thank you for the info, Jamie."

I finished my scanty breakfast, slipped him the usual pourboire, and set off for the office wondering what significance the change of staff at the Gottschalk home might have. I doubted it was meaningful but I have come to realize even the smallest details sometimes prove important.

I dimly recall a homicide case of many years ago. A husband took his wife to Niagara Falls by train to celebrate a tenth anniversary at the place where they had enjoyed their honeymoon. The wife fell into the river and was swept to her death. A tragic accident, the police decided—until they discovered the husband had purchased one round-trip ticket and one one-way ticket.

Moral: If you're planning murder, don't economize.

By the time I arrived at my orifice (why do I keep spelling it that way?) at the McNally Building, I was beginning to emerge from my funk and hoped I might live to see the turn of the century and perhaps even learn to play the sweet potato. (I have already mastered the kazoo.)

I was lighting my first ciggie of the day when I heard a respectful knock on my locker door. Rare. *Very* rare. Visitors are usually announced and fellow employees ordinarily come barging in, reckoning their work is of more moment to McNally & Son than mine. How right they are.

I opened the door to greet Judd Wilkins. He appeared as

loopy as ever, so physically relaxed I wouldn't have been a bit surprised if he suddenly melted into a boneless heap on the floor.

"Hi, Judd," I said. "Come in and make yourself comfortable in my coffin—if such a thing is possible."

"Nah," he said. "This won't take long and I've got to get back to my machinery. One of the partners wants a rundown on autoworkers who have sued because they were fired for excessive flatulence on the assembly line. That's interesting, isn't it?"

"Not very," I said. "And I wish you hadn't mentioned it."

"Anyway," he went on, "what you asked about—the Fish and Wildlife Service and their Division of Law Enforcement—I can't find all their publications on line but they're available in print. Like five pounds of books, pamphlets, laws, regulations, international treaties, and so forth. Is that what you want?"

"Good lord, no!" I said.

"Didn't think so," he said. "I could get it all from other sources but the printout would fill your office."

"A paperback book would fill this office. Any suggestions, Judd?"

"No problem," he said. "We're tied into nets that can provide any info you want—for a price of course. If you could be more specific, tell me exactly what you need, I could query the nets. Even bulletin boards. If the stuff exists I can download it. But I'll need a few words or a phrase—the shorter the better—to get results."

My mind worked at blinding speed. No? Will you accept "quickly"?

"Parrots," I said.

He looked at me with his dreamy eyes. "Parrots?"

"Parrots," I repeated firmly. "Those squawky, ill-tempered birds who befoul their cages, bite friends and strangers, and recite verses by Edgar Guest. Where do these creatures come from? Are there parrot farms? More importantly, is there a trade, possibly illicit, in rare species? Are parrots being smuggled across our borders along with cocaine and counterfeit Calvin Klein underwear? In other words, is jiggery-pokery going on?"

He wasn't at all flummoxed by my outrageous requests. "No problem," he said. "If it's out there, you've got it."

He departed abruptly. I confess his technological skills humbled me. He was not a nerd, definitely not, but a member of a totally new generation with which I had little in common. I suffered a small pang of *Weltschmerz*, wondering when the world had changed and why I hadn't changed along with it.

I had plans for that Tuesday, activities which might possibly help unsnarl some of the tangles of the Gottschalk homicide. For instance, I hoped to persuade my father to reveal to me the details of the decedent's will. I could think of no good reason why *mein papa* would refuse to divulge this information, since the testament would soon be filed for probate and become public knowledge.

I was about to call his office, begging a few moments of his valuable time, when my own phone rang. The caller was Sgt. Al Rogoff.

"I'm coming over," he said without preamble.

"You shall be welcome of course," I said. "But may I inquire as to the purpose of your visit. Is anything wrong?"

"Wrong?" he said with a brittle laugh. "What could possibly go wrong in this best of all possible worlds? You told me that."

"Never," I said. "You're confusing me with Dr. Pangloss."

"Whatever," he said. "See you in twenty minutes or so." And he hung up.

A half hour later he was occupying the one folding steel chair I'm able to offer guests. It's alongside my desk and excruciatingly uncomfortable, especially to one of Rogoff's bulk. He overflows it and every time I see him planted there I expect the steel to buckle at any moment.

He took out his fat little notebook, stuffed with scraps of paper and bound with a thick rubber band. That alerted me. Al rarely makes notes. When he does I know he considers the matter of sufficient import to warrant a written record.

"Emma Gompertz and Anthony Sutcliffe," he said tonelessly. "They've been located."

"That's a relief," I said.

His face was expressionless. "Not really. They're dead. Their bodies were found in the Everglades early this morning. Both had been shot through the back of the head. Assassinations. Both have been positively ID'd."

I closed my eyes. I couldn't speak.

"It came over the wire about two hours ago," the sergeant went on. "I called but the usual jurisdiction squabble is going on. They don't yet know if the bodies were found in Dade or Broward County. Who handles it? Which sheriff's office? Or the state troopers? The FBI has an oar in too. It'll all get straightened out eventually and whoever takes over will trace Sutcliffe and Gompertz back to West Palm Beach. But I want to stay ahead of the curve and offer what I have as soon as possible. You agree?"

I nodded.

"But I need to know more about them. You think their murders might have a connection with the Hiram Gottschalk homicide?"

"I do," I said, my voice sounding to me like a weak croak.

"They worked as clerks in Parrots Unlimited?"

"Correct."

"How did they get along with the late owner?"

"Fine, as far as I know."

"And how did they get along with the new manager, Ricardo Chrisling?"

"Apparently there was enmity there. He fired Tony, and Emma quit in sympathy."

"The two lived together?"

"Yes."

"Married?"

"I doubt it."

"Do you know what the disagreement was about—the hostility between Chrisling and Sutcliffe?"

"No, I don't know, Al." He had asked me if I *knew* and I didn't. If he had asked me what I suspected I would have told him.

"Do you know of anyone else who might have a reason to abduct and kill Gompertz and Sutcliffe?"

"No, I don't," I said angrily. "They were nice, pleasant kids."

"Kids?"

"Anyone younger than I is a kid."

His smile was bleak. "Yeah, me too. What about the relations between the victims and the rest of the Gottschalk tribe: Peter, the twins, the housekeeper?"

"Their relations? I'd judge they were friendly but distant. Gompertz and Sutcliffe were at the party celebrating the twins' return from a European trip. But all the employees of Parrots Unlimited were invited. Nothing special there."

"What was your take on Sutcliffe and Gompertz. Druggies?"

"No. As I told you, they were just two nice, pleasant kids."

"You don't get a bullet in the back of the head for being a nice, pleasant kid."

The sergeant had been making brief notes as I answered his questions. Now he paused and looked up. "How do you know Chrisling fired Tony Sutcliffe?"

"Binky Watrous told me."

Rogoff was astounded. "Binky Watrous? The Village Idiot? How did he know?"

"He works part-time at Parrots Unlimited."

"Watrous *works?* Since when? I thought all he does is chase centerfolds. It's said he won't go out with a woman unless she's got staples in her belly. How come he's got a job at Parrots Unlimited?"

"I finagled it," I admitted. "After Gottschalk claimed his life was threatened, I decided I wanted an undercover operative in the store."

"Binky is an experienced undercover operative all right," Al said. "Under the blanket and under the sheet. Did he come up with anything?"

"He certainly did," I said loyally. "Most of what I've told you during this rigorous interrogation is the result of Binky's observations."

"I wish you had told me he was working there."

"It slipped my mind."

"Sometimes I think your entire mind has slipped. Is he still working at Parrots Unlimited?"

"As far as I know."

"Good. Keep him there. Has he told you anything else you haven't had the decency to reveal to me?"

"Nothing of any importance."

"Let me be the judge of that."

"After Sutcliffe and Gompertz left, Ricardo Chrisling hired a married couple to take their places. Binky doesn't like them."

"Oh? Why not?"

"He says they lurk."

The sergeant sighed. "They lurk," he repeated. "Whenever I get involved in one of your discreet inquiries it turns out to be fruitcake time."

"Al, is it okay if I tell Binky about the murders of Gompertz and Sutcliffe?"

He thought a moment. "I don't see why not," he said finally. "It'll be on the radio and TV tonight and in the papers tomorrow."

"Binky will be devastated," I said. "He and Bridget were pals of Emma and Tony."

"Who's Bridget?"

"Bridget Houlihan, a colleen who also works at Parrots Unlimited. She and Binky have an *in vivo* romance. And they have a theatrical act. Binky does birdcalls while Bridget accompanies him on the tambourine."

Rogoff stared at me, then cast his eyes heavenward. "Why hast thou forsaken me?" he inquired plaintively.

23

M Y QUANDARY NOW, while not intractable, was troubling: How was I to inform Binky of the deaths of Tony and Emma? A phone call would have been unfeeling—don't you agree? The distressing news had to be delivered in person. Over lunch? And if so, before or after the food was served? A silly predicament, I admit, but important to me. I finally decided there was no completely satisfying solution to such a trying problem.

I had a vague recollection, possibly mistaken, that Binky had told me he didn't clean birdcages on Tuesdays. But even if true, his work schedule may have been revised by the new manager. In any event I thought it best to phone him first at his home. My call was answered by the Watrous houseman.

"Master Binky is not available at present," he informed me in sepulchral tones. "You may reach him at his office."

I thanked him and hung up much bemused by "his office" and wondering if Binky had convinced the Duchess he had become a tycoon of birdland. I then phoned Parrots Unlimited and found him there.

"Lunch?" I suggested.

"Uh," he said.

"What does that mean—'uh'?"

"Well, we have to ask when we can leave and for how long."

"Oh-oh," I said. "Boot camp?"

"Something like that."

"I'm inviting you and Bridget to lunch. See if you can finagle it. I'll hang on."

It must have taken almost five minutes but eventually he came back on the line.

"All right," he said breathlessly. "Bridget and I can get out together for lunch."

"For how long?"

"Half an hour."

"Beautiful," I said. "Where?"

"There's a pizza joint across the street we go to."

"Fine. What's it called?"

"The Pizza Joint."

"Love it," I said. "Back to basics. Twelve-thirty?"

"Okay," he said hastily, and disconnected. I thought he sounded distraught, and what I had to say at lunch wasn't going to help.

Sadness does not ordinarily play a major role in my life. I mean I am by nature a cheery bloke, always looking for rainbows during drizzles. And the task of conveying bad news is not one I 'relish. But this was something I had to do, and I had no idea of how to handle it other than blurt out the truth. One can't tenderize death, can one?

So there we were—Bridget, Binky, and your rattled scribe seated at a Formica table awaiting the arrival of our King Kong Special (cheese, eggplant, sausage, anchovies, and button mushrooms), when I told them.

"I'm afraid I am the bearer of bad news," I plunged. "Emma Gompertz and Anthony Sutcliffe are dead. Their bodies were found early this morning in the Everglades. Both had been murdered."

They stared at me. "You're kidding," Binky said with a sick smile.

I was infuriated by his comment, implying I would joke about such a tragedy. Then I realized he was stunned by my disclosure and his reaction was an attempt to deny reality.

"It will be on radio and TV tonight," I went on. "And in the newspapers tomorrow. They were killed by gunshots to the head."

I had expected Bridget to dissolve and Binky to comfort her. I should have known better. It was he who collapsed, hunching over trying to stay a sob. Bridget put an arm about him, hugged him close, kept murmuring, "There, there." What a brave lass she was!

Binky finally regained control and wiped his bleary eyes with a paper napkin. Our King Kong Special arrived at that moment and we said nothing as we began scarfing, gulping beers to sluice down the spiced mélange. I wondered if tragic news increases hunger: a need to eat and postpone mortality. It's a concept much too recondite for me to understand. But why are wakes such an enduring tradition?

"What should we do, Archy?" Bridget said finally. "Quit?"

"Absolutely not," I said firmly. "Continue working at Parrots

Unlimited. I'm sure the police will come around asking questions. Answer them honestly."

Binky glanced up. "It's not right," he said stoutly. "It's just not right. Emma and Tony were good people."

"Of course they were," I agreed. "And that's why you and Bridget must be on the qv. Not only to help solve this horrendous crime but to watch your own backs. Be careful. More than that, be cautious. As Dr. Doyle might say, 'Evil is afoot.' "

Bridget looked at me. "You think the murders of Emma and Tony have something to do with the death of Mr. Gottschalk?"

She asked me that, not Binky. She was, I realized, smarter than he. But then who isn't?

"Yes, I believe so," I told her.

"Are Binky and I in danger?"

"Possibly," I said. "Don't take chances. Look about. Lock and bolt doors. And windows. Reject the approach of strangers. Very antisocial but necessary."

"Archy," she said, "will all this be cleared up?"

"Of course it shall," I said heartily. "Just a question of time. And sooner rather than later," I added.

I think I convinced them. Oh, if I had only convinced myself.

On occasion I have been accused of being a devious lad—justifiably I might add. I do have a taste for the Machiavellian and sometimes indulge in such conduct even when not necessary, simply to keep in practice. During the drive back to the McNally Building I concocted a cunning stratagem that might or might not yield results but was certainly worth a try.

The moment I was in my office I got on the horn to Lolly Spindrift. We exchanged rude greetings. Of course I made no reference to the funeral he had attended the previous day.

"Lol," I said, "I owe you one and it's payola time."

"Goody," he said. "What have you got for me?"

"Early this morning the bodies of a young couple were found in the Everglades. Both had been shot to death. I'm sure your news desk has the story by now."

"So why are you telling me?"

"Because the victims were Emma Gompertz and Anthony Sutcliffe, employees of Parrots Unlimited, the West Palm bird store presently managed by Ricardo Chrisling. He was, you'll recall, the subject of your recent item and our more recent conversation."

I heard his sudden intake of breath. "And Parrots Unlimited was formerly owned by Hiram Gottschalk who himself was stabbed to death."

"You've got it," I said.

"You believe there's a connection between the three murders?"

"I do believe."

He sighed. "It's not my cup of oolong, sweetie, but I'll report it to the news desk. They'll be delighted with the local angle. It should earn me some brownie points."

"That's why I called."

"Tell me something, luv: What's your edge on all this?"

"I'm a troublemaker," I told him. "I want to cause trouble for the killer, whoever he, she, or they may be. I want them to know the law is aware something dreadful is going on at Parrots Unlimited."

Spindrift laughed. "What a sneaky chap you are!"

"You have no idea how sneaky I can be when it's called for."

"Then it's part of one of your discreet inquiries, I presume."

"You presume correctly."

"I hope you'll scurry to me with all the gory details when it's over."

"Lolly, you'll be the first to know," I lied cheerfully.

My second call was to my father's office for I was still intent on learning the details of Hiram Gottschalk's will. I was answered by Mrs. Trelawney, pop's antiquated (and raunchy) private secretary. She reported the master had left for a luncheon conference with a commercial client and did not expect to return that afternoon.

After that I had nothing to do but brood, trying to sort out all the ramifications of the Gottschalk puzzle. Meanwhile I smoked two cigarettes and resolved never to light another until Connie called. It was liable to be an effective vow to ensure eternal withdrawal.

Ms. Garcia didn't phone but Dr. Gussie Pearlberg did.

"I can't talk long, dollink," she said briskly. "Busy, busy, busy. But I wanted you to know your friend came in. Peter Gottschalk."

"Not quite a friend," I said cautiously. "More of an acquaintance."

"A very meshuga acquaintance. Poor boy. I now believe I was right: he is manic-depressive. I have sent him to a good man who specializes in such things. This condition can be controlled with proper medication and frequent monitoring. That is the first thing to be done. But also Peter has another problem and this might not be so easy to solve. You understand?"

"A psychiatric problem?" I ventured.

"I cannot discuss it," she said severely. "But after his manic-depression is stabilized he has promised to return to me and talk some more. I think I can help him. I am calling to tell you what I told him. He is not to drink alcohol or use drugs if he expects his condition to improve. I want you to impress that on him. Definitely no alcohol and no drugs."

"Dr. Gussie," I protested, "I see him infrequently. I am not his keeper."

"But you'll do what you can?"

"Of course. I know you can't go into details but could you give me a hint of the nature of Peter's psychiatric problem?"

Her laugh was short and harsh. "Family," she said. "What else?"

That did it. I had heard enough wretchedness for one day and needed a respite from the gloom. I drove home, roughhoused with Hobo for ten minutes, and left him exhausted while I went upstairs to change into swimming togs: Speedo trunks in such a virulent orange I was sure to be spotted by a rescuing helicopter if I collapsed during my two-mile wallow.

The sea was delightfully warm and calm. I vary my swimming techniques: crawl, breaststroke, and backstroke. Of the three I prefer the second because it sounds so nice. I emerged from my dunk with eyes smarting from the salt but feeling much relaxed and happy. I had time for a short nap before dressing for the family cocktail hour.

Dinner that evening was a feast of hors d'oeuvres with no main dish. We had marinated grilled scallops wrapped in bacon, Oriental barbecued chicken wings, and tiny meatballs in a curry sauce. The salad was endives (my favorite) with a raspberry vinaigrette dressing. Father and I had Pouilly-Fumé. It was an okay wine, not great but okay. Mother had her usual glass of sauterne. It was her preference but I thought it similar to drinking Yoo-Hoo with oysters.

I went upstairs to my journal after dinner and spent an hour recording the day's events relating to the murder of Hiram Gottschalk. Finished, I reviewed my notes and decided it was time to question my father. "Beard the lion in his den" isn't quite an apt expression but it comes close.

If you must know the truth (and I presume you *must*,) I find my father a rather intimidating man. It is simply part of his nature and doesn't diminish my love for him. But I confess I approach our one-on-ones with some trepidation, fearing I may say something or do something to convince him his male offspring is a twerp nonpareil.

The door to his study was firmly closed and I overcame my apprehension sufficiently to rap the portal smartly. I heard his "Come in," and entered to find him settled behind his magisterial desk and, as usual, smoking one of his silver-banded James Upshall pipes. Also as usual, there was a glass of port on his desk blotter alongside an open book. I recognized it as a leather-bound volume from his set of Charles Dickens. From its bulk I guessed it to be *Little Dorrit* and wished him the best of luck.

"Father," I said, "may I speak to you for a moment?"

He nodded but didn't ask me to be seated. It's his way of telling me to keep it brief.

"It concerns my inquiry into the murder of Hiram Gottschalk," I started. "I feel I am making progress, but slowly, and it might help if you would tell me the major beneficiaries in Mr. Gottschalk's will."

He listened to my request gravely. But if I had mentioned I had a hangnail he would have listened just as gravely. Levity was foreign to him. He thought life a very serious matter indeed, and sometimes I wondered if my own frivolousness was a revolt against the pater's sobriety. He was not a dull man, you understand, but lordy he was earnest. What a scoutmaster he would have made! I could picture him demonstrating how to start a fire by rubbing two dry sticks together to a group of tenderfeet all of whom carried Zippo lighters.

"I see no reason to withhold that information," he said finally.

"It will soon become a matter of public knowledge. It is an odd testament but as I told you, from the beginning I found Mr. Gottschalk a rather eccentric gentleman. But of course his wishes had to be respected."

"Of course," I said, and waited patiently.

24

"THERE ARE A number of minor bequests," he began. "To old friends, employees, distant relatives, and members of his domestic staff. His home with its furnishings is left to Yvonne Chrisling, his housekeeper. The store, Parrots Unlimited, and the not inconsiderable plot of land on which it is located go to Ricardo Chrisling. The remainder of his assets are to be divided into three equal shares to his son Peter and twin daughters Judith and Julia." He paused to give me a chilly smile. "All this after the payment of estate taxes of course."

"Will there be much left after the tax?"

"A great deal," he said briefly. "If his children invest their inheritance wisely it should support them comfortably for the remainder of their lives."

"Sir, you mentioned minor bequests to his domestic staff. His chef and maid, Got and Mei Lee, have recently left the Gottschalk household. Will their leaving affect their legacy?"

"No."

"You also mentioned bequests to his employees. Father, have you listened to the local news on radio or TV tonight?"

"I have not. Why do you ask?"

"The bodies of a young couple, former employees of Parrots Unlimited, were found in the Everglades. Both had been murdered, shot to death at close range in what was apparently an assassination-type slaying."

He stared at me, his expression growing increasingly bleak. "You believe there is a connection between their deaths and the murder of our client?"

"Yes, sir, I believe that—and so does Sergeant Rogoff."

He was silent a few moments while he went into his mulling mode, mentally masticating information received, comparing it to past experience, essaying various explanations and hypotheses, and eventually arriving at his considered judgment. I would never dare attempt to hurry this process. It would be like urging a sphinx to get his rear in gear.

"Archy," he said at long last, "are you suggesting this unfortunate couple may have been slain because they were included in Mr. Gottschalk's will? If so, I believe you are mistaken. Their bequests are five thousand each. People are not murdered for that sum."

"They've been killed for less," I said tartly. "But no, I do not believe they were shot because of their inclusion in our client's will. I doubt if their killers were even aware of it. I think another motive was at work. I cannot even guess what it might be but I have no doubt all three homicides are linked and were committed by or effected by the same person or persons."

(Why, after a few moments of conversation with Prescott Mc-Nally, Esq., do I begin to mimic his prolixity?)

"Do you have any leads?" he asked.

"Several but nothing substantive. I believe the key to the puzzle will eventually be found in the store."

He hoisted one bristly eyebrow. "The store? But all they sell are parrots."

"I'm aware of that, father, but Parrots Unlimited seems to be the nexus of all the deviltry going on."

He terminated me abruptly. "Very well," he said. "Keep at it." He picked up his glass of port and I departed.

Being somewhat miffed by his cold dismissal, I treated myself to a brandy after climbing to my chamber. I sat at my battered desk and considered what he had revealed. He had described Mr. Gottschalk's will as "an odd testament" but that was lawyerly opinion. He did not consider what those bequests might signify. He was deliberately an unemotional man because he felt in his profession emotion could not contravene reason.

But emotion was my realm. It really was what I dealt with—all those sealed cans labeled love, hate, revenge, envy, jealousy, spite, fury, and so forth. And so I interpreted our client's bequests as an index of his heart rather than his head. If you wish to call me Old Softy, you're quite welcome.

Leaving his home and its furnishings to Yvonne Chrisling—what did that signify? It was a munificent gift.

Just as generous was his bequest of Parrots Unlimited to Yvonne's stepson, Ricardo. Surely there was a hidden reason for that. The lad was, after all, merely an employee. Or was he more than that?

The division of the major portion of his net worth to his three children seemed straightforward enough. But I had learned from experience the most beautiful Red Delicious apple might prove to be mealy.

Sighing, I propped up my feet and started reading the entire record of the Gottschalk affair from the beginning. And you know, I found a tidbit that enlightened me. I am not pretending to be a Master Sleuth, because I have played fair and square and casually mentioned the item to you previously.

I wouldn't want you to think I'm cheating. Why, you'd never speak to me again.

The following morning did not begin auspiciously. I do possess an electric shaver but I customarily follow my father's traditional practice of using a porcelain mug containing a disk of soap, badger-haired brush, and single-edged safety razor to depilate the lower mandible. It was a fresh blade and I sliced my jaw. A styptic pencil saved me from exsanguination but I trotted downstairs to breakfast looking like a nineteenth-century duelist from the University of Heidelberg.

"Did you cut yourself, Archy?" mother inquired solicitously.

"A mere nick," I assured her.

"Perhaps you stood too close to the razor," father remarked.

I find his attempts at humor somewhat heavy-handed, don't you?

We had a satisfying morning meal (blueberry pancakes with heather honey) and discussed plans for Thanksgiving Day, fast approaching. Mother suggested it would be nice to enable the Olsons to enjoy a private holiday by not requiring Ursi to provide the usual turkey feast. Unexpectedly father concurred, and it was decided the family would gobble a gobbler at a restaurant that had the sense to serve a sauce of whole cranberries rather than an effete jelly.

"You might invite Connie," mother said, beaming. "If she has no other plans I'm sure she'd love to join us and we'd like to have her."

"Yes," I said. "Thank you."

I drove to the office intending to spend a few hours creating my expense account for the month. I cannot compose madrigals and my expertise at heroic couplets is limited but when it comes to expense accounts I am a veritable Jules Verne. Imagination? You wouldn't believe!

I was happily at work, wondering if I might charge McNally & Son for a haircut, when I heard a tentative rap at my office door. I rose to open it and found Judd Wilkins. He was bearing a roll of bumf bound with a low-tech rubber band.

He looked at me with his dreamy eyes. "What happened to your chin?" he asked.

"Attempted suicide," I said.

He accepted that. "Here's the download you wanted," he said, proffering the bundle. "About parrots."

I was astounded. "So soon? I asked for this stuff just yesterday."

He gave me a glance I could only interpret as pitying. "It's not snail mail you know. There may be some late factoids coming in but I think you'll find what you want here."

"Interesting?" I asked.

"I thought so."

"Anything illegal going on?"

"Yep," he said cheerfully.

"Judd, thank you for your fast work. I appreciate it."

"No problem," he said, and was gone.

I put aside my expense account and began reading the information he had gleaned from cyberspace. It required concentration because the printouts contained misspellings, ellipses, and abbreviations foreign to me. I read the entire record twice to get a general feel of the material and then perused it a third time with close attention to those elements I thought might be significant in solving the Gottschalk puzzle.

Up to that point my interest in matters psittacine had been limited. I mean parrots are beautiful birds, no denying it, but I am usually concerned with more weighty subjects—such as whether or not to drizzle vinegar on potato chips. But after studying the computer-generated skinny provided by Judd Wilkins I became fascinated by the fate of those gorgeously feathered creatures and I hope you will be similarly intrigued.

Here is the gist of what I learned:

The U.S. is signatory to the Convention of International Trade in Endangered Species of Wild Fauna and Flora, a mouthful usually mercifully shortened to CITES. Under that agreement more than a hundred nations attempt to regulate transnational commerce in plants and animals threatened or potentially threatened with extinction.

In addition, our federal and state governments maintain lists of endangered species, about a thousand in number. Overseeing all the multitudinous regulations is the Department of Interior's Fish and Wildlife Service, and their Department of Law Enforcement when needed.

It has been estimated that 250,000 parrots are imported annually and legally into the U.S., despite the numbing quantity of permits required. Many of these birds become part of domestic breeding programs by legitimate and licensed parrot farmers.

But there are approximately fifty species of wild parrots whose importation is verboten. And that's where the smugglers take over. Rare and expensive birds are sneaked in from Brazil, Australia, and Africa. Main ports of entry are Miami and Los Angeles. One authority guesses this illicit trade probably exceeds $25 million annually.

The smugglers' methods are gruesome. Fully grown and fledgling parrots are hidden in luggage, stuffed into plastic piping, concealed in furniture and machinery, buried in mounds of grain, even sealed in ventilated cans. The mortality rate is horrendous. There is a tale of a smuggler apprehended at L.A. who was wearing a specially constructed vest of many small pockets each of which contained the egg of an endangered Australian cockatiel.

Allow me a spot of editorializing.

Apparently in our enlightened land there are people willing— nay, eager—to pay any amount for a brilliantly colored wild parrot, the rarer the better—with no interest whatsoever in the exotic bird's antecedents or how it arrived on our shores. It becomes a status symbol, not a pet.

One of Judd's contributors remarked that parrots suffer when taken from the wild, deprived of their mates, and thrust into a cage. Many of the captured birds develop neuroses, adopt self-destructive habits, or become aggressive. They sometimes bite and claw their new owners. Bully!

It really is a depressing record. As I've told you, I have no special fondness for parrots but the cruel trapping, smuggling, and profitable sale of wild and endangered species seem to me a particularly heinous practice. Especially since so many of those birds die shortly after being wrenched from their homes and imprisoned.

It was time for lunch and I fled to the Pelican Club as relieved as a schoolchild anticipating recess. The joint was sparsely occupied and so I was able to sit at the bar and order a gin and bitters from Simon Pettibone. Our estimable bartender and club manager gave me a quizzical look.

"Feeling ginnish this morning, Mr. McNally?" he inquired.

"Feeling bitterish," I replied. He served my drink and I said, "Mr. Pettibone, I know you to be a man of vast erudition and experience. Tell me something: What do you think of birds?"

"Love 'em," he said promptly. "Chickens, ducks, turkeys, all roasted, fried, or broiled. Any which way. I once ate a pigeon and very tasty it was."

"Oh, I concur," I said, "but I framed my question awkwardly. I was not referring to edible species raised for the table. What do you think of birds kept in cages? As pets or sometimes just as interior decoration."

"Ah," he said, suddenly serious, "that's something else again. I don't hold with caging dumb creatures. I've never had a bird as a pet and never will. It's cruel to my way of thinking. Ever see an eagle soar? Now that's something."

"I understand what you're saying but it's a difficult moral choice, isn't it? I mean I enjoy a roasted duck with a nice sauce of wild cherries as much as you. Never give the poor fowl's fate a second thought. But the idea of keeping a bird in a cage turns me off."

He looked at me. "No one keeps a duck in a cage, Mr. McNally."

"I hope not. But I'm thinking about parrots. Especially beautiful and rare parrots taken from the wild and put behind bars."

"No," he said firmly, "I don't hold with that."

"Thank you, Mr. Pettibone," I said gratefully. "I respect your opinion."

Then I lunched alone but, *mirabile dictu*, I cannot recollect what I had. This is astonishing, even shocking to relate for I have almost total recall of past breakfasts, brunches, luncheons, dinners, and late suppers. Why, I distinctly remember an excellent braised oxtail I consumed in 1984.

The reason for this memory lapse, I think, is heavy and insistent pondering as I scarfed. The knowledge that rare birds were captured in the wild, smuggled abroad, and sold to moneyed collectors distressed me. For the moment, I put aside how this illegal trade might possibly affect the homicides I was investigating. I was disturbed by the birdnapping itself.

I have, I suppose, a very limited personal code of moral conduct. To wit: I strive to behave in a manner that gives me pleasure but doesn't harm anyone else. I mean I'm a live-and-let-live bloke. I've never been an -ist of any sort, not sexist, racist, leftist, rightist, idealist, realist, and so forth. Well, on occasion I act as an egoist—but only on occasion.

What my dilemma amounted to was something you may find ridiculous and I admit had a slightly farcical tone. If I objected to the capture and imprisonment of birds for profit, how could I justify my enjoyment of a baked free-range chicken, much more flavorful than the factory-raised variety?

I agreed with Mr. Pettibone that it was okay to feast on domesticated fowl but wrong to ensnare and incarcerate exotic parrots. But they're all birds, aren't they, and where is the moral justification for the difference in their treatment?

Finally I gave up on my mental maunderings. I could find no way out of the maze of imponderables. It was, I decided, a question with no final answer. Similar to the problem of whether brandied apples or broiled oranges go better with a roasted goose.

25

I ARRIVED BACK AT the McNally Building to find on my desk
a handwritten note from Yvonne Chrisling. It was an invitation
to attend a "joyous tribute" to Hiram Gottschalk to be held that
evening beginning at eight p.m. Not to mourn, she wrote, but
to remember and celebrate the life of a wonderful man. "I want
it to be more like a cheerful wake," she added.

Uh-huh.

She finished with a fanfare: "Archy, I'll be devastated if you
don't come. I want so much to see you again!"

Double uh-huh. I wondered again what game the Dragon
Lady was playing and determined to present myself in all my
sockless glory at the soiree that evening at the Gottschalk manse.
It might, I reckoned, prove as educational and entertaining as a
visit to a zoo.

I phoned Sgt. Al Rogoff and was put on hold for at least three minutes. He finally came on the line.

"What took you so long?" I asked. "Finishing an anchovy pizza and a can of Sprite?"

"Close but no cigar," he said. "Actually I was beating a suspect with a short length of rubber hose. What's up?"

"That's why I called. Anything happening?"

"Nope. Nothing of any great interest."

"C'mon, Al, you must be doing *something*."

"Just routine. We got an alleged eyewitness who lives in the same condo as Sutcliffe and Gompertz. She claims she saw the two of them leaving at night with two guys she describes as 'goons.' She says the four of them got in a car and drove away."

"Is this eyewitness a middle-aged lady carrying a ton of mascara?"

"You've got it. You know her?"

"Met her briefly during my last visit. She let me in—a stupid thing to do. I thought her a bit loopy."

"That's the word."

"Can she identify the car they used?"

"Says it was white. Isn't that beautiful? How many white cars are there in South Florida—a zillion?"

"Possibly more. Al, does the apparent abduction and murder of Gompertz and Sutcliffe take Peter Gottschalk off the hook for the killing of his father?"

"Well . . . maybe," he admitted grudgingly. "I can't find anything linking him to the Everglades cases. But that's assuming all three homicides are somehow connected."

"You believe it, don't you?"

"Yeah," he said, sighing heavily, "I guess I do. Have you come up with anything?"

"Parrots," I said. "I think parrots may be the key to the whole megillah."

Short silence. "Parrots," he repeated. "Archy, have you ever considered a brain transplant?"

" 'O ye of little faith.' Believe me, parrots hold the answer."

I was hoping he wouldn't say it but he did.

"That's for the birds," he said, laughed, and hung up.

I tried to get back to fiddling with my expense account but found I had lost interest. My creative juices were still flowing but whereas, at lunch, I had put aside the Gottschalk puzzle to ruminate on the moral implications of gnawing a chicken's crispy drumstick, now I postponed my monthly raid on McNally & Son's bottom line to concentrate on the perplexities of my current discreet inquiry.

I went back to fundamentals, the start of everything. It all began with the acts of personal terrorism and vandalism that frightened Hiram: the slashed photograph, the mass card, the strangled mynah, the shattered phonograph record. They were all deliberate acts of cruelty. If I could determine the motive involved I might be able to identify the perpetrator.

Dr. Gussie had said the destroyed photo was an attempt to eliminate Hiram's happy memory. The same could be said of the smashed Caruso recording, a gift from his beloved wife, now long gone. The posted mass card and killing of his favorite bird were more serious: warnings of a possible impending doom. Those explanations made a grisly kind of sense but led precisely nowhere. They yielded no clues as to who might be responsible for inflicting such grievous pain.

Just as puzzling was the manner of his death. It seemed obvious the killer had chosen to stab the hapless victim through the eyes because he had seen too much. In some benighted countries the hand of a convicted thief is lopped off. Mr. Gottschalk's eyes were destroyed and his life taken because his slayer could not endure his continued observation or witnessing of—what?

But again, all that might be an explanation but it was not a solution, was it? I wrestled with the riddles for the remainder of the afternoon, doodling on a pad of scratch paper and finding myself making crude drawings of eyes and birds. I waited for an inspired flash of insight that never arrived. And so I closed up shop and went home wondering if I might be better suited for another profession. Stuffing strudel was one possibility.

During the family cocktail hour at twilight I casually mentioned I was attending a memorial service for Hiram Gottschalk that night. Father paused in his preparation of our martinis.

"Your mother and I were invited," he said stiffly. "But I thought it best we not accept."

"Sir, would you prefer I didn't go?" I asked him.

"No, no," he said. "Represent McNally and Son. And perhaps you may learn something to further your inquiry."

"Perhaps," I said, thinking, Not bloody likely—which proves how mistaken a sleuthhound can be.

After dinner I went upstairs to change. I decided to wear a *suit*. Can you believe it? Yep, my jacket and trousers matched: a black and tan glen plaid in a windowpane design. Classic but jaunty. I lightened the formality further with a knitted sport shirt of Sea Island cotton in hunter green. Cordovan loafers with modest tassels. The final effect, I decided, was assertive without being aggressive.

I must confess my getup was an attempt to trump Ricardo Chrisling's Armani elegance. Didn't someone once say you can cure a man of any folly except vanity?

It was a so-so night hardly worth mentioning, but I shall. The sky was totally overcast, making for a heavy darkness, and what breeze existed came in fits and starts. I was aware of an unusual odor on the air. Not quite fishy. Not quite sewer gas. Brimstone? Nah. That was my imagination galloping amok.

There was a plenitude of cars already parked on the slated driveway of the Gottschalk estate as I drove in. I spotted Binky Watrous's dented antique M-B cabriolet and was happy my gormless aide would be present. I was sliding from my fire engine–red quadriga when Peter Gottschalk came out of nowhere, hand outstretched. He was grinning. Not a drugged grin or a sappy grin. Just a nice natural expression of pleasure.

"Hiya, Archy," he said. "I was hoping you'd show up."

I shook the proffered paw. "Peter, good to see you again. How are things going?"

"Listen," he said, "I've got to thank you for steering me to that shrink."

"Dr. Pearlberg?"

"Yeah. I went to see her. She's something, she is."

"I concur. A marvelous woman."

"Anyway, she sent me to another doc—a *doctor* doc, not a mind bender—and he's got me on medication."

"Any results?"

"Not yet but I feel better knowing I'm getting help. I'm off the booze and the weed and that's a drag. But I can stand it if my brain starts functioning."

"Good for you," I said. "Coming inside?"

"In a while," he said. "Not right now. I just want to walk around and look at things. It's like I'm seeing them for the first time. That's goofy, isn't it?"

"Not so. Very understandable. Peter, what is this shindig all about? A sort of delayed wake?"

"It's supposed to be but it's just a party. My sisters' idea. They love a bash."

"Tell me something: Do you always know which is which?"

"Oh sure. It's easy. Julia wears Chanel Cristalle perfume and Judith uses Must de Cartier."

I laughed. "I had never considered that method of identification. But what if they switch scents?"

He shrugged. "So what? Who cares? They're a couple of airheads anyway. See you later."

Then he was gone. I stayed a moment thinking of the sobriquet he had used to describe his sisters: airheads. It had been my initial impression also, but now I was beginning to think there was another trait the twins shared. It was darker and far less superficial than their fondness for partying.

The front door of the Gottschalk home was wide open. I entered and paused to glance about. Yvonne Chrisling came bustling up to give me a tight *abrazo* and press a warm cheek against mine.

"Archy!" she exclaimed. "I am *sooo* happy you have arrived. What a delight to see you!"

My ego is of the stalwart variety, as you well know, but her effusion startled me. I do like to fancy I am a reincarnation of Ronald Colman, but I could not believe I had captivated this woman to the degree she displayed in speech and manner.

"Come along," she said in her hearty contralto voice, "and let me get you a drink. You prefer vodka, do you not?"

She grasped my arm and led me to a portable bar set up by the caterer handling the affair. She made certain I was supplied with a heavy Sterling on the rocks with a slice of lime. Then she toyed with my left ear.

"Now I must act like a hostess," she said, managing a girlish pout, "but you and I shall have a nice long talk later."

She moved away, leaving me a bit rattled. I had no doubt the lady was coming on to me, as she had before, and I could not guess her motive. That it was not overwhelming passion I was well aware. And I doubted if she even knew of my store of scabrous limericks. So why was she being so *physical?* It could of course be merely a case of chronic flirtatiousness—but I didn't think so.

I stood at the bar watching her stroll slowly through the throng of guests, pausing to chat, patting shoulders, stroking cheeks, clasping hands. She really *was* physical.

I think "dolled up" would be an apt description of her costume: a strapless sheath of shimmering pink pallettes. Her black hair hung in a glossy sheaf. A diamond choker encircled her strong neck. The effect of those glittering rocks against her dark skin was striking.

As she sauntered slowly but purposefully I suddenly realized she was not acting "like a hostess" as she had said, she was playing the role of chatelaine, entertaining in *her* home, greeting *her* guests. Then I knew, *knew* she was aware of her inheritance. This rumpled mansion, its furnishings and grounds, were now all hers. *Hers!* To do with as she willed. No wonder she was chockablock with brio.

I wandered away from the bar searching for Binky. I finally located him seated in a cozy corner holding hands with Bridget Houlihan. Their heads were close and when I said, "Hello, kids," they looked up vacantly as if I had just interrupted a shared dream.

"Oh," Binky said. "Hi."

"Hi," Bridget said.

"Hi," I added, "and I trust that concludes the 'hi's' for the evening. Having a good time?"

They looked at each other and I wondered if they were fully aware of where they were, so lost they seemed to be in their private world.

"Binky," I said, "have the police come to the store?"

He nodded. "They showed up today. Two detectives."

"Asking questions about Emma and Tony," Bridget said sorrowfully. "We couldn't tell them much."

"Did they talk to Ricardo?"

"He wasn't there," Binky said. "He's away on a business trip."

"Oh?" I said. "Is he here tonight?"

"I haven't seen him," Bridget said. "Have you, lover?" she asked her swain. *Lover?!* Calling Binky Watrous a lover is similar to labeling Caligula an Eagle Scout.

"Haven't seen him," my unpaid helot replied. "He's away a lot."

"The new employees," I said. "The ones replacing Tony and Emma—are they present tonight?"

"They're here but you won't like them," Bridget advised. "Riffraff."

"The riffest of the raffest," Binky added.

I expressed thanks and left. There were more questions I wanted to ask but I felt I was intruding on their twosomeness (I think that's a new word I just coined). I confess I was envious. I wondered where Connie Garcia was at that moment and what she was doing. Stubborn, mulish, obstinate woman! Grrr.

26

I WISH I COULD tell you I had a blast at Hiram Gottschalk's memorial, but I did not. All the other guests, and there were many, seemed to be having a high old time. The decibel count rose as more drinks were consumed, laughter became raucous, and I even witnessed the sight of a middle-aged man putting a fringed lampshade on his head and attempting an imitation of Carmen Miranda. Yes, I actually saw it.

But despite a second vodka I remained subdued if not dejected. A series of events contributed to my angst.

I met the new domestic staff hired to replace Mei and Got Lee. They were an unprepossessing couple with none of the cheery charm of their predecessors. They were obviously foreign-born and I overheard them conversing in a language I could not positively identify although I recognized a few French words. I finally guessed they were speaking Creole, which might explain their wariness. They acted as if an agent from the Immigration Service might tap them on the shoulder at any moment.

Just as off-putting were the man and woman employed to take the place of Tony Sutcliffe and Emma Gompertz at Parrots Unlimited. I introduced myself and found them a singularly surly and uncommunicative couple. They stood stiffly, full glasses gripped tightly. They seemed totally divorced from the revelry around them and, having put in an appearance, were eager to depart as soon as possible.

"How's the parrot business?" I asked the man genially, trying to jolt him into even the merest semblance of casual conversation. I think his name was Martin something.

"You're interested in parrots?" he said, staring at me suspiciously.

It was all I needed—a challenge like that.

"Well, I'm not," I said briskly, "but my dear old grandfather is absolutely dotty about them. Must have at least twenty, give or take, and he's still collecting. They'll probably outlive him—right?"

"Probably," the woman said. I think her name was Felice something.

"He owns some rare birds," I burbled on. "Beautiful specimens. His ninety-second birthday is coming up and I'd like to buy him a special gift. Do you have any unusual parrots in your shop? I mean something he's not likely to have in his attic."

Martin thawed. A little. "I think we can supply a rare and lovely bird," he said. "Expensive of course."

"Of course," I said.

"Stop by the store and I'll show you what's available."

"Great!" I said. "I know it'll make gramps happy."

I gave them an idiotic grin. Did I know what I was doing? No, I did not but it was a gambit worth a try.

I was beginning to think it was time to make a surreptitious departure, when I observed a pas de trois being performed across the thronged living room. My view was frequently obscured by the mingling of guests and I heard nothing of what was being said. The rising volume of gibble-gabble prevented that.

Peter Gottschalk was seated in the center of the tattered velvet love seat. Crowded in were the twins, Julia and Judith, pressing him between them, a slender dun volume held tightly by two garish bookends. There was a bottle of what appeared to be red wine on the cocktail table before them, and each of the three held a full glass.

From my distance it was a scene in mime but I had no doubt what was happening. The sisters urged him to drink. He resisted. They laughed and whispered into his ears. He laughed. They lifted their glasses. A toast. He took a sip. They gulped and nudged him. He drank more. They all laughed.

I didn't know if the twins were fully aware of their brother's condition but I thought their behavior abhorrent. I wanted to push my way through the mob and strike the glass from his hand. But I couldn't do that, could I? People would think me drunk or insane, and the three principals involved would be outraged by my officiousness. And so I did nothing. Just watched, saddened by the sight of the sisters clutching his arms, petting him, keeping his glass filled. I saw it as a kind of corruption.

Then I did leave, sneaking away and hoping my departure was unobserved. No such luck. I was standing alongside the Miata, looking upward and happy to see the sky was clearing—a few stars were winking at me—when Yvonne Chrisling came running to slide an arm about my waist.

"You naughty boy," she said. "Leaving without a good-night kiss."

"I apologize," I said. "I wanted to thank you for an enjoyable evening but you were busy with your guests."

"I wanted everyone to have a happy time," she said in such a simpering tone I was tempted to utter a blasphemy. "Did you have a happy time, Archy?"

"I did indeed," I assured her. "My only regret is your stepson wasn't present. I was looking forward to chatting with him."

"Ah, poor Ricardo," she said. "On a business trip. He works, works, works. He is so determined to make the business a success."

"I'm sure he shall. But I did have a chance to talk with Peter for a few moments. He seems in much better shape." I watched closely for her reaction.

She sighed. "Such a problem, that one. He's going to doctors, you know, for help in curing his depression and stopping the crazy things he does. But I'm afraid he will not do what they say or take his medication. Peter is so weak, so weak. Are you weak, Archy?"

"Only physically, mentally, and emotionally," I told her. "Other than that I am a tower of strength."

She smiled. "May we sit in your car a moment? I need a few moments away from the hullabaloo."

"Of course," I said.

So there we were, side by side in the parked Miata. I do not believe she was using a perfume but I was conscious of her scent, deep and musky. And disturbing I might add. Dim starlight gleamed on bare shoulders. The diamond choker seemed reflected on dark skin. I thought it a bit chill for her costume but she made no complaint. Perhaps she generated her own warmth, an inner furnace never extinguished. (Oh, McNally, you're *such* a poet!)

She turned sideways and took my hand. "Do you think you shall ever marry?" she asked suddenly.

I was startled. "I honestly don't know, Yvonne. How can one possibly predict something like that?"

"Take my advice and don't marry," she said.

"Oh? Why do you say that?"

"You're not the type."

"You mean there's a marrying type of man and natural-born bachelors who smoke a pipe, keep a cat, and sew leather patches on the elbows of their Harris tweed sport jacket?"

She was kind enough to laugh. "Let me tell you something, Archy. It's a secret but I shall reveal it to you. Every smart woman in the world knows if she had been born a man she would never marry."

"What a cynic you are," I said.

"Oh no, but I am realistic. And I know marrying or not marrying is not so important. A piece of paper. What is important is how a man feels about a woman and how she feels about him. You agree?"

"I do," I said with the uneasy feeling this woman knew more about everything than I knew about anything.

She began fondling my right ear. She seemed to have a thing about ears. That's okay. I have a furtive fondness for the backs of female knees. And it is said the Japanese admire an attractive nape. One never knows, do one?

"Age means nothing," Yvonne continued. "And really, physical attractiveness is not, ah, crucial. It's the stirring one feels."

She pressed closer. I began to appreciate how a trapped ferret must feel.

"Also," she said, "it is necessary a man and a woman who are simpatico do not hurt each other. It is very necessary. You wouldn't hurt me, would you, Archy?"

"Of course not," I said staunchly without the slightest idea where this woman was coming from. She was speaking words that made little sense unless she was implying a meaning I could not fathom.

"I know you won't," she said, and I was immediately aware she had switched from "wouldn't" to "won't." "And I won't hurt you. And so," she concluded with a sigh of content, "there is no reason you and I cannot enjoy an intimate relationship and make each other happy."

Then she enveloped me. I can't think of a more fitting verb for I felt engulfed, surrounded, swallowed as she lurched to enfold me in her arms and plaster my mug with wet, passionate kisses. What a scene! Acceptable in a boudoir certainly but in an open car parked on a crowded driveway? I mean, how louche can you get?

I touched her hair cautiously, fearing I might find a nest of snakes. But it was pure gloss. Was I tempted to respond to the bold advances of this intense woman? Of course I was tempted. I am, after all, not whittled of oak. But if my glands were energized the bowl of Cheerios I call my brain sent forth a warning alert.

She wanted something from me, I guessed, and then I reckoned it was possible she was playing the siren because there was something she *didn't* want from me. Her operatic seduction (opera buffa, not grand opera) might be an attempt to persuade me to inaction. She wanted me to cease and desist. It was an intriguing hypothesis.

Rejection without giving offense to the rejectee is a delicate art. I weaseled of course, as is my wont, and explained to Yvonne as gently as I could that while we undoubtedly were kindred spirits, this was neither the time nor the place for continued intimacy. But our moment would arrive, I assured her, when our new and delightful relationship could come to glorious fruition. In other words, I stalled her.

She disengaged far enough to peer into my eyes. "You promise?" she asked huskily.

"I do not take promises lightly," I told her. It was, you may note, a classic example of a dissembler's talent. Not a lie but not a definite pledge, either.

"When?" she persisted.

"As soon as possible," I replied, which gave me plenty of wriggle room. "I'll call you."

"Very soon," she said, and gave me a final kiss. What a wicked tongue she had! "And if you don't, I shall call you. Frequently."

She may not have meant it as a threat but I took it as such. She was not in the habit of being denied. She gave my ear one last tweak, slid from the car, and stalked back to the party. I watched her go, admiring her erect posture and the way she seemed to thrust herself forward. I could not believe she ever had a doubt in her life.

I drove home at a relatively early hour, congratulating myself on escaping from what might have been a sticky situation. I believe I hummed "Does Your Chewing Gum Lose Its Flavor (on the Bedpost Overnight)?" but it could have been Mozart's Violin Concerto No. 3 in G major. Whatever, I found I had recovered from my brief spasm of *Weltschmerz* earlier in the evening. I wasn't exactly chipper, you understand, but in a relaxed, ruminative mood.

I disrobed in my adytum (there's a lovely word; look it up!), sorry my glen plaid suit hadn't had the opportunity to compete with Ricardo Chrisling's Armani. I donned a new pongee robe embroidered with Chinese characters. I had been told by the merchant the calligraphy could be translated as: "May you have a happy life." But I suspected it meant, "Suffer, you miserable schlub," or some other invidious imprecation.

I poured myself a wee marc and settled down behind my desk for a period of pondering before surrendering to the need for eight hours of Z's. I found myself smiling because I recalled my father's comment at the family cocktail hour. He had urged me to attend the Gottschalk party, saying, "Perhaps you may learn something to further your inquiry." I had doubted it but the senior had been proved right again. Was the man never wrong?

I *had* furthered my inquiry at the squirrelly and totally unnecessary "joyous tribute." Nothing momentous, you understand, but bits and pieces which might prove of value. I had met the new employees of Parrots Unlimited and was not impressed. The recently hired domestic staff was even more questionable.

But those meetings were of peripheral interest. There had been two developments of more significant concern. To wit:

I had seen with my own peepers Julia and Judith encouraging, nay urging their brother to swill wine. The sight had disturbed me but I was willing to give them the benefit of the doubt and assume they didn't know he was under a doctor's care.

But then Yvonne Chrisling had revealed she was aware of Peter's condition, and so it was reasonable to assume he had also told his sisters he was on a no-alcohol, no-drugs regimen. Yet they were plying him with the fermented grape. Just high spirits on the part of the twins and not deliberate conduct? I didn't think so. Attributing their behavior solely to their kicky dispositions was enough to dash a balder.

My second observation of note was—you guessed it—the diamond choker worn by Yvonne. You didn't believe I missed it, did you, or forgot the mention of a diamond choker by Lolly

Spindrift when he was detailing the evidence he had of Ricardo Chrisling's career of Don Juanism?

There are many diamond chokers in the world of course, most of them in Palm Beach. But still I thought it a mind-tickling coincidence that Ricardo had recently purchased a choker on Worth Avenue and now Yvonne was wearing a gemmy circlet—to smashing effect I might add.

Even assuming the diamond choker purchased by Ricardo was the one worn by Yvonne—so what? It could well have been a present from stepson to stepmother, perhaps to celebrate a birthday or some other family occasion. But it was such a lavish gift I found myself questioning the motive of the giver and what the recipient might have done to deserve such largesse.

I went to bed about an hour later still musing on the horrid murder of Hiram Gottschalk and the two immutable laws of human existence:

1. Life is unfair.
2. It's better to be lucky than smart.

27

HAVE A VAGUE recollection of Thursday starting as a zingy day. It could not have been the weather, for it was droopy, with heavy rain forecast for the afternoon. I suspect my Joy D'Veeve (a stripper I once met at the Lido in Paris) was due to a solid night's sleep and the fact that I didn't slice myself while shaving.

After breakfast with my parents I emerged into a drizzly world but my élan was not diminished, because Hobo came trotting up for a morning pat. His coat was glistening with moisture but he seemed not at all daunted by the damp. I checked his condo to make certain it was dry and snug.

While I was examining his house Jamie Olson came wandering, gumming his old briar.

"Morning, Mr. Archy," he said.

"Good morning, Jamie. Hobo's been behaving himself, has he?"

"Yep," he said. "The hound amazes me and Ursi. Smarter than most people we know. About a week ago, mebbe two, three in the morning, it was storming hard. Thunder, lightning, everything. Squall woke me up and I heard a scratching at our door over the garage. It was Hobo. He had got flooded out and come up the stairs to our apartment. I let him in, dried him off, spread an old piece of carpet for him. Suited him just fine. Didn't misbehave or anything, if you know what I mean. Next day it cleared and he went outside again and hasn't moved in with us since."

"Knows enough to come in out of the rain," I observed.

"Yep, and he knows a lot of other things he ain't telling. That dog is *deep.*"

I drove to work pleased my faith in Hobo had been justified. I was no sooner in my cubicle when a knock on the door announced a visitor. It was Judd Wilkins, our computer whiz.

"I asked the security guard to give me a call when you showed up," he said without a greeting. "Got a minute or two?"

"Sure I do," I said. "Come on in."

This time he sat in the steel chair alongside my desk. I thought I detected a certain tenseness in his manner. His eyes had lost their dreaminess. He seemed distant, as if he were concentrating on solving the puzzle of the Pyramid Inch.

"What's up, Judd?" I asked him.

"We've been hacked," he said.

I had absolutely no idea what he meant. "Hacked?"

"Invaded," he said. "Someone's got into our computers and is rummaging around."

It didn't, at first, seem to me a matter of great concern. Although, as I've mentioned, I'm a computer illiterate, I am aware cyberspace does not provide complete privacy. PCs offer a tempting target for hackers, thieves, competitors, or innocent tyros attempting to expand their keyboard expertise.

"I thought we had a security system," I said.

"Model-T," Judd said. "I've sent a dozen memos saying we've got to upgrade and get state-of-the-art firewalls. No response."

"Doesn't everyone with a computer on his or her desk have a private password?"

He grimaced. "Passwords? Not worth diddly-squat. One of our senior partners—know what his password is?"

"What?"

" 'Password.' That's his personal, private password: 'Password.' "

"Beautiful," I said.

"Your father has a PC. He doesn't work it but his aides do. Want to know his password?"

"Tell me."

" 'McNally.' "

I groaned. "Why didn't he make it 'Open Sesame'? Judd, are you certain we've been tapped?"

"Absolutely. Someone is inside us and searching around."

"How do you know?"

"I just *know*," he said definitely. "Some stuff has been switched, some is out of order or jumbled, tallies of references are out of sync with past records. Look, it's like someone got into your closet and shuffled your suits. You'd know it, wouldn't you?"

Suddenly the import of what he was saying sank in and I was shaken. "Are you telling me a stranger now has access to all our personal files? Wills, contracts, trusts, agreements, litigation, partnerships, the affairs of our clients, even our personnel records and tax returns?"

"Everything," he said.

"Oh lordy," I said. "My father will have a conniption. You want me to break the bad news? Is that why you're here?"

"Part of it," he said. "I want you to tell him what's happened and how we've got to put more muscle in our security. But there's something else."

My morning vivacity, already diminished, now seemed doomed. "Let's have it," I said, expecting the worst. It was.

"I'm guessing now," Judd said, "but there's a good chance I'm on target. We've been computerized for almost five years with no security problems. I kept warning it could happen but all the fuds said who would want to hack a South Florida law firm. Well, now it's happened. I hate to tell you this but I think you're responsible."

"What?" I cried.

"Not you personally. But you asked me to go on line and see what I could get on parrots, especially anything illegal. It couldn't have been more than twenty-four hours after I queried the nets that we got invaded. Like I said, I'm guessing but I think the parrot inquiry brought in the cyberpunk. I could be wrong but I believe I'm right."

We stared at each other, unblinking. I was, I admit, stunned by his disclosure. My first impulse was to phone immediately for a one-way airline ticket to Shanghai. First-class of course. But my cravenness was vanished by the remembrance of a long-ago incident when, not completely sober, I was confronted by a would-be mugger in New Haven. He was wielding a knife that appeared to be just slightly shorter than a scimitar.

I had looked at him sadly, wagged my head, and said, "Somewhere a mother's heart is breaking."

He was so disconcerted by my remark I was able to escape. At full speed I might add.

The recollection of this daring act enabled me to face the current crisis with some aplomb. "All right, Judd," I said. "I shall urge my father as strongly as I can to install more formidable security in our computer system. Now about your belief my inquiry about parrots sparked the break-in—I don't doubt it for a moment."

He suddenly relaxed, slumping in the hellish steel chair, gratified by my response.

"I know little about computers," I continued. "As I'm sure you're fully aware. But is there any way we can discover who is trespassing and sharing our secrets?"

His eyes closed slowly, remained shut for a moment, then popped open again. "It can be done," he said, "but I can't do it. Don't have the software or the know-how. But I'm exchanging E-mail with a guy down in Miami. He's a real tech-head, the nerdiest of the nerds. He works for a computer security outfit and I'll guess he's their house genius. I'm betting he could track our virus to its source."

"Can we hire him?"

"He's out of everything unless it comes in bytes. I mean he knows nothing about free-lance work, contracts, fees, and so forth. But we could hire the company he works for with the understanding their first job is to find who infected us. If they succeed we can promise them the assignment of redesigning our whole setup to beef security. How does it sound?"

"Great," I said. "Let's do it."

"That's a go-ahead?"

I bit the bullet. "Yes," I said. "A definite commitment from McNally and Son. I'll take the responsibility."

His look wasn't doubtful but it was wary. "Your father will go along?"

"I'll convince him," I said with more assurance than I felt.

He departed and I phoned Mrs. Trelawney immediately, fearing if I dallied my resolve would simply ooze away. I asked for an audience with m'lord but she said he was busy with a client. When he was available she would inform him I had called and relay his reaction.

"Tell him it's a matter of life and death," I said.

"Whose life?" she asked. "And whose death?"

"All of us," I said hollowly. "And I kid you not."

I settled back to await her call. I shook an English Oval from the packet but didn't light it. I just fingered it as a satiated infant might fondle a pacifier. The fog I had been in since the death of Hiram Gottschalk was beginning to dissipate. Not whisked away but softly shredding. And what I saw wasn't pretty.

My summons arrived sooner than expected and I climbed the back stairs to my father's sanctum with some trepidation. After all I wouldn't be the first messenger in history executed for bringing bad news.

I found him seated in his swivel chair before his antique rolltop desk. He waved me to a seat on the green leather chesterfield. He seemed in a genial mood.

"Mrs. Trelawney tells me you wish to discuss a matter of life and death," he said with some amusement.

"A slight exaggeration, sir," I said, "but very slight."

I then reported what Judd Wilkins had told me. I left nothing out, including the probability of my inquiry about parrots being the cause of the invasion.

When I finished, he stood and began striding about his office, hands thrust into his trouser pockets. I do not believe a stranger or even a casual acquaintance would have recognized the depth of his wrath. He was a disciplined man, a controlled man, and loath to display his emotions. But he was my father; I knew him as well as he knew me and I saw the signs of his fury: a hardening of the eyes, a grim set to the jaw, a stiffness in his neck. He was riven by anger and doing his best to conceal it.

"What you're telling me," he said tonelessly, "is that a stranger is now privy to all the confidential data of this firm."

"Yes, sir," I said. "Wills, trusts, litigation, contracts—the whole caboodle."

He stopped his pacing to stare at the floor. "The world is too much with me, Archy," he said. "I know less about computers than you do, I'm sure, but the more I read about the digital revolution, the more I am convinced it means the end of privacy. We could have been burglarized before computers, of course. Documents could have been stolen or copied. But now a teenaged desperado fiddling at a keyboard is able to enter and share our very existence: past, present, and future. It is an obscenity."

"I agree, father," I said. "But there is no need to surrender meekly to electronic assaults without fighting back."

I told him I had authorized Judd Wilkins to hire a computer security company with the understanding that if they were able to identify our assailant they would be given a contract to redesign our computer setup with state-of-the-art safeguards.

Since Prescott McNally, Esq., could not confront the information superhighway with any hope of response, he decided to concentrate his rage and frustration on his mild-mannered scion: me.

"You did *what?*" he demanded in a tone I can only describe as glacial.

I repeated my commitment of McNally & Son. I then arose from my slump on the leather couch and stood erect. If we were to have an altercation I had no wish to be in a subservient physical position.

"You had no right to make such an agreement," he said sternly.

"The decision was mine to make and you should have obtained my approval before obligating us to an unspecified expense."

"Father," I said, "be reasonable. You want to ensure everything be done that can be done to prevent future break-ins. And I want to do all I can to obtain the name of the person who is so curious about my interest in parrots. The solution to that mystery may possibly lead to the identity of Hiram Gottschalk's killer. It seems to me the expense I approved is justified by the results we hope to obtain."

"It's not the money," he said, still steaming, "it's the principle of the thing."

(*Nota bene:* When people say it's not the money it's the principle, it's the money.)

"Sir," I said, "I do not feel I exceeded my authority. It was important to get things moving as quickly as possible. If I had delayed until I received your permission, what would have been accomplished? Surely you would approve the hiring of computer security experts, would you not?"

"That's not the point," he said testily.

"Then what *is* the point?" I asked, becoming just as heated as he. "That I went over your head? If it disturbs you unendurably you may have my resignation as soon as I can write it out."

He glared at me. "Oh, don't be such an ass," he said grumpily. "All I'm suggesting—*strongly* suggesting—is you consult me in the future before committing McNally and Son to an expensive and problematic course of action."

I had won a small victory but it was not enough. "No, father, I cannot promise that. Situations may arise similar to the present matter when I feel it best to make an instant decision before clearing it with you. Either you trust my judgment or you do not."

He looked at me with what I can only describe as a sardonic

smile. "The apple never falls far from the tree," he observed.

And that inanity reminded me of an undergraduate jape I've mentioned before: The turd never falls far from the bird.

"I will not undo what you have done," he pronounced in a frigid voice, turning to his desk. "Now go back to work."

28

I RETURNED TO MY office in a mood I can only label as festive. I had climbed into the cage with the king of beasts and tamed him—temporarily at least. But then, on further reflection, my coup was moderated. I became conscious my relationship with my father had been subtly altered during our wrangle. It was not a sea change, mind you, but perhaps the beginning of one.

I was about to resume inventing my expense account when Binky Watrous phoned. He seemed joyous, bubbly in fact.

"Binky," I said, "are you calling from Parrots Unlimited?"

"No, boss, I am not," he said with a giggle. "I have been fired. Along with Bridget."

I gulped. "When did this happen?"

"About an hour ago. Ricardo showed up, back from one of his business trips, and gave both of us the old heave-ho."

"Did he offer any reason?"

"Said the business couldn't afford a sales staff of four—which is a crock. The store is doing a booming business. I mean we weren't just standing around. The place was always busy. In fact, Bridget and I are thinking of opening a bird store of our own. Not just parrots, you know, but all kinds of chirpy pets: canaries, mynahs, swans, penguins."

"Swans?" I said, startled. "Penguins? Why not an ostrich or two?"

"Why not?" he said gaily.

"Listen, Binky, how about you and Bridget meeting me for lunch at the club. Around noonish. You can tell me all about your sacking and your plans for the future."

"Ripping idea. We'll celebrate our release from gainful employment."

I hung up puzzled by this new development. It was apparent Ricardo was revamping Parrots Unlimited, as he had every right to do since he was now the manager and, after Mr. Gottschalk's estate was settled, would be the sole owner. I just wondered what plans he had for the psittacine emporium. A discount store? Something like a feathered Kmart?

I finished my expense account and dropped it onto the desk of Raymond Gelding, our treasurer.

"Oh, goody," he said. "Just what I wanted. I haven't read any really exciting fiction lately."

"To quote a former president of our great republic," I said loftily, "I am not a crook."

"And you know what happened to him," Ray said. "But I must admit I admire your chutzpah, Archy. You are the only employee of McNally and Son who has ever attempted to charge the firm for a purchase of Extra-Strength Excedrin."

"A legitimate business expense," I assured him, turning to leave. "Headaches are an occupational hazard."

"What about my ulcer?" he yelled after me.

I arrived at the Pelican Club at precisely the same moment Binky's battered Mercedes came chugging into the parking area. He and Bridget alighted by sliding out the door on the driver's side, the one closed with a loop of twine. The passenger's door was so tightly jammed only a small explosive charge might have opened it—but I doubt it.

I greeted the kids and we all entered the club and went directly to the dining area. Priscilla came sauntering over to take our order. I asked for Kir Royales for the three of us.

Pris winked at Binky. "You've got a live one today," she told him.

"I hope so," he said. "Bridget and I have just been fired."

"Some people have all the luck," she sighed, and went off to fetch our drinks.

I asked Binky for more details of what had happened but there was little he could add to what he had already related. Ricardo Chrisling appeared an hour after the store opened, called Bridget and Binky into his private office, and canned both of them forthwith. He promised each two weeks' severance and requested they leave immediately.

"What was his mood?" I inquired. "His manner?"

Bridget answered. What a charming young woman she was: saucy, energetic, with a brisk wit. She reminded me in many ways of Connie Garcia. You remember Connie, don't you, McNally? Of course you remember, you poltroon!

"Ricardo was an icicle," Bridget said decisively. "All business.

Binky and I were just numbers in a ledger. And bad cess to him. He needed us more than we needed him."

"Hear, hear," Binky murmured.

"The new people," I said. "What are their names . . . Martin and Felice? Yes. They know nothing about parrots?"

"They know," she admitted. "But they treat the birds like products. A box of cornflakes. No warmth there, no sympathy. They had no favorites and sometimes they could be mean."

"Plebs," Binky added. "Definitely plebs."

But then our drinks arrived and I raised my glass in a toast. "To your freedom," I said.

They responded most heartily and I was happy to see they were not at all disheartened by their sudden termination. Relieved, as a matter of fact. I wondered if they envisioned a future on the Las Vegas stage as a duet featuring birdcalls with tambourine accompaniment.

If you're interested in matters gustatory, and I presume you are, our lunch was a gargantuan seafood salad served in a wooden bowl large enough to hold a hippo's hip. In addition to the greens, onions, black olives, bell peppers, mushrooms, and radishes, it contained shrimp, crabmeat, lobster, scallops, and a few chunks of pepperoni for the fun of it. Leroy had prepared a creamy lemon-and-dill dressing. Excellent. We had a chilled bottle of Sancerre. Also excellent.

As we gorged on this healthful repast, Bridget and Binky regaled me with the tale of an incident I found diverting and hope you will too even though it has little connection with the discreet inquiry inspiring this narrative.

It concerns a remarkable happening at a nursing home in Stuart where The Busy B's were entertaining the residents. Binky was giving the coo of the mourning dove and Bridget was spanking her tambourine when an oldster lurched from his wheelchair, hobbled to the center of the floor, and began to perform an arthritic jig in time to the "music."

His impromptu dance elicited such an enthusiastic response that Bridget and Binky determined to revise their repertoire and reproduce or suggest dance rhythms in their act. The results were startling they assured me. At subsequent nursing home performances they had geriatrics attempting jigs, clogs, waltzes, polkas, even a slow-motion Charleston.

You may think this activity by the elderly as exciting as group flossing but I find the idea of gaffers and gammers kicking up their heels invigorating. I trust when I am toothless and spavined I will have the spirit to essay a rumba.

During the remainder of the luncheon I queried my guests on the daily routine at Parrots Unlimited: who fed the birds, who was responsible for totaling the day's receipts, how often inventory was taken, etc. Their answers revealed nothing of significance. Several days passed before I realized I hadn't asked the right questions. This is a frequent failing of detectives and suspicious wives.

We finished, left the Pelican Club, and were standing in the parking area when I felt it necessary to warn them again.

"Please," I said, "do be careful. Emma and Tony were fired and I know I needn't remind you what happened to them. Now you have been sacked. Be extra-cautious."

They assured me I had nothing to worry about; they were perfectly capable of ensuring their own safety.

"If any bullyboy attacks us," Bridget said, "I'll bounce my tambourine off his noggin."

"And I shall befuddle him with the hoot of the barn owl," Binky added.

We all laughed and I watched them depart, wondering about the derivation of the phrase "babes in the wood."

I returned to my sepulcher at the McNally Building and found on my desk two messages reporting phone calls taken by our lobby receptionist. My first callback was to Sgt. Al Rogoff. He sounded desperate.

"Anything?" he asked.

"Nada," I said. "Except Binky Watrous just got fired from Parrots Unlimited. There goes my mole."

"A perfect mole. They're blind, aren't they?"

"Not completely but most of them wear bifocals."

"Very funny. Did you get any skinny from Watrous?"

"Not much," I admitted. "But I wanted someone inside. Now I'm stymied. You?"

"The same," he said glumly. "In spades. The only news to report is Peter Gottschalk is back in the hospital."

It wasn't a great shock. I think I had expected it. "When did this happen?" I asked Rogoff.

"Early this morning. A call to nine-one-one. Too much booze, I guess. Not fatal but they're keeping him under observation. What a saphead the lad is."

"But not a killer."

"I guess not," the sergeant said. "But if not him, then who? Listen, Archy, you really think the Gottschalk homicide is connected to the blasting of those kids in the Everglades?"

"I do and thought you did too."

"I did but now I'm beginning to wonder. Everything's getting cold and we're getting nowhere. You know how solution rates go down as time passes. Have you got anything you can throw me? A crumb?"

I paused a moment, wondering if it was worth a gamble. I decided it was, because if it proved out I would benefit and so would the sergeant.

"Want to take a chance, Al?"

"A chance? Right now I'll listen to some Gypsy with a crystal ball. Sure I'll take a chance."

"You told me an eyewitness stated she saw Emma Gompertz and Tony Sutcliffe being hustled into a white car she couldn't identify."

"That's right."

"Show her a color photo of a white four-door Ford Explorer and ask her if it could be the vehicle involved."

"Who owns a white four-door Ford Explorer?" he demanded.

"I'm not going to answer that; I don't want to involve an individual who may be totally innocent. You wanted a crumb, I'm giving you one. Are you going to do it or not?"

"I'll do it," he said, not at all happy. "What choice have I got? There's nothing else. But if this lays a big fat egg, you and I will pretend we never met. Okay?"

"Suits me," I said, and hung up as surly as he.

I could empathize with the sergeant. He was a professional and I was merely a semipro but I shared his frustration. A devious criminal was outbraining us and I believe we both considered it a sneering attack on our investigative skills. Ego, ego, all is ego.

But when Al said, "There's nothing else," he wasn't speaking for me. I did have a few minor scents I hadn't mentioned to him because they were too vaporous.

Item: The hacking of McNally & Son's computer after I had initiated an inquiry about parrots.

Item: A diamond choker worn by Yvonne Chrisling that might or might not be a gift from her stepson.

Item: What seemed to me a deliberate attempt by the Gottschalk twins to intoxicate their brother even though they were aware of his illness.

But what would be gained if I reported such ephemera to Rogoff? I knew his reaction would be: "So what?" He wanted facts, sworn testimony, hard evidence. He wanted to cut knots open with knife or scissors. I had the patience to untangle, picking endlessly. I really had no choice, did I?

My second caller had been Ricardo Chrisling phoning from Parrots Unlimited. The person who answered was abrupt, almost churlish, and I began to question the efficiency of the new staff. But when Ricardo came on the line he couldn't have been more congenial. Señor Charm himself. A definite change from his previous distant manner.

"Sorry I missed you at the to-do last night," he said breezily. "Had to go out of town on business. Good party, was it?"

"Very enjoyable," I lied.

"Listen, Archy, I've been hoping to get together with you for some time now but I've been so busy since Hiram passed I haven't had time to do what I *want* to do. I know this is short notice but could I treat you to dinner tonight? There's a new Mexican restaurant on Dixie Highway. It's called the Alcazar, which is a laugh because it's really a hole-in-the-wall with no more than ten tables. But the food is something special. No tacos, enchiladas, or any other Tex-Mex garbage. This is classic Mexican cuisine and it's really something. Also, they serve the best margaritas in Florida. How does that sound?"

"I'm salivating already."

"Then you can meet me around seven?"

"Sure."

"One drawback: I'll have to cut and run by nine o'clock. Some friends are flying into Miami from South America and I want to be there to meet them. But we'll have time for a nice leisurely dinner. Okay?"

"Of course."

He gave me the address of the Alcazar and hung up before I had a chance to ask if I should wear a sombrero.

It was a strange invitation, was it not? Totally unexpected, and setting a time limit for "a nice leisurely dinner" seemed to me rather infra d.

This lad, I decided, had a strong penchant for things Hispanic. He had given me Mexican brandy, he was taking me to a Mexican restaurant, he was leaving early to meet friends flying in from South America. And suddenly I recalled Lolly Spindrift telling me Ricardo had been involved in an imbroglio at a local boîte. It had been a private party of *sudamericanos*. And there had been violence, someone had been shot. Now wasn't that intriguing?

But how could I condemn Ricardo Chrisling for his friendship with Latinos? Was not Connie Garcia, a Marielito, my very own light-o'-love? Even though she seemed determined to turn off the light.

29

H E WAS RIGHT; it *was* a hole-in-the-wall and required a spot of searching. I finally located the Alcazar at the rear of a mini-mall. It appeared to be a narrow establishment with no advertising other than the name in hammered iron script over a weathered oak door. I was only a few moments late but Ricardo was waiting for me at a tiny stand-up bar to the right of the entrance. He shook my hand heartily, a totally unnecessary long-time-no-see grip.

I had given up hope of competing with his Armani elegance and wore my silver-gray Ultrasuede sport jacket with black gabardine slacks. I was happy to see he was just as informally attired, although his terra-cotta jacket and taupe trousers were both in a nubby raw silk. But the man was without a single wrinkle. I had a mad fancy he had his clothes pressed daily—with him in them.

"Glad you could make it, Archy," he said, and made it sound sincere. "Now you must try a margarita—the house specialty."

"I'm willing."

He ordered from a mustachioed bartender and turned back to me. "How was your day?" he asked. He was trying hard to be genial and I appreciated the effort. But I sensed it was exactly that—an effort.

"My day?" I said, and flipped a hand back and forth. "Half and half. Rough and rugged until you called. Then I decided to pack it in. Went home, had a swim in the ocean, took a short and delightful nap, shared a cocktail with my parents, and here I am. Things are looking up."

"This will help," he said as our margaritas were served in glasses large enough to hold a baby coelacanth. I took a sip and he looked at me expectantly.

"Marvelous," I said. "Absolutely top-notch."

He glowed as if he had mixed them himself. Actually they were excellent drinks but couldn't equal Simon Pettibone's margaritas, which were ne plus ultra. I think Mr. Pettibone's secret was the sea salt he used to rim the glass but I may be mistaken. I am occasionally incorrect, you know. As when I persuaded Binky Watrous he could easily consume a platter of fried rattlesnake meat without suffering a gastric disaster. Wrong!

"What do you think of the place?" Ricardo asked.

I looked into the dining area. Definitely small. As he had said, no more than ten tables. It was a stark room with minimal decoration. There was a single bullfight poster on a whitewashed wall. The matador pictured, Belmonte, bore a striking resemblance to Chrisling: haughty, elegant, severe. Both man and poster gave the impression of repressed passion.

"It's a bit spartan," I admitted, recalling the soft luxury of his apartment. "But I like the way the tables are dressed. Fresh flowers are always welcome."

"We may be eating them later," he said. "Served with cilantro."

His wit wasn't dry; it was desiccated.

I shan't attempt to describe our meal in detail since my palate is not discerning enough to identify subtle flavorings. I know we had a remarkable avocado salad with lime juice; mussels with scallions, white wine, and cream; and a main dish of salmon fillets with garlic and chilies. We agreed to skip dessert since we were both surfeited after more than ample portions of those luscious vittles.

Our choices had been spicy but not too hot and the service was admirable. I told Ricardo how much I had enjoyed it and I hoped we might return to try other examples of Mexican haute cuisine. "Next time you'll be my guest," I said.

"Sure," he said. "But if I can't make it and you want to ask someone else, just mention my name to get a table. The Alcazar has become an *in* spot."

I didn't doubt it for by the time we finished, every table was taken and several patrons were waiting at the bar, each gripping one of those huge margaritas. Ricardo and I were draining final glasses of a flinty Mexican sauvignon blanc when he glanced at his Rolex.

"Sorry," he said, "but I've got to run. Listen, Archy, if you'd care to stay and have a brandy at the bar, by all means do. I have an account here and I'll tell the maître d' to put it on my tab."

"That's very kind of you," I said, "but I think I'll leave as well. Thank you for a most enjoyable feast."

We both rose to depart and it was then the tenor of the evening changed. Later it seemed to me to consist of two distinct acts: the dinner and what followed. I had the notion of a curtain being lowered and being raised again on a totally different scene.

A young woman pushed through the throng at the bar and came hurrying to confront us.

"Hi, Dick," she said breathlessly. "You haven't seen Paul tonight, have you?"

I glanced at Ricardo and saw him wince. You may adjudge me a simpleton but at the moment I thought his discomfort came from being addressed as Dick. But why should he be dismayed? Ricardo is another form of Richard, and Dick is a generally accepted diminutive. My name is Archibald but I have no objection to Archy. However I do have an aversion to Arch, which I feel is more adjective than name.

But then his obvious disconcertment may have been due to the lady's physical appearance. She was attractive enough in a Betty Boopish kind of way, but it was more her costume than her looks or manner which might have caused Ricardo's distress. She was clad in a tarty outfit of flaming red leather, jacket and skirt, the latter so short her bare knees were completely revealed, each a perfect image of Herbert Hoover.

"No, Sonia, I haven't seen Paul," Chrisling said stiffly. Then, remembering his manners, he uttered a swift introduction. "Sonia, this is Archy. Archy, Sonia." No last names.

"Hi, Archy," she said brightly.

"Hi, Sonia," I said just as brightly. Did I have a choice?

"I've got to leave right now," Ricardo said, "or I'll never get to the Lauderdale airport in time to meet my friends. Archy, do me a favor, will you? Treat Sonia to a drink at the bar. And don't forget to put it on my tab."

He fled and I was left with Ms. Miniskirt. "Would you care for a drink?" I asked gamely.

"Why not?" she said. "I already et."

Most of the waiting customers had now been seated and we were able to find room at the zinc-topped bar. Sonia ordered a margarita of course but I asked for a brandy. I was served a Presidente, the same brand Chrisling had given me.

"Have you known Ricardo long?" I asked casually.

"Dick?" she said. "Sure, we're old friends. He's the handsomest guy I've ever met. Don't you think he's handsome?"

"I do indeed," I assured her. "But what about Paul? The man you're looking for." I meant it teasingly but she became suddenly morose.

"My ex," she said darkly. "A real stinker. He's a week late on the alimony check. That's why I'm looking for him. I'll clean his clock. It's not he ain't got the bucks."

"Ah," I said. "He's gainfully employed?"

"Sure he is. A good job. He's a naval architect."

"He designs navels?"

She looked at me. "Boats," she said. "He designs boats."

"Oh," I said.

"Listen, Archy, I've got a great idea. Why don't you buy us a bottle of something somewhere and we'll go back to my place, let down our hair, and tell each other the stories of our lives. Then we'll see what happens. Okay?"

"Oh, I don't think I could do that," I said hastily.

"It doesn't have to be a big bottle," she told me. "A pint will do."

Our conversation was beginning to take on a surreal quality, and if this tootsiesque young lady had suddenly launched into a dance routine from a Busby Berkeley musical I wouldn't have been a bit surprised.

"Sonia," I said earnestly, "I do thank you for your kind invitation but I'm afraid it's impossible tonight."

"You don't like me? I don't turn you on?"

"I *do* like you," I declared, "and you *do* turn me on. But I have an important errand of mercy to perform tonight. My dear old grandmother is in the hospital and she's depending on me to stop by to read the latest financial report on her investment in pork belly futures."

Look, I wasn't going to let her outgoof me. I could be just as mentally anorexic as she.

"What's wrong with your grandmother?"

"I'm afraid it's a terminal case of flagrante delicto."

"Oh lordy, that sounds awful."

"It is. Endless suffering."

"But listen, couldn't you come over to my place after you visit your grandmother? I mean it's just the shank of the evening. I'll wait for you."

She was being awfully persistent and I think it was at that moment I realized this was quite possibly more than a casual pickup. Despite her fey conversation she was intent on her purpose: to lure me to her lair.

"Sonia, I'd love to," I said with what I hoped sounded like a sigh of ineffable regret. "But after I visit grandmama I'm so wrung out emotionally I'm not capable of fun and games. You understand, don't you?"

"I guess," she said.

"But I want to see you again," I said eagerly. "Perhaps we could make it another night. May I ask for your telephone number?"

That seemed to enthuse her. "You betcha," she said, fished in the pocket of her leather jacket, and came out with a tube of lipstick.

Before I was fully aware of what was happening she had grasped my left hand, turned it over, and scrawled her telephone number on my palm in virulent red lip gloss.

"There!" she said triumphantly. "How's that? I have an answering machine. If I'm not in, leave a message."

"I certainly shall," I said feebly.

"Soon?"

"As possible," I said, looking at the number smeared on my palm with loathing. I prayed Brillo and Ajax might do the trick.

She finished her margarita and leaned forward to give me a kiss and a wink. Then she was gone with a creaking of leather. I gulped my brandy hurriedly, fearing she might return.

"Mr. Chrisling has taken care of the bill, sir," the mustachioed bartender said gravely.

I thanked him and handed over a sawbuck gratuity. He gave me a grateful smile I prayed was sincere. At the moment I was desperately in need of unambiguity.

I drove home slowly, thoughts awhirl as usual, and pulled into my slot in our three-car garage. I switched off engine, lights, and just sat there in the darkness. After a moment I heard a gentle scratching, leaned to open the door, and Hobo leaped into the passenger bucket. I think he wanted to lick my schnozz but I wouldn't let him; I'd had enough unsolicited affection for one night. But I did pet him, stroking his head and back. A few minutes later he curled up on the leather seat and closed his eyes. Lucky dog.

I wished I could sleep as easily and instantly as he, but I could not. All the rusty McNally neurons were in overdrive and the ferment was almost painful as I tried to figure out exactly what had happened that night. I strove to think logically—which you may feel is similar to my attempting a fifty-foot pole vault.

I started by assuming Ricardo Chrisling's invitation to dinner was not simply to have a sociable get-together; the man had an ulterior motive. And it had appeared in red leather. I refused to believe Sonia's intrusion was merely a chance encounter. He had arranged it.

Perhaps it was one of those macho things. Here's a willing chick you should meet and you'll have a great time. But I did not think Ricardo capable of such crassness. He was wilier than that.

Putting aside his scheming for the nonce, I concentrated on the conduct of Sonia.

It would be understandable if she, a not so gay divorcée, was lonely and yearned for companionship, even if it lasted no more than one night. Possible but not probable.

Or she was engaged in Murphy's game, one of the oldest cons in the history of scams. A chippie, real or faux, entices a john to her digs with the promise of instant gratification. Once inside her door the victim is confronted by her alleged husband, boyfriend, pimp, or perhaps an armed plug-ugly hired for the occasion. The mark is robbed and forcibly ejected from the premises. Was that Sonia's script? Possible but not probable.

Which brought me back to Ricardo's role in this farrago. If he had written the scenario, planned I was to meet the available lady with the bees' knees, what in the name of Jehoshaphat could be his reason?

I left Hobo snoozing in the Miata and went into the house, up to my hideaway, still puzzled by Ricardo's behavior and wondering if I was not being paranoid. The man had really done nothing suspicious. He had invited me to a splendid dinner. An acquaintance had unexpectedly appeared. So why was I impugning his motives, searching for any evidence of deception?

I was disrobing, preparing to spend an hour or two bringing my journal up to date, when I stopped suddenly. I think I may have grinned. Because a short memory loss was restored and I recalled something Ricardo had said during the evening. I shall not dignify it by calling it a "clue," but I thought it significant.

Surely you know what I'm writing about, don't you? You picked up on it before I did—not so? If not, you must be patient and be assured your temporarily prideful scribe will reveal Ricardo's slip at the proper time.

Stay in touch.

30

Before I retired on Thursday night I laboriously expunged Sonia's lipsticked telephone number from my palm. A bit of scouring powder helped. But first I copied the number into my daybook. As an amateur sleuth I had learned God is in the details. Or is it the Devil who is in the details? I can never remember which.

Regarding the next morning . . .

There is an anecdote about W. C. Fields—or perhaps it was Jimmy Durante—who was called upon to make a daybreak appearance at his movie studio. As he staggered through the dawn's early light he came upon a lofty tree laden with sleeping and nesting birds. Immediately he began kicking the tree and whacking it with his walking stick.

"When I'm up," he shouted, "everybody up!"

I recalled the story after Sgt. Al Rogoff shattered my deep slumber with a phone call at eight o'clock on Friday morning. Ungodly hour.

"When you're up," I grumbled, "everybody up. Have you no mercy?"

"Not me," he said curtly. "I'm working my tail off and I expect the same from you. Listen, I showed a color photo of a white Ford Explorer to the gooney lady who claims she saw Tony Sutcliffe and Emma Gompertz being hustled away. She says yes, she thinks that was the vehicle used. She *thinks* it was but she isn't certain. A defense attorney could easily demolish her testimony but it's good enough for me. Like I told you, I got nothing else. So what was Ricardo Chrisling's car doing there when the ex-employees of Parrots Unlimited were abducted?"

It staggered me for a sec. "I didn't tell you it belonged to Chrisling."

He was indignant. "You think I'm a mutt? After the loopy dame made a tentative identification I checked the cars of everyone connected with this mishmash and came up with Chrisling. You think he's our hero?"

"I just don't know," I said truthfully. "But I'm happy my tip yielded results. Now you owe me one—right?"

"Oh-oh," he said resignedly. "All right, what do you want?"

"I have a telephone number and a woman's first name. I'd like to know if she's got a sheet."

"This is personal? You're looking to romance the lady?"

"Don't get cute, Al. She's a friend of Chrisling."

"In that case I'll go along."

I told him her name was Sonia and, after a moment, I found her number in my professional diary and repeated it to Rogoff.

"I'll let you know," he said.

"When?"

"ASAP. I think the ice is beginning to break."

He hung up and I went back to bed for another thirty minutes of sweet somnolence. I finally did get to work that morning—late but in an energetic mood. I decided Sgt. Rogoff had been correct; the ice pack was cracking. I hadn't grasped the infamous plot earlier because I underestimated the villainy of the people involved. It's a constant fault; I can never acknowledge the power of sheer evil.

I had two phone calls to make. The first was to the Gottschalk home. I was finally put through to one of the twins. Don't ask me which one although she claimed to be Judith. I inquired as to the condition of her brother.

"Oh, Peter's been released from the hospital," she said breezily. "Right now he's on his way to visit some quack. What a twerp he is!"

I thanked her hurriedly and hung up. I had no desire for an extended conversation. I might get suckered into hosting a champagne brunch.

Before I could make my second call I received one—from Yvonne Chrisling. "You naughty boy," she said reprovingly. "You promised to phone and you didn't."

"Yvonne, we spoke only a day or so ago. I really intended to contact you." Liar, liar, pants on fire.

"No matter," she said, suddenly brisk. "I must see you at once. It's very important."

"Lunch?"

"No," she said authoritatively. "Not in public. And not in my home."

"*My* home": I loved it. A few weeks ago it had been Hiram Gottschalk's home. *Sic transit* . . . and so forth.

"Would you care to come to the office?" I suggested.

"No." She was quite decisive. "I might be seen."

I wanted to ask, "By whom?" but didn't.

"If this is to be a confidential meeting," I said, "as you apparently wish, perhaps we might get together at the McNally residence. We can talk inside or during a walk on the beach—whichever you prefer."

She didn't hesitate a mo. "Yes," she said, "that will do. In an hour. You will be there?"

"I shall. You have my address?"

"Of course," she said. "I'm so looking forward to seeing you again, darling."

I am hypersensitive to tones of voice and I thought her last declaration had a wheedling inflection. Curious for a woman of her resolution.

I had time to make my second call before leaving for a tête-à-tête with the Spider Woman. So I phoned Binky Watrous and found him at home in an excitable mood.

"Do you know anything about yellow-shafted flickers?" he demanded.

"Of course," I said. "Some of my best friends are yellow-shafted flickers, several of whom have been incarcerated for exhibiting their proclivity in public."

"Archy," he protested, "they're birds! Woodpeckers. And they attack anything even resembling a tree. They hammer at it with their beaks. I bought a recording of their hammering and I've been practicing imitating it. It's great, even better than calls. Bridget says with her tambourine and my hammering of the yellow-shafted flicker we'll have a classic. A *classic*, Archy!"

I should have replied, "A classic *what?*" But I couldn't rain on his parade; he was so up.

"Binky," I said, "the reason I called was to ask you about Martin and Felice, the recently hired employees of Parrots Unlimited."

"I already told you. Definitely below the salt."

"Useless, are they?"

"Well, they're not bird mavens, for sure, for sure."

"Then what do they *do?*" I persisted. "The man, Martin, for instance. He does feedings, cleans cages, and similar scut work?"

"Never saw him lift a hand. Sold a bird occasionally but he spent most of his time in the boss's office fiddling with the computer."

My heart leaped like an intoxicated gazelle. "Thank you, my son," I said huskily. "Your skinny may prove of inestimable value. Now go back to your hammering and don't blunt your beak."

I hung up in such an ebullient mood I wanted to chortle—if only I knew how to chortle. Things were coming together, wouldn't you agree? But there were surprises to come I hadn't anticipated. The picture puzzle was not quite complete. Stick with me, kid, and you'll be wearing diamonds.

I drove home hastily and waited only ten minutes on our graveled turnaround before Yvonne Chrisling appeared in a new Cadillac DeVille. And I mean *spanking* new. It was a forest green, a color much in vogue at the time, and had such a gleam it looked as if it had just been driven from the showroom. As the Mad. Ave. pundits advise: If you've got it, flaunt it.

She emerged from the yacht wearing stonewashed jeans and a white canvas bush jacket. I realized I had never before seen her dressed so informally. I liked it; she seemed softer, more vulnerable.

But my impression was quickly dispelled. She gave me a dim smile and then looked about at the McNally estate: our ersatz-Tudor main house feathered in ivy, garage, greenhouse, potting shed, and Hobo's abode.

"Very antique, isn't it?" she said sniffishly.

"True," I said, refusing to be riled. "We planned it so."

"Not to my taste," she pronounced, and it was then I became fully aware of what a snarky mood she was in. "Is there anyone about?" she asked abruptly.

"Probably my mother and the staff."

"Then let's go down to the beach."

"Would you care for a drink of something first?"

"No," she said tersely, and I had a premonition this meeting was going to be as much fun as the extraction of an impacted molar.

I conducted her across Ocean Boulevard, down the rickety wooden staircase to the sand. She took up a firmly planted station in the shade of some palms and showed no inclination to move farther.

"A walk?" I suggested. "Perhaps a wade in the water?"

"I don't think so," she said. "I hate the beach and the ocean."

It was too much. "Then what on earth are you doing in South Florida?"

"Circumstances," she said, which told me nothing. "Archy," she went on determinedly, "I need legal advice."

"Whoa!" I said, holding up a palm. "I am not an attorney. I do not have a law degree or license to practice. I think you better consult my father or another qualified lawyer."

"But you know a lot about the law, don't you?"

"Some," I admitted, cautiously forbearing to tell her the story of why I was booted out of Yale Law.

"This isn't for me," she said. "It's for a friend who has a problem."

She looked at me so wide-eyed and sincere I knew she was lying. Besides, everyone in the legal profession has heard the old wheeze from a client: "I have a friend with a legal problem." Hogwash. The attorney knows immediately it's the client's problem.

"What is it, Yvonne?"

"My friend, a woman, has knowledge of a crime. She wasn't involved in any way, shape, or form but she knows who did it. What should she do?"

"Immediately report what she knows to a law enforcement agency," I said promptly. "She is obligated to do so. If not she may find herself in deep, deep trouble. Concealing knowledge of criminal behavior is not a charge to be taken lightly."

Yvonne showed no indication of surprise or shock. I reckoned she already knew what I had told her.

"But it's not so simple," she said, turning her gaze out to sea: a true thousand-yard stare. "First of all, the individual who committed the crime is close to her. Very close. It would pain her to be an informer."

I shook my head. "She has no choice."

"Another factor . . ." Yvonne continued, looking at me directly again. "My friend is afraid of what the reaction might be of the person she accuses."

"Afraid? Of physical retaliation?"

"Yes."

"She can ask for police protection. She can move, change her phone number, take on a new identity. Whatever will ensure her safety."

"But she must tell what she knows?"

"Absolutely."

"She is entirely innocent, you understand, and now she is trapped in this terrible dilemma and she is frightened. You can sympathize with that, can you not?"

"Of course I can, Yvonne."

I had said the right thing, because her manner was suddenly transformed. She melted, became almost flirtatious.

"How happy I am to have asked for your advice, Archy," she said in a lilting voice. "I knew I could depend on you. We are so compatible. We must see more of each other. You agree?"

"Oh yes."

"*Much* more," she chortled. *She* knew how to do it. "And I shall tell my friend everything you have said. Thank you, sweetheart."

She took my hand as I led her back to the parked Cadillac. She couldn't have been more affectionate. Well, she could have been but I resisted, fearing Hobo might be observing us from his kennel. "Thank you again, darling," she caroled just before she drove away. "What a treasure you are!"

I watched her wheeled castle depart, thinking, There goes one very brainy lady. But more of that later. At the moment I was famished and hustled into the kitchen. First things first.

No one was present and I presumed Ursi and perhaps mother were on a shopping expedition to replenish our larder. I opened the fridge and inspected the contents to see what I might use to concoct a modest, nutritious lunch.

A bag of Walla Walla sweet onions caught my eye. When Vidalias are not in season we send for Walla Wallas or Texas sweets. Admirable onions, no doubt, but I still prefer the distinctive flavor of Vidalias. But one must make do and so I constructed a toasted bagel sandwich holding a thick slice of Walla Walla slathered with Dijonnaise. You've never had an onion sandwich? The mother of all sandwiches. Especially when accompanied by an icy bottle of lager.

I ate slowly with much pleasure, resolutely refraining from thinking about my conversation with Yvonne Chrisling. I finished after stoutly rejecting an urge to make and devour a duplicate—and stoutly is the right word. I then phoned the office, spoke to Mrs. Trelawney, and found my father would be absent all afternoon conferring with a client in Lantana. It meant my necessary meeting with him would have to be postponed until the evening. I must admit I was relieved.

I uncapped another bottle of lager, took it upstairs to my atelier, and settled down for a deep think. Yvonne Chrisling . . .

I recognized she had heavy, heavy motives for initiating our chat on the beach. Her ploy of asking legal advice for a friend was a transparent fraud. She was pleading her own case. And unless she considered me a complete dolt—and I trusted she didn't—she knew I identified her as the troubled woman involved.

But why devise such a Byzantine plot to enlist my sympathy?

It took me almost an hour and the second bottle of lager to arrive at what I considered a logical reason. The lady was, in effect, attempting to cop a plea or cut a deal. She realized or sensed the running wolves—in the shape of Sgt. Al Rogoff and yrs. truly—were baying at her sleigh and coming closer.

"Save yourself" was the belief, the faith governing her existence. Now, feeling threatened, she was moving boldly and shrewdly to protect herself. I didn't want to but I had to admire her effort. It is no easy task for anyone to claim innocence, even the guiltless.

I was convinced I had her pinned. It gave me no joy. It would be simplistic to label the people involved as weak. They were not weak. They were strong, venomous characters who had made a cold, reasoned choice of corruption and its rewards.

Saddened by the perfidy existing in one family, I began to reread my entire scribbled record of the affair. And I arrived at what I believed to be a reasonable (and depressing) explanation of all that had occurred in the Gottschalk nest of vipers.

I intend to complete this penny dreadful as quickly as possible. I know you want to go to bed.

31

M Y FATHER is more gourmand than gourmet and so I was delighted our Friday night dinner was pot roast with potato pancakes—his favorite. I hoped it might put him in a felicitous mood during an interrogation I simply had to make. Sometimes in our Q&A sessions he adopts a prickly you-have-no-need-to-know attitude which makes me want to run away from home.

"Could I have a few moments of your time, sir?" I said as we left the dining room after a dessert of lemon sorbet and pralines.

"And what is your definition of a few moments?" he asked genially enough.

"Ten, perhaps fifteen minutes."

"Concerning what?"

"My inquiry into the death of Hiram Gottschalk."

He nodded and led the way into his study. "A peg of brandy?" he inquired.

"That would be welcome, thank you."

He did the honors, pouring each of us a small snifter. It wasn't his best cognac but I made no complaint. He didn't ask me to be seated and he also remained standing. It was his way of ensuring our meeting would be brief.

"Well?" he said.

"Father, I have been reviewing my notes regarding the Gottschalk case, beginning with the initial assignment. At that time you mentioned you had discussions with him regarding the creation of a foundation in order to reduce his estate tax. Am I right?"

One hairy eyebrow was hoisted aloft. "Archy, I admire the thoroughness of your records. Yes, you are correct. I had several conversations with Mr. Gottschalk concerning the establishment of a nonprofit foundation."

"Could you tell me what he had in mind?"

"He was rather vague about it but it seemed he was interested in financing a sort of aviary in which research and breeding would help ensure the continued existence of endangered species of birds, particularly parrots."

"If he had lived long enough to set up such an institution, it would have reduced his net worth?"

"Naturally. And given him the tax advantages of a sizable charitable contribution, I might add."

"If the foundation had been in place prior to his death would it have limited his bequests to his heirs and beneficiaries?"

He pondered a long time, taking two tastes of his cognac. "Perhaps limited is the wrong word," he said finally. "Heirs and beneficiaries would have profited handsomely even if the foundation was in existence. Specific sums would be bequeathed. If the foundation did *not* exist at Mr. Gottschalk's death, as it does not, those bequests will be larger."

"Much larger?" I persisted.

"Appreciably," he said dryly.

"Father, do you know if Mr. Gottschalk informed his heirs and beneficiaries of his intention to establish a charitable foundation?"

I think he was puzzled by my question. "I have no idea. Why don't you ask them, Archy?"

"I doubt if I'd get a straight answer. Will you venture a guess, sir. Did he tell them or didn't he?"

Again he mulled, finishing his brandy. "I'd guess he told them," he said at last. "Our late client was a very outgoing man. Eccentric but trusting. Is that all?"

"A final question. . . . In the event an heir is deemed incompetent for mental or physical disabilities to handle his or her personal and financial affairs, who is appointed guardian?"

"A court of law would make the decision on the heir's incompetency after hearing testimony from physicians and other relevant witnesses. If the heir is adjudged mentally and/or physically unable to handle his or her affairs, I'd say the most likely guardian to be appointed by the court would be the closest family member."

"Or members," I said.

"Or members," he acknowledged.

"Thank you, father," I said, draining my brandy. "Have a pleasant evening."

"I hope to," he said. "Is this disagreeable business winding down, Archy?"

"I believe it is, sir. With good luck."

"Luck?" he repeated. "We make our own luck."

"Not always," I informed him. "Sometimes we benefit from other people's bad luck."

Profound—no? But I wasn't sure what I meant.

I went upstairs full of beans. After what father had told me, I exulted, I had everything. It wasn't long after that—a short session at my desk flipping through my journal did the trick—I realized I had nothing. Oh, I conjured a marvelous hypothesis elucidating all—including the 5th Problem of Hilbert. Watertight, one might even say, and I do say it. But I had no proof, and without what Al Rogoff calls "hard evidence" it was all smoke and mirrors.

What I needed, I concluded disconsolately, was a deus ex machina. And because I live a clean life and have a pure heart it arrived about an hour later in the form of a telephone call from the crusty sergeant himself.

"You're awake?" he said. "And sober?"

"Of course I'm awake and sober," I said. "And working I might add. 'Neither snow, nor rain, nor heat, nor gloom of night stays these couriers from the swift completion of their appointed rounds.' "

"You work for the post office?"

"It's Herodotus, Al."

"Thank you. I won't forget it for at least five minutes. Listen, about the bimbo you asked me to check out."

"Sonia. What's her last name?"

"She's got about six of them. Take your pick."

"She told me her ex-husband is a naval architect."

"The last time we had her in she told us her ex is a brain surgeon. I think he used liposuction on hers."

"You mean she's got a record?"

"Archy, she's a toughie. Many, many charges. Probations without end. And she did six months for loitering."

"Loitering for what?"

"For the purpose of singing hymns, idiot boy. She's a friend of Ricardo Chrisling?"

"Right now," I said, "I think she's more an employee than a friend. Al, where are you calling from?"

"Headquarters, about to leave."

"Have you had dinner?"

"Of course."

"What kind of pizza?"

"Anchovy."

"Then you must be thirsty. How about stopping by my place on your way home."

"Why should I do that?"

"Two cold bottles of Rolling Rock."

"Be there in about thirty minutes," he said.

The half hour gave me time to kick my cerebral cortex into high gear and decide to limit my revelations to Rogoff. There were things he needed to know to further his investigation of three homicides and things concerning only my own discreet inquiry. Admittedly the two intermixed to some extent but I hoped to keep them distinct. Hopeless hope.

I was downstairs when his pickup skidded to a stop with a scattering of gravel. I uncapped two bottles of beer, brought them outside, and clambered into the cab alongside him. He had been smoking a cigar but mercifully laid it to rest in a huge ashtray attached magnetically to the dash. But the atmosphere remained yucky enough to spur me into lighting an English Oval in self-defense.

He took a heavy gulp of his first beer and sighed. "Manna," he said. Then: "What do you want?"

"Al, why do you think I want anything?"

"Why else would you be bribing me with a couple of brews?"

"Well, it's true I need your cooperation but in return I am about to give you a gift beyond compare."

"Yeah? And what might that be?"

"Listen to this. . . ."

I must have talked steadily for at least ten minutes, detailing my certainty that Ricardo Chrisling was the murderer of Hiram Gottschalk and deeply involved in the killings of Emma Gompertz and Anthony Sutcliffe.

1. Chrisling has close ties to Mexican and South American banditos engaged in the smuggling of endangered birds, particularly parrots, into the U.S.

2. He serves as one of several retail dealers selling these expensive birds to collectors.

3. Hiram Gottschalk became aware of what Ricardo was doing and vowed to expose him. And so Hiram was eliminated.

4. Tony Sutcliffe and his companion met the same fate when they accused Chrisling of the prohibited trade in rare species.

5. Ricardo uses the computer setup at Parrots Unlimited to keep track of his purchases, sales, and customers. The same computer was used to query the net on the subject of parrots, and Chrisling became aware of the interest of McNally & Son in the smuggling of the birds.

I paused to light another ciggie as Rogoff started on his second beer.

"I'll buy it," he said unexpectedly. "It ties in with Chrisling's car being used to grab Gompertz and Sutcliffe. And among the papers I took from their apartment were copies of letters written to the Division of Law Enforcement of the Fish and Wildlife Service. They were about the smuggling of birds on the proscribed list, how the smuggling was done, ports of entry, penalties, and so forth. So Sutcliffe must have suspected something rancid was going on at Parrots Unlimited."

"He didn't suspect," I said, "he *knew*. And like the innocent he was, he confronted Ricardo and probably announced his intention of informing the authorities. And so he and Emma got their brains blown out in the Everglades. Pretty?"

The sergeant took a deep breath. "It all listens," he said. "A very neat solution and I believe every word of it. There's only one thing wrong with it; it's all ozone. You know? Not a thing we can take to the state attorney."

"Al, I've got an expert working on the invasion of McNally and Son's computer. We may be able to prove the break-in originated at Parrots Unlimited."

"So what? Chrisling would claim an employee was doing a little unauthorized hacking just for the fun of it, and he'll promise to fire the guy. Then where are we? Archy, we've got no proof of anything—let's face it."

"I've already faced it," I told him. "And there's only one way to resolve this stalemate: entrapment."

"Don't use that word!" Rogoff cried. "It means my pension."

"All right, then let me put it this way: It's a slim chance of snagging Ricardo Chrisling. It's a gamble, I admit, but you're a gambler, aren't you?"

"Would I be a cop if I wasn't?"

"I think 'if I weren't' is the correct usage."

He sighed. "Always the professor. Okay, let's hear your gamble."

"It involves Sonia, the hidebound vixen. From what you've

told me about her I'm convinced she's a pro. I'm also convinced Ricardo plotted what was apparently a chance meeting. The man warned me on the phone he'd have to leave early to drive to the Miami airport to greet arriving friends. But at dinner he said he must rush off to meet those friends at the Fort Lauderdale airport. An innocent slip or change of plans? I don't think so. He was lying and he forgot his original lie. A good memory is absolutely essential for successful prevarication. Ask me; I know."

"All right," Al said, "let's assume he set up your meet with the hustler. What was his purpose? To provide you with a night of fun and games? Maybe he even paid her—a little after-dinner gift."

"I doubt it," I said. "Ricardo has more pride than that. I think she was instructed to play Murphy's game, as designed by Chrisling. I was to accompany the lady to her home, full of good food, Mexican brandy, and unutterable longing. At a designated moment one or more yobbos would appear and whisk me off to the Everglades, where I would meet the same fate that befell Gompertz and Sutcliffe."

"Very dramatic," Rogoff said. "But why should Chrisling want to put you down?"

"I told you," I explained patiently. "Ricardo's computer maven had already discovered McNally and Son was investigating the smuggling of parrots. Chrisling may be a villain but he's no fool. He guessed why I was nosing around—to identify the killer of Hiram Gottschalk. And in addition I was now making inquiries about his criminal and very profitable business activities. He's a direct man, Al; murder solves all his difficulties."

The sergeant fished his cold cigar from the ashtray and ignited it again. And so I had to light another cigarette to match him puff for puff, fume for fume.

"Supposing you're on target," he said, "what's your gamble?"

"I want to phone Sonia, make an appointment for tomorrow night. I think she'll leap at the chance because she struck out the last time. She'll inform Chrisling and the original scenario will be resurrected. But you and your stalwarts will be waiting outside. Concealed of course. And when the ruffians march me out for a one-way trip to the Everglades you'll be able to grab them. And Sonia as well."

He turned to stare at me. "You're a complete and total loony," he said. "You know that, don't you?"

"Al, I told you it's a gamble but I think the odds are in our favor. If it works you'll have Sonia and the muscles in custody. You know the hoods will probably have sheets longer than Sonia's. If you lean on them I wager one or more will spill to cop a plea. They'll tell you Ricardo Chrisling was the boss and masterminded the whole schmear."

"And if it doesn't work?"

"You mean Sonia turns out to be merely a hardworking entrepreneur eager to make a buck? I can handle that situation and beat a graceful retreat with my innocence intact. And you and your crew will have lurked a few hours in the darkness with no result. Is that so awful? You've been on unproductive stakeouts before, haven't you?"

He didn't answer immediately. He was silent a long time and I didn't know if his decision would be yea or nay.

"Okay," he said finally. "I'll play your nutty game. Nothing ventured, nothing gained."

"How true, how true," I said. "And a rolling stone gathers no moss."

"Go to hell," he said. "You'll set it up for tomorrow night?"

"If I can," I told him. "I'll let you know as soon as my dalliance with Sonia is confirmed. Where can I reach you tomorrow? Will you be at headquarters?"

"No," he said. "At home. I start a forty-eight at midnight."

"Sorry about that, Al."

He shrugged. "It comes with the territory. Thanks for the beers."

32

CLIMBED OUT OF his pickup and waited until he pulled away. Then I went upstairs to wonder if what the sergeant had called my "nutty game" had a chance to succeed. It did, I assured myself, it did, it definitely did. And so I phoned Sonia, the femmy fatally in this circus.

I didn't speak to the lady herself but I reported to her answering machine. "Sonia," I said in what I hoped were fervid tones, "this is Archy. We were introduced by Ricardo Chrisling at the Alcazar—remember? I'd like very much to accept your kind invitation to visit you at your home. I'll bring the refreshment. Could we make it at nine o'clock tomorrow? Nine on Saturday night. Please let me know. I hope you'll say yes. It means so much to me."

I concluded by giving my unlisted phone number. It is not

something I ordinarily care to do but I had no choice. I hoped she might return my call before noon the next day, when I had a golfing date with a trio of buddies including Binky Watrous. I prayed he wouldn't wear his plaid tam-o'-shanter, which looked like a Spanish omelette flapping about his ears.

I was sound asleep when I was awakened by the insistent shrill of my phone. I roused sufficiently to look at my illuminated bedside clock through bleary eyes. It was almost three a.m. and I feared what ghastly news awaited me. I picked up the phone with a trembling hand.

"Hiya, Archy," she said cheerily. "This is Sonia. I got your message and you're a sweetie to call. Of course I want to see you at nine tomorrow."

"Your address," I said in a sleep-slurred voice. "I don't know where you live. Wait a mo until I locate pen and paper."

She gave me her address and I scrawled it down as best I could.

"Ooh, I can hardly wait until tomorrow night, darling," she cooed. "We'll have such fun. By the way, I like gin."

She hung up and I rolled groaning back into bed, hoping to resume the dream I had been having of rescuing Joan Blondell from a burning building.

When I awoke about eight-thirty on Saturday morning the first thing I did was don my reading specs to make certain my torpid penmanship of the night before was readable. It was; Sonia's address was legible. Then horror struck. I realized she lived only a few doors away from the abode of Consuela Garcia. What a way to start a new day!

I phoned Al Rogoff and informed him my date with Sonia was set for nine p.m. I gave him the address. He grunted. I had the feeling his joy was underwhelming.

Actually it turned out to be a snappy and invigorating Saturday. After a few moments of worried reflection I concluded the

chances of Connie spotting me sneaking into the lair of a local
Mata Hari were practically nil and I could safely ignore the danger. Also, it was a super day, climatically speaking, and because
I'm so attuned to the weather I found it impossible to be gloomy
when the sky appeared dry-cleaned and the sun looked like a just
minted one-ounce Golden Eagle.

The golf game was a joy. Binky and I were paired and won easily, earning a nice piece of change. Then we all adjourned to the
Pelican Club for a raucous lunch of barbecued ribs and suds.
After the gorge we played darts and again I won. Custom decreed
the victor buy drinks for the losers, so my triumph cost more than
my winnings. Silly, isn't it? But I didn't care; I took my luck at
golf and darts as a harbinger of more good fortune to come.

The remainder of the day passed swiftly: the lazy, hazy dream
of every Palm Beach layabout. I returned home, had a slow, languorous swim in a soup-warm sea, took a sweet nap, dressed, and
joined my parents at the cocktail hour. After dinner I changed
my duds to a more sportif costume I thought might impress
Sonia. Then I set out on the night's venture, wondering if this
was the way C. Auguste Dupin got his start.

Sonia had requested gin and my first inclination was to buy
the cheapest corrosive available, since if my prediction of what
was to happen proved correct we wouldn't be lifting a celebra-
tory glass. But then I reproved myself for such a non-U decision.
It indicated a shocking lack of noblesse oblige. And so I bought
a bottle of Beefeater and toted that to the island of our very own
Circe, who, as we all know, turned men into swine.

I parked a few streets away and wandered back no more fear-
ful than if I were scaling the north face of the Eiger. I looked
about warily but saw no signs of skulking miscreants. Nor did I
spot Sgt. Rogoff and his army. I could only hope they were present.

I had no problem gaining entrance to Sonia's den. She was listed on the directory as Sonia Smith. Innocent enough. I pressed the button opposite her name, identified myself on the intercom, and was immediately buzzed in. I rode a rather tatty elevator to the sixth floor, walked down a tattier corridor, and was greeted at the opened door of 6-E by the grinning hostess, who promptly gave me a noisy smooch I could have done without.

"It's happy time!" she cried, and yanked me inside, locking, bolting, and chaining the door behind me. I wondered if I'd get time off for good behavior.

I was pulled into a living room decorated in South Florida Renaissance: glass tables supported on driftwood, milky paintings of conch shells, and tinted mirrors. Lots and lots of mirrors. I saw myself reflected from every angle: a depressing sight. Was I really beginning to sprout a dewlap?

Sonia was wearing a stained denim jumpsuit zippered from hither to yon. She looked as if she were ready to change the oil on your Winnebago. She grabbed the brown paper bag from my hands, extracted the bottle to glance at the label.

"Yummy!" she yelped. "My favorite. Now you make yourself at home while I slip into something more comfortable."

She disappeared with the gin, leaving me bemused. "Slip into something more comfortable." How long has it been since you've heard that line? It was a favorite in the movie romances of the 1930s and 1940s, usually murmured by Ann Sheridan. At the moment I would have liked to slip into something more comfortable, like a flak jacket atop a bulletproof vest.

My foreboding proved accurate when Sonia did not reappear but instead two gross creatures, seemingly as broad as they were tall, came lumbering from the rear of the apartment. They planted themselves stolidly and stared at me.

You must believe it when I tell you fright was not my first re-action. Instead I felt a surge of satisfaction at having correctly an-alyzed the situation and predicted what was likely to occur. But then, as gratification ebbed, terror took over.

"Good evening, gentlemen," I said with a silly laugh.

"Let's go," one of them growled.

"Go where?" I inquired reasonably enough.

"A little trip," the other said.

"Why on earth should I take a trip with you?" I asked. "I have no desire to travel at the moment."

"Here's why, jerko," ruffian #1 said, and withdrew a snub-nosed revolver from his jacket pocket. He pointed the muzzle at me.

"Well, yes," I admitted. "A sufficient invitation. May I bid a fond farewell to Sonia?"

They didn't bother replying. I was marched out of the apart-ment, both thugs crowding me so closely I was aware of their scent: something like a geriatric flounder. We waited for the el-evator.

"If someone's on it," one of the brutes said, "behave yourself. We don't want to hurt innocent people."

"I'm innocent," I observed.

They looked at me.

Fortunately the elevator was empty and we descended to a lobby apparently just as vacant. My escorts prodded me outside and suddenly it seemed we had stepped onto a floodlighted Broadway stage.

Three cars were drawn up in an arc, and as we exited, their headlights went on and I was tempted to ask my abductors if they'd care to join me in a soft-shoe routine, perhaps to the rhythm of "Shuffle Off to Buffalo."

While we stood frozen in the brilliance, two police officers in mufti came from the lobby behind us and stuck weapons into the ribs of my captors. Their arms rose slowly, just floated up.

What amazed me most about this beautifully executed operation was the total absence of speech. I mean there were no shouts of "Freeze!" or "Hands up!" or even "Eat dirt, turkey!" But then Rogoff and his cohorts were professionals. And so were my escorts—professional hoodlums. There was no need for dialogue; everyone knew what was going down.

The two schtarkers were relieved of their guns, cuffed, and hustled separately into two of the parked cars. Headlights were dimmed and the sergeant came strolling toward me, juicing up a fresh cigar. I think he was trying hard not to grin.

"You okay?" he asked.

"Tip-top," I assured him. "Or will be when the tremors in my knees subside. It was nicely done, Al, and I thank you. But why aren't any of these vehicles police cars? They all look like they're privately owned."

"They are," he said. "If I had asked for an official go-ahead on this chancy game the brass would have thought I'd blown a fuse. So I had to recruit a few go-for-broke guys who'd play along just for the fun of it."

Then I realized the career risk he had taken on my behalf and I was grateful. What a fortunate SOB I was. That stands for son of a barrister of course. "I owe you a big one," I told Rogoff.

"Sure you do," he agreed. "Now let's go up and collect the airhead."

"I don't think she'll let us in," I said.

"Why not?" he said. "We're nice people. Sonia Smith—right? I checked the directory earlier today."

He pressed the button and when she answered on the intercom, her voice sounded a mite shaky. "Who is this?" she asked.

"Ma'am, this is Sergeant Al Rogoff of the Palm Beach Police

Department. May I have a little conversation with you, please? It won't take long."

"I'm busy at the moment," she said. "Could we make it tomorrow?"

"On the other hand," he said pleasantly, "I could order up a SWAT team and have your door blasted open with a nuclear rocket. Would you prefer that, Sonia?"

Short pause. Then the buzzer sounded and we entered.

"You do have a way about you," I said admiringly.

He shrugged. "What's the point of having a potsy if you can't use it?"

Sonia opened her door with a bright smile that faded when she saw me. Al displayed his ID. She stood aside to let us enter. She was still wearing the denim jumpsuit but defiance had replaced her former élan.

"Is this a bust?" she demanded. "If it is, you got to read me my rights and I ain't saying a word until I talk to my lawyer."

"Nah," Rogoff said, "this is no arrest. I just think it would be to your advantage if you'd come down to headquarters with me and answer a few questions. If you don't want to, I'll have to go through the business of getting a warrant and pulling you in. It's really unnecessary. If you decide to come along you can always change your mind, clam up, and call your lawyer. It's a very small thing, Sonia. We don't suspect you of a supermarket massacre or anything like that. All we want is a little information on a minor matter. You're not being charged with anything. And if you cooperate you get a gold star next to your name on your records. Might help you in the future—right? How about it? Will you help us?"

He was very persuasive and it didn't take her long to decide. "Okay," she said. "Do I have to stay overnight?"

"Maybe," Rogoff admitted.

"Let me get my handbag," she said, and the sergeant followed her into the inner room. He didn't miss a trick.

When they emerged Al was rummaging through her bag. He held aloft a vial of pills. "What's this stuff?" he asked her.

"Aspirin," she said.

"Now they're making purple aspirin?" the sergeant said. "Crazy. Come along, luv. You'll be home again before you know it."

We let her lock up the apartment. We were waiting for the elevator when Sonia looked at me directly. "Archy," she said reproachfully, "I *trusted* you." Al and I were convulsed. Wouldn't you be?

Rogoff escorted her to the remaining car, keeping a firm grip on her arm. I followed and watched her safely installed in the back seat alongside a cop who offered her a stick of Juicy Fruit.

"Al," I said before he climbed behind the wheel, "may I call you tomorrow to find out what you've dragged out of the creeps?"

He finally lighted the cigar he'd been carrying. "Sure. But make it late. It'll be Sunday and things won't go fast. All the lawyers will be playing golf. Hey, it turned out to be a blast, didn't it?"

"A superblast," I assured him. "And thank you again."

"A big one!" he shouted back as he drove away. I thought at first he was referring to the recent action. Then I realized he was reminding me of my vow: "I owe you a big one." I intended to honor it.

Nerves still jangling, I decided a stop at the Pelican Club was called for. I hoped it would be a peaceable retreat where I could sit quietly at the mahogany and down a cognac or two to reduce my level of adrenaline. No such luck. The parking area was crowded and when I peeked inside I saw a boisterous mob of Saturday night revelers. Not for me; I just wasn't in the mood.

About to depart, I was stopped by the sight of the parking lot jammed with all kinds of wheels from sleek BMWs to hunky Harley Hogs. I called police headquarters on my cellular phone, identified myself, and asked to speak to Sgt. Al Rogoff. It required many minutes and many dollars before he came on the line.

"Now what?" he demanded.

"Al, how did those louts get to Sonia's apartment and how were they going to whisk me away? Did you look around for a vehicle they may have used?"

"You think I'm a Binky?" he said indignantly. "Of course we toured the neighborhood, and found a parked white Ford Explorer registered to Ricardo Chrisling. You like?"

"Very much," I said happily. "The final nail."

He sighed. "Get real, Archy," he advised. "Try thinking like a rat. Ricardo will claim he loaned his car to a friend or it was stolen. It doesn't prove a thing. Well, maybe it's a small piece but not enough to rack him up for murder-one."

"Where will you be tonight?" I asked him.

"Right here. There is going to be an all-night, five-star production with interrogations, lawyers coming and going, endless paperwork, conferences, black coffee, and burgers."

"Sorry about that."

"Sure you are. Now go home, go to sleep, and call me never. Some of us toil and some of us spin. I toil; you spin. Good night. I hope."

He hung up and I drove slowly home, charged by what he had told me of the presence of Ricardo's van at the scene of my escapade. Al seemed to take it lightly; I thought it meaningful. I decided a muscular brandy followed by sleep might provide the answers to all my questions. Or at least supply eight hours of for-getfulness.

But my crystal ball had cracked; the night didn't turn out as I anticipated.

One never knows, do one?

33

I GARAGED THE MIATA and noted the lights were on in my father's ground-floor study. It probably meant he was sipping port and doggedly continuing his self-imposed task of reading his way through the entire *oeuvre* of Chas. Dickens. It pleased me that in a world of senseless greed and gratuitous violence boredom still exerted its peculiar attraction. A somnifacient, I suspect.

Hobo had roused and come to the entrance of his house when I arrived. I gave him a wave and wished him a sweet slumber. He rewarded me with a single tail thump, then lay down with his chin resting between his paws and closed his eyes. I hoped to emulate him shortly—but it was not to be.

I was upstairs preparing an injection of 80-proof plasma when my phone rang. I think I may have repeated aloud Sgt. Rogoff's querulous query: "Now what?"

"Good evening, Archy," Ricardo Chrisling said. "I hope I'm not disturbing you."

"Not at all," I made myself say.

"Something came up and I thought of you immediately. Martin, my assistant, mentioned you were interested in obtaining a rare parrot."

"True," I said. "A gift for my antiquated grandfather who's a demon collector of birds, the rarer the better." (*I* remembered *my* lies.)

"I've been able to locate a Spix's macaw," he went on. "I don't know if you're familiar with the species but it's an extremely uncommon Brazilian bird. Only thirty-two known to exist. Collectors would love to have one but since we're friends I thought I'd give you first chance. It's a healthy male and very attractive. Dark blue with a gray-blue head. Yellow eyes. Interested?"

"I am indeed," I said, certain the bird he described would be an endangered species.

"I should warn you it's expensive."

"No problem," I assured him.

"What I'd like to do if I may is pop over to your place, show you a color photo, and we can discuss it. Is that convenient?"

"Of course."

"Be there in about twenty minutes," he said. "I think you'll like this bird, Archy." He hung up leaving me excited by the prospect of confirming his illicit trade in parrots on the proscribed list.

Those twenty minutes gave me time to ingest a brawny slug of Presidente brandy. Thus fortified I descended to our driveway and awaited the arrival of Ricardo Chrisling. I cannot to this day believe I never doubted his story about the Spix's macaw. Which only proves, I suppose, that although I may know the details of the Peloponnesian Wars, when it comes to more quotidian matters I am a complete dope.

He drove up in a new, dark green Cadillac DeVille, and it set an alarm bell chiming softly. The last time I had seen the car it was driven by Yvonne Chrisling. I assumed it was hers. But perhaps he borrowed it. Perhaps not. Perhaps it was his. Perhaps they shared it. At the moment I was flummoxed by an excess of perhapses and hadn't the time to sort them out.

Ricardo alighted, paused, and seemed to spend an inordinate time inspecting the premises, including the lights burning in my father's study and Hobo snoozing in the doorway of his condo. Then he came toward me with a flinty smile, hand outstretched. We shook: one hard, wrenching clasp.

"Archy," he said.

"Ricardo," I said. "I see you have new wheels."

"Not mine," he said. "My mother's."

Note the "My mother's" rather than "My stepmother's."

"Ah," I said, all my perhapses resolved—if I could believe him. "Would you care to come inside? We can have a drink and talk."

He came closer and looked at me strangely. "I tried," he said sadly. "I really tried to be your friend."

Realization arrived. It was slow in coming, I admit, but suddenly there it was: This man was my enemy and intended to harm me.

"You didn't try hard enough," I said just as sadly.

Lordy, he was fast. His hand snaked into his jacket pocket and came out with a bone handle. He pressed a button and a thin, naked blade swung out and clicked into a locked position. He moved a step closer.

Earlier in the evening I had faced a loaded revolver and was frightened. But it couldn't compare to the fear I felt at the sight of that bare, shining sliver of steel. I can't explain it. A gun can wound or kill as surely as a knife but the latter terrorizes more. Don't ask me why.

"The weapon you used to murder Hiram Gottschalk?" I asked, and my voice sounded quavery even to me.

He didn't reply. He was close enough to thrust at my midriff but not so close I wasn't able to knock his arm aside and grapple. For a moment or two we hugged, straining and swaying. Then he put a heel behind one of my knees, pushed violently, and dumped me onto the ground. He leaned over, stiletto poised, and I regretted I hadn't apologized to Consuela Garcia for any real or fancied hurt.

It was at that precise instant Hobo came charging, paws scrabbling at the gravel. He was a smallish terrier but he attacked like a fifty-pound pit bull. Marvelous, wonderful, magnificent dog! And the sounds he was making! Bloodcurdling, ferocious growls, lips drawn back, fangs showing. I do believe he was slavering in anticipation.

He launched himself upon my assailant, apparently with the intent of ripping out his throat. Ricardo gave a shrill cry of fear and stumbled back, raising his arms to protect himself. The knife fell from his grasp. I scrambled to my feet and kicked it away. I watched with satisfaction as Hobo's assault continued. Chrisling had fallen and was churning and writhing on the gravel to avoid those ravening jaws.

Finally I shouted, "Hobo! Enough!"

He stopped his attack but remained astride his recumbent victim and began barking and snarling ferociously. He sounded murderous but made no attempt to bite.

The ruckus was enough to disturb everyone within hearing distance and so it did. My father came to the back door wearing a maroon velvet smoking jacket and carrying one of his James Upshall pipes. He surveyed the scene and uttered a classic line I shall never forget.

"What is the meaning of this?" he demanded.

With a great effort of will I refrained from hysterical laughter. "Father," I said, "I have just been the victim of a knife attack by Ricardo Chrisling. May I request you call nine-one-one and ask them to send police officers as soon as possible. Also, I would appreciate it if you'd phone Sergeant Rogoff—he's presently at headquarters—and tell him what happened."

I thought my voice was steady. Papa wasn't going to outcool me.

He nodded and went back inside. His place was taken by mother clad in nightgown and robe, fluffy mules on her feet. Then came Ursi and Jamie Olson from their apartment over the garage. Jamie was carrying an iron crowbar and I had no doubt he'd use it as a lethal weapon if necessary.

I can only describe the next hour as organized confusion. Two squad cars appeared, followed soon after by Al Rogoff in his pickup. Eventually there were ten of us surrounding Ricardo, who was still lying supine on the gravel, eyes closed. His face was remarkably calm.

No one wanted to touch him. But when Rogoff arrived he hauled Chrisling unceremoniously to his feet. He was searched, handcuffed, and taken away in one of the squads. Meanwhile Hobo had been shooed back to his house and I had recited an abbreviated report of what had occurred at least three times, the last to the sergeant.

He nodded. "You'll have to dictate a statement," he told me.

"Delighted."

He had taken possession of Chrisling's snickersnee and he fiddled with it, levering the slender blade back into the bone handle and then pressing the button to watch the steel spring out and lock into striking position. It looked as skinny as an ice pick.

"Could be," he said, looking at me.

I knew what he meant. "Not could but *is*," I said firmly.

"No proof," he said. "There's got to be a thousand shivs like this in South Florida."

"Anything from Sonia?" I asked him.

"Oh yeah," he said. "She claims Ricardo hired her just to get you up to her place. She didn't know what for—she says. So where does that leave us? The two slobs are letting their lawyers talk for them. Maybe we can cut a deal, maybe not. Anyway, we've got Chrisling for assault with a deadly weapon with intent to commit murder. That's something. He'll do time."

"Not enough," I said angrily.

"You're right," Al agreed. "Not enough. It still leaves me with three open homicides. Archy, please don't call me again tonight. Your life is beginning to resemble *The Perils of Pauline.*"

Finally everyone departed. The only reminder of the hullabaloo was Yvonne Chrisling's Cadillac still parked in the center of our turnaround. I looked about and there was Hobo sitting quietly outside his mini-mansion. I went over and looked down at him. He looked up at me.

"You're something you are," I said. "The smartest, spunkiest dog who ever lived." I got down on my knees, leaned close, put a palm on his head. "How can I repay you?" I asked him. "Broiled tournedos with green peppercorn sauce? No? A raw sirloin? No? How about your very own package of Pepperidge Farm Milano cookies?"

He yawned. I laughed and lightly touched my nose to his. Sickeningly sentimental? Of course it was. But I had to restrain myself from hugs and kisses. I owed him a big one, just as I owed Al Rogoff. I was becoming a habitual debtor.

But I could repay my marker to the sergeant and knew how to do it. The night's events—two escapes from an early demise—had given me the confidence of P. T. Barnum and his reliance on flimflam. I went up to my barracks and exchanged my Technicolored threads for a suit of navy tropical worsted. Definitely a somber costume. Almost funereal in fact. Exactly the impression I wished to convey.

I phoned Yvonne Chrisling. It was then shortly before midnight.

"Yvonne," I said in solemn tones, "this is Archy McNally. Please forgive me for calling at such a late hour. I hope I didn't wake you."

"Oh no," she said. "No, no. I've been reading a novel. What is it, Archy? You sound so serious."

"It concerns a serious matter. About an hour ago your stepson attempted to stab me to death."

"What?!"

I repeated my statement. I thought her shock was genuine.

She mewled. "Are you injured?"

"Fortunately not."

"Where is Ricardo now?"

"In police custody."

She sighed. "He is such a hothead; you wouldn't believe. I'll call the authorities first thing in the morning."

"I'm afraid it might be too late. You may be involved. You know what police interrogations are like."

I hoped to spook her with visions of thumbscrews and truncheon blows to the kidneys. Apparently it worked, for her voice became shaky.

"Why should I be involved?"

"Because he used your car to come to my home and assault me. The Cadillac is still parked in our driveway."

"The fool!" she cried wrathfully. "Can you bring it back here and then I'll drive you home."

"No, Yvonne, I cannot do that. The police are presently checking the registration and will want to photograph the car in position to prove it was used in the commission of a vicious crime." All pure fudge of course.

Silence. Then she wailed, "What shall I do, Archy?"

"I suggest I come over to your place now and we discuss the situation. Perhaps we can find a solution to your predicament."

"Oh yes!" she said, instantly relieved. "Come to me immediately, darling."

I hung up grinning. Zorro strikes again!

I had trouble maneuvering the Miata from the garage; Yvonne's phaeton was blocking the way. But I finally slid free and drove slowly to the Gottschalk home, slowly because I needed time to rehearse my role. And if my tardy arrival made the lady anxious, so much the better.

But she was not my first encounter with one of the dramatis personae. I parked, approached the entrance, and found Peter Gottschalk slumped on the top step. He looked up at me.

"Archy!" he said. "Just the man I wanted to see. I was going to phone you but I lost my nerve."

"It doesn't take nerve to call me, Peter," I said. "A whim will do. How are you feeling?"

"I'm getting there. I've been walking the straight and narrow. No booze, no grass. I'm taking my medication and I go twice a week to get monitored."

"Bravo!" I said. "Keep it up."

"Listen, I guess you thought I was bughouse, didn't you?"

"No, I didn't believe that," I told him. "You were seriously ill and acting irrationally."

"I've been doing a lot of heavy thinking lately," he went on, "and now I can see things clearer than I ever saw them before."

"Such as?"

"My dear sisters. They were trying to keep me wacko so they could control my share of pop's estate. Am I right?"

I knew he was but I said nothing.

"At first, when I realized what they were up to, I wanted to kill them. Then I figured they weren't important enough to kill. Just a couple of greedy bubbleheads. The best revenge is to get healthy and let them keep buying junk until they run out of funds."

"Yes," I said. "A wise decision."

"While I'm letting my hair down," he continued, putting a hand over his eyes, and I wondered if it might be to hide his weeping, "I might as well tell you it was me who slashed the photograph of my mother and father. And then I broke the phonograph record she had given him. Because I loved my mother so much, and I didn't like the way he was behaving. I know now what I did was totally goofy."

"You were ill," I consoled him. "Wild mood swings. Did you tape a mass card inside your father's closet door?"

"No, I didn't do that."

"Did you strangle the mynah?"

"Dicky? Not me. I liked that bird."

I nodded and started toward the door but he held up a hand for a final confession.

"I told you I hated my father, Archy. Maybe I did at the time. But I don't hate him now. He was just human, wasn't he? I mean he wasn't a god without sin or without weakness. None of us are."

Except *moi* of course.

"You've got it," I said. "I'm going to call you and we'll have a nonalcoholic lunch and trade X-rated jokes."

He smiled weakly, wiping his eyes. "I'd like that."

I left him there, sitting alone on the steps of what had formerly been his father's home. I hoped he was recovering from his illness, but he seemed so forlorn. His physical condition might be improving but his spirit seemed sodden. I thought I might call

Dr. Gussie Pearlberg to ask if there was anything she could do to rejuvenate his *joie de vivre*.

I was grateful for our brief conversation but he had really told me little I hadn't already guessed. I knew his sisters, Julia and Judith, were willing victims of the most common of the seven deadly sins: covetousness. The avaricious twins were quite capable of posting the mass card after they learned of their father's plan to establish a foundation. And for the benefit of parrots! Horrors! He was going to give away their inheritance. It was not to be endured and he had to be warned of the danger of retribution. Stupid? Of course it was. But that's the power of greed.

Most interesting of all were Peter's comments about his father. He had slashed the photograph and shattered the phonograph record, he said, because he loved his deceased mother and didn't like the way his father was behaving. More grist for the McNally mill.

I rang the bell of the Gottschalk home—soon to be the Yvonne Chrisling home—wondering if I might qualify for a Nobel prize awarded for Unprovable Conclusions.

34

SHE WAS WEARING a khaki pantsuit of military twill. I was surprised it didn't sport epaulets, a name badge, and two rows of campaign ribbons. I mean the lady was dressed in a uniform. Give her a swagger stick and she'd have made a splendid drill instructor at Sandhurst or Parris Island.

She clutched my hands. "Archy!" she exclaimed. "Sweetheart! My savior!"

A bit much wouldn't you say? I disengaged myself and gave her a sad smile. At least I hoped it was a sad smile and not a smirk, for I was in a smirky mood.

There are two things I must tell you from the outset about the conversation to follow in the disordered living room. First, we both remained standing and neither suggested things might go more smoothly if we were seated instead of confronting each other like warring gamecocks.

Second, I was aware she paused a brief instant before answering my questions. Her hesitations didn't last long, just a beat or two, but I reckoned they gave her time to consider her replies. She was too brainy to be a blurter. Every action, every speech was calculated.

"Archy, have you any idea why Ricardo attacked you?"

"Of course, Yvonne. He knew I had discovered he was dealing in endangered and smuggled parrots. Surely you knew of his criminal activities."

"I wasn't sure but I suspected. I know so little about business."

That should have earned her a hearty guffaw. She knew as little about business as she did about breathing. She was a shrewd bottom-line lady.

"He'll be fined and may serve time for parrot smuggling," I went on. "I doubt if you will be accused of involvement in that scheme. Of course it would help if you provide what corroborative evidence you can."

She was puzzled. "But when you phoned tonight you said I might be involved."

"You are," I told her. "But in a much graver matter. Dick will probably be charged with the murder of Hiram Gottschalk and possibly the slaying of Anthony Sutcliffe and Emma Gompertz."

I had used Ricardo's diminutive deliberately in hopes of eliciting a response and I won.

"Dick," she repeated with a small moue of protest. "He hates that nickname. He wants always to be called Ricardo. As for killing Hiram and those other people, it's just nonsense."

"I don't think so," I said. "You came to me not too long ago asking advice for a woman who had knowledge of a crime committed by someone close to her. The woman you described was obviously you. I urged you then to inform the authorities immediately. I now repeat my recommendation, Yvonne. Go to the police at once and make a voluntary statement. Ricardo is in custody and cannot harm you. But faced with a charge of homicide, he may hope to avoid the electric chair by cooperating with the state attorney and implicating you."

"He would never do that!" she cried.

"Wouldn't he?" I said, and we stared at each other.

"Besides," she said, and I thought I detected a note of franticness in her voice, "what proof do they have? They have no proof."

I improvised boldly. "His car was used to transport Gompertz and Sutcliffe to the Everglades where they were slain. The knife he used to attack me tonight is the same weapon he used to stab Mr. Gottschalk through the eyes." I thought my repetition of "used, used, used" would spook her and it did.

"But his motive," she said desperately. "What could possibly have been his motive? Did he think Hiram suspected his connection with parrot smuggling?"

"It may have been part of it," I conceded, "but I doubt it. Mr. Gottschalk was not a suspicious man; he was a naive man. Even more, he was a good man and could not comprehend others might be evil. No, I think Ricardo's motives were more complex."

"More complex?" she repeated. "I don't understand."

"Sure you do. Now I must say things I would prefer not to say but I must. You were intimate with Hiram Gottschalk, were you not? You shared his bed."

She accepted my pronouncement calmly. This woman never ceased to amaze me. But she had no idea of what I had in store for her.

"It is true," she said equably. "Hiram and I were intimate."

"Believe me," I said hastily, "I do not condemn you. I see nothing wrong in your comforting the waning years of a widower. But Ricardo knew what was going on and was jealous, was he not?"

"Ricardo loves me," she said simply. "And he is a very passionate boy."

"And too frequently his passion erupts in violence," I added. "He was furious about your relationship with Mr. Gottschalk—correct? He knew Hiram had eyes for you. He knew Hiram saw you naked in the bed alongside him. The vision enraged him."

She took a deep breath. "I told him he was courting disaster," she said.

"Courting disaster"? Don't you just love it! I wondered what novel she had been reading.

"There was more to it than just jealousy," I said, playing my trump card. "There was also rivalry. For at the same time you were sharing Hiram's bed you were also romping with your stepson."

She slapped my face.

I trust you will recall that was the opening line of this narrative. And now a repetition. I had to wonder if I was becoming the favorite punching bag of the female sex. An unnerving prospect.

"What a despicable thing to say!" Yvonne spat at me. "I told you Ricardo loves me and I love him. But it is an affectionate love. There has never been anything physical between us. You have no reasons for saying such a detestable thing."

No reasons? Well, perhaps no ironclad proof, but indications I found convincing.

Item: The decoration of Ricardo's apartment, which displayed a woman's influence.

Item: The diamond choker purchased by Ricardo and presumably given to Yvonne.

Item: The report in Lolly Spindrift's column of Ricardo's romantic activities being merely a blind to conceal a secret infatuation.

Item: Yvonne's new Cadillac. Who had provided the funds for that bauble?

"There is absolutely nothing sexual between Ricardo and me," she repeated sternly.

"If you say so," I said, a wishy-washy comment if ever I heard one. I had hoped for a full confession but I was prepared for denial. "Disregarding Ricardo's motives for the moment, consider the facts as they exist. Your stepson is accused of being a murderer. He is presently under arrest and is being questioned. I told you the evidence against him is strong. You don't know what he might say in an effort to lessen his punishment. I urge you to forestall him by making your own statement to the police as soon as possible. Yvonne, save yourself!"

She gave me a look dark and hard enough to stop an attacking hyena. Then she turned from me and began stalking about the room hugging her elbows, head lowered. She was obviously considering her options. I waited patiently, knowing this was make-or-break time. Finally she stopped her pacing and came forward to face me again.

"All right," she said, her voice tense, "here is what happened. . . ."

She had left Hiram's bedroom to return to her own adjoining bedchamber. It was true she and her employer were having an affair but they slept separately. She heard sounds coming from Hiram's room: footfalls, a gasping cry. She hurried back, fearing he might be ill, perhaps suffering a heart attack.

She found her stepson, dripping knife in hand, retreating from the room, leaving behind the body of Hiram Gottschalk, his eyes bloodied.

"I was shocked," Yvonne wailed. "I didn't know what to do."

Ricardo, she claimed, was as distraught as she. He seemed totally disoriented and she was forced to take command even though she was torn between horror at what he had done and her desire to protect a stepson she loved. And so she had helped him to escape from the house. They had, in their agitated state, broken the glass of the patio door, hoping the police would think the murder had been committed by an intruder.

It was, she admitted, a foolish thing to do. Then, after Ricardo had departed, she waited perhaps thirty minutes, weeping, before she called the police and roused the household.

"And that's exactly what happened," she concluded, putting a hand on my arm. "You believe me, don't you, Archy?"

"Of course I believe you," I said. Did I? C'mon, do you take me for a dunce? The lady's story had more holes than a wedge of Emmentaler and the police would spot them as easily as I did.

How had Ricardo gained entrance to the Gottschalk home? There was no reason for him to have a key. Why hadn't the other residents—the twins, Peter, the staff—been awakened by the sounds from Hiram's bedroom Yvonne had described, as well as her conversation with Ricardo? And why hadn't she called 911 immediately in hopes of saving Hiram? How did she know he was dead? She had said nothing of examining the victim's condition.

Oh, her story was not a complete falsehood, you understand, but it was a half-truth. She had put her own spin on reality in an effort to protect herself. It was understandable but would be wasted on Sgt. Rogoff just as it had been on me.

What had actually happened? You know, don't you? Of course

you do. The two of them, stepmother and stepson, lovers, were in it together. The crime had been planned. Yvonne had unlocked the front door to allow Ricardo to enter, after making certain Hiram and everyone else in the house was asleep. The murder was perpetrated noiselessly. The smashing of the patio glass was a mistake but a minor one. The killer departed as silently as he had arrived. Yvonne gave him time to get away and then called the police and went into her grief-stricken act.

Their motive? Remember the song "Money, Money" from *Cabaret?* The lyrics state "money makes de vurld go round." And so it does. With Hiram Gottschalk dead Ricardo would inherit a successful business and a convenient outlet for his nefarious activities. Yvonne would have a home of her own and the two of them would live happily ever after. Why did they need the old man?

"May I call Sergeant Al Rogoff now?" I asked her gently. "He's a friend of mine and I'm sure he'll treat you with respect."

She nodded. She wanted respect. I used her phone and eventually was put through to Rogoff.

"You again?" he said, groaning. "You promised no more calls tonight."

"Sergeant," I said formally, "I am with Yvonne Chrisling at the moment. She wishes to come to headquarters and make a voluntary statement."

He picked up on it immediately, realizing the woman was present and listening to me.

"A voluntary statement?" he repeated. "Regarding the Gottschalk homicide?"

"Correct."

"Bring her in," he said, and could not hide the exultancy in his voice. "I shall await your arrival with open arms."

I was about to say, "That's better than with bated breath," but said nothing and hung up. I gave Yvonne a small smile. "Let's go," I said.

I drove her to headquarters in my Miata. We did not speak during the trip. Rogoff and a female officer were waiting for us. Just before Yvonne exited she leaned forward to kiss my ear.

"When this is all over and I am free," she said in a sultry voice, "you and I must spend a wonderful night together. Not so, Archy darling?"

I was tempted to ask, "A down payment on a lifetime of ecstasy?" but again I bit my tongue and said only, "Of course."

Then I turned her over to the cops.

I drove home in a pensive mood, not as eager for sleep as I thought I'd be, considering the hour and the harrowing events of a tumultuous day. When I was safe in my own sanctum, slowly disrobing, I was still pondering the role I had played in bringing to justice the killer or killers of three innocent people. I wished I could have done more but I was satisfied with what had been accomplished. The final solution now rested with Sgt. Rogoff and his colleagues.

They had two prime suspects in custody and I knew how they would proceed. They would interrogate Yvonne and Ricardo separately of course, suggesting to each that her or his partner in crime was talking freely and condemning the other. "Yes, Yvonne, but he says . . ." "Yes, Ricardo, but she says . . ." The two would find their "love" shriveling away as they attempted to save themselves. The same would be true of their legal counselors, who would urge each to shift the guilt as much as possible in order to cut a more advantageous deal. Justice can be messy. But you already knew that, didn't you?

There was one final puzzle in need of a solution: Who strangled Dicky, the mynah? I thought I knew, but had no intention of mentioning it to my father or Al Rogoff. Both would think I had gone completely crackers. But I shall tell you because I hope you may be more understanding and agree, "Yes, it could have happened as you say."

I believed Ricardo killed the bird because of its repeated squawk, "Dicky did it, Dicky did it." Not only was the use of the diminutive an affront to Ricardo's amour-propre, his insistence on the use of his full first name, but "Dicky did it" was also a constant, disturbing reference to the crimes he was committing and those he planned to commit.

It was a theory but I thought it valid. Ricardo's misdeed was senseless. But we all occasionally act in a manner others may find irrational. I myself have been known to add sliced radishes to a bowl of sour cream.

35

D ID I SLEEP in on Sunday morning? Late, later, latest! By
the time I awoke, my parents and the Olsons had departed for
their churches. I put together a skimpy breakfast: a couple of
toasted muffins with slices of sharp Muenster and two mugs of
black caffeine. Okay but dull; definitely not animating.

I was still feeling logy and decided I needed a Bloody Mary to
get me up to speed. I very rarely drink anything alcoholic before
noon but this, I told myself, was a special occasion. A discreet inquiry was being resolved and I deserved a small reward. But the
drink didn't get my corpuscles dancing; I was still feeling feeblish
when my parents returned.

I cornered my father before he could settle down with his
five-pound Sunday newspaper.

"A few moments, sir?" I asked.

He nodded and led the way into his study. He was not, I could tell, in a sunshiny mood.

"What a ridiculous sermon," he said angrily. "Archy, do you really believe 'Ask, and ye shall receive . . .'?"

"It hasn't worked for me," I said, and he laughed. "Father, I want to give you a summary of the investigation into the murder of Mr. Hiram Gottschalk. I'll make it as brief as possible."

I delivered an account of everything that had occurred since my last report. I told him Yvonne and Ricardo Chrisling were presently being held by the police and I strongly suspected they were both guilty of homicide. Ricardo could certainly be convicted for his attack upon me and his involvement in the smuggling and illicit trade in endangered birds.

The pater interrupted. "Have you been able to determine if our security was invaded by the computer at Parrots Unlimited?"

"No, sir, I have not yet heard from Judd Wilkins. But I think it's now moot. I believe the police will ignore the smuggling charge and the felonious assault and go for a murder-one indictment."

He nodded. I expected him to say, "A dreadful affair," but he said, "A dreadful matter." Well, I was close.

"I shall be in touch with the authorities," he stated, "and determine how these arrests, charges, indictments, and so forth may affect the probate of Mr. Gottschalk's last will and testament. Thank you for your assistance, Archy."

He began to shuffle through his *New York Times* and I was dismissed. I went back upstairs and because I had made no golf or tennis dates for the day I set to work completing my journal record of the Gottschalk case, relieved my psittacosis was ended.

I was interrupted only once, by a phone call from Al Rogoff, and marveled he could still be awake and in such a buoyant temper.

"It's going as planned," he reported happily. "Sonia, the two punks, Yvonne, Ricardo—everyone's singing. We really need a choral director. They all want to cut deals."

"Al, do you have enough to convict?"

"I think so. Maybe no one will fry but Yvonne and Ricardo will do hard time. It'll be a while before we decide who takes the heaviest hit. The mills of the law grind slowly."

I sighed. "The correct reference is to 'the mills of God' but I'll accept hard time for those disgustful creatures."

"Yep," he said cheerily. "Me, too. Stay tuned."

Al's call should have lightened my spirits but it did not. And I knew the cause of my depression. When I was lying defenseless on the gravel, Ricardo's dirk at my throat, I did not think, Mother-of-pearl, is this the end of Archy McNally? No, what might have been my last thought was regret I had not made amends for my disagreement with Consuela Garcia, the cause of which was lost in the mists of history.

I did not gird my loins—not knowing exactly how it was done—but I dealt my ego a sharp blow to the solar plexus and summoned up the courage to phone her, unable to endure my despondency another moment.

"Hello?"

"Ms. Garcia?"

"Yes. Who is this?"

"Archibald McNally."

"I don't recognize the name," she said coldly. "What is this in reference to?"

"It is in reference to a poor, miserable wretch calling to express his most abject apologies and plead for your forgiveness."

"Plead," she said, still chilly but thawing.

"I have acted like a complete rotter," I said. And then overcome by the pleasure of confession I added, "An utter scoundrel. There is no reasonable excuse I can make for my execrable conduct. It was folly and all I can do now is ask for mercy. I know you are a kindhearted woman and I pray you will be generous enough to pardon my stupidity and give me another chance to prove my fidelity."

Short silence. Then: "Perhaps. What did you have in mind?"

"I would appreciate the opportunity of apologizing to you in person rather than over the phone. And I feel it should be a meeting à deux, not in a restaurant or at a bar. I would like to come to your apartment as soon as possible. I would also enjoy bringing sufficient provisions for a light but nourishing Sunday dinner."

"Very well," she said. "Come ahead. But I am still very cross with you, Archy."

"As you have every right to be," I assured her, and hung up, mad with delight.

I had neglected to shave that morning but I did so then. I also changed to more informal duds, including a linen shirt of alternating aqua and lavender stripes which I knew Connie admired. During these preparations I thought of playing a tape of Louis Armstrong singing, "I Can't Give You Anything but Love." Then I decided, under the circumstances, the sentiment expressed was just too hokey. So I put on Satchmo's rendition of "I've Got the World on a String." Much better.

Let's see, what else did I do in the following hour? I phoned Leroy Pettibone at the Pelican Club, hoping he would be there preparing the luncheon menu. He was present and I explained my problem: I wanted to buy five pounds of stone crabs but knew local retail fishmongers would not be open on Sunday.

"No problem, Archy," he said. "Our wholesale supplier works

on Sunday getting ready for Monday deliveries. I'll give him a call and tell him to take care of you. He'll probably charge you retail price and it wouldn't hurt if you slipped him a few extra bucks."

"I'll give him an additional fin," I promised. "Perfect for a fish dealer."

"I've heard better jokes than that," Leroy said.

"Who hasn't?" I said, and he gave me the address of the supplier.

I went down to the kitchen and found Ursi Olson preparing our Sunday dinner. I told her I would not be able to join my parents and she was disappointed.

"Oh, Mr. Archy," she said, "it's a leg of lamb with fresh thyme."

"One of my favorite legs," I said, "but duty calls and I regret I cannot share the feast. But if there are any leftovers, Ursi, be sure to save them for me. I may be in dire need later tonight."

I rummaged through our pantry and found a bottle of a decent muscadet and a jar of mustard sauce. It was a commercial product and not half as good, I knew, as the homemade but it would do. I packed both wine and sauce in an insulated bag with plenty of ice cubes and was on my way.

I found the fish supplier in West Palm Beach with little trouble and walked into a wild, noisy scene of rubber-aproned workers busily unloading newly caught fish from iced cartons and cutting, scaling, gutting, slicing, filleting, and repacking portions into plastic bags stuffed with ice. I was finally able to find the bearded foreman and identified myself.

"Oh sure," he said. "Leroy's pal. You want five pounds of stone crabs—right? You want them hammered?"

"Please," I said humbly, having no idea whether or not Connie had the tools to break the heavy shells.

So he swatted the thick claws enthusiastically with a wooden mallet on a butcher-block table. Then he bundled the cracked stone crabs into a plastic bag which I added to my insulated carrier. I paid what he asked for and added what I considered a generous tip. He must have thought so too, for he winked at me.

"Have a nice crab," he said.

I wasn't certain how to interpret that but I thanked him and sped directly to Connie's condo.

She opened the door of her apartment wearing brief cutoff jeans and a T-shirt imprinted with a large crimson question mark. No smile. I thought she looked smashing. Her manner was a bit on the frosty side.

But she could not resist the stone crabs with mustard sauce and by the time we finished half the muscadet things were going smoothly, and we had almost fully regained our former mateyness. Connie is not vindictive; she is a jolly woman who'd much rather smile than frown. But she does require continual stroking.

I shall not repeat the details of our conversation that Sunday afternoon—some things are sacred. But when the wine was finished (with enough stone crabs left for a nibble later) she looked at me intently and asked, "Have you been faithful to me, Archy?"

I was tempted to quote Dowson—"I have been faithful to thee, Cynara! in my fashion"—but thought better of it. Instead I said, "I have been true-blue, Connie, and will swear to it on the Boy Scout Handbook."

She gave me a roguish smile and I reached for her.

She didn't slap my face.